To Janet

THE B TEAM
A HORSE RACING SAGA

ALAN MINDELL

SUNBURY PRESS

Mechanicsburg, Pennsylvania USA

Published by Sunbury Press, Inc.
50 West Main Street
Mechanicsburg, Pennsylvania 17055

www.sunburypress.com

For information about special discounts for bulk purchases, please contact Sunbury Press Orders Dept. at (855) 338-8359 or orders@sunburypress.com.

To request one of our authors for speaking engagements or book signings, please contact Sunbury Press Publicity Dept. at publicity@sunburypress.com.

ISBN: 978-1-62006-595-2 (Trade Paperback)
ISBN: 978-1-62006-596-9 (Mobipocket)

Library of Congress Control Number: 2015937822

FIRST SUNBURY PRESS EDITION: April 2015

Product of the United States of America
0 1 1 2 3 5 8 13 21 34 55

Set in Bookman Old Style
Designed by Crystal Devine
Cover by Amber Rendon
Edited by Amanda Shrawder

Continue the Enlightenment!

To Missy.

May she forever rest peacefully in canine heaven.

ACKNOWLEDGMENTS

The author would like to thank:

Devra Mindell, Jerry Mindell, Bobbi Lona, Claudia Yost, Paula Halicki, Judy Brown, Judy Bishop, Kea Warner and her San Diego Area Writers' Workshop, Tom Robbins, Rich Perloff, Richie Silverstein, Brad Pegram, Mike Smith, Dean Pederson, Jobi Mindell, Joe Mindell, Barry Bernstein, Jack Allen, Fred Shatsky, Linda Luke, Leslie Moffett, Heather Fritz, Daniel Levy, Ed Alston, Jon Udell, Bon Temp Social Club of San Diego, Greg Benusa, Jan Maxted, Margaret Sohn, Garry Todd, Carole Osborne, San Diego Swingcats, Lisa Wolff, Bonnie Owen, Nick Nichols, Hope Weissman, Laura Barbanell, Lorraine Etkin, Dave Sanderson, Debbie Klein, Marvin Zuckerman, Therese Tanalski, Ginny Burt, Barbara Bruser, Debbie Hecht, Tom Mckee, Deanna Fountain, Judy Shapiro, Liz Bell, Anne Richardson, Ed Idell, Bill Gifford, Christine Candland, Lawrence Knorr, Amanda Shrawder, Amber Rendon, Barbara Crisler, Barbara Fowler, Monica Omark, Debbie Lynn, Monica Sujan, Fred Close, Eva Close, Karalee Austin, John Southworth, Lynn Eames, and Gary Dolgin

ABOUT THE AUTHOR

Alan Mindell has owned and bred racehorses for many years. His horses have raced at many tracks, including Santa Anita, Hollywood Park, Del Mar, Golden Gate Fields, Emerald Downs, Turf Paradise, Arlington Park, Tampa Bay Downs and Canterbury Park. A former standout baseball player at the University of California, Berkeley, he won four gold medals as a sprinter in the 2012 San Diego Senior Olympics and is a world-class 400 meter runner in his age group.

Also by Alan Mindell:

THE CLOSER (2013)

PART ONE

TURF PARADISE

CHAPTER 1

COOKIE JUMPED UP ON THE BED. The instant Cory Andrews felt her next to him, he knew what would come next. He could save his small black and white cocker spaniel the trouble, but this afternoon he simply didn't feel like moving. Instead, he just lay still and waited. Almost immediately he got what he expected—a wet, juicy lick across the side of his face.

Cookie could tell time. There was no other explanation. Five minutes before the alarm on his old clock was to go off, she would wake him. He remembered setting it for two thirty. Thus the time now was exactly two twenty-five.

She was his snooze button, too. Five minutes past the alarm setting, she'd lick him again. If he didn't get up within ten minutes of the second lick and walk her, she'd begin barking—a loud, penetrating bark incongruous with her refined appearance. After turning off the alarm button, Cory tried to avoid the latter components of her wake-up service by struggling off the bed and slipping on some jeans.

Okay, he was willing to concede that she could tell time. But read the alarm hand on his clock too? And subtract five minutes. Then add five minutes after the alarm rang. Or maybe she counted ten minutes from the first lick until she licked him again. And another ten minutes to her first bark. Whatever, he could only shake his head at all this.

Cory had good reason to nap this afternoon. It was plainly too hot to do anything else. Today's forecast was a hundred and two. Outrageous for early April, even in Phoenix. Besides, he didn't sleep well last night. Nor this afternoon, for that matter. Not unusual for him before one of Rugged Landing's races.

Cory knew better than to get attached to one of the horses he trained. Probably his father's foremost advice. But how could he not feel sentiment for a horse that had won seventeen races for him? A professional racehorse, in every sense of the phrase. Even at nine—old to still be racing—and running today in an eight-thousand-dollar claimer. Simply put, if there was any way he could beat you, he would.

The same could be said for Cory's father, who had died three months ago from cancer. It wasn't unexpected, yet Cory hadn't come close to accepting it. Things just hadn't been the same since. Not that their relationship was without friction. His father had been very demanding and quick to anger. But he also had that strong will to win, probably his single most defining characteristic.

His father was a jockey virtually all his working life. Mostly at gritty Midwestern tracks like River Downs, near Cincinnati, and the long defunct Ak-Sar-Ben, in Omaha. Turf Paradise, in Phoenix, didn't come until later in his career, about twenty years ago, following the death of Cory's mother from emphysema. When his two older brothers stayed behind for good jobs with an Ohio construction company, Cory, in his late teens at the time, was the only family member who came west with his father.

Never possessing the ability for the big leagues of American horse racing—Kentucky, California, New York, Florida—Cory's father probably eked out a living less on riding skill than talent for cashing wagers. As injuries and failing health slowed him in recent years, he depended almost exclusively on shrewdness at the betting windows, Cory often accompanying him.

Cookie jumped off the bed. Cory watched her go to their front door, take her leash in her mouth and bring it to him. After attaching it to her collar, he followed her onto the grass outside the small apartment. He quickly concluded that the forecast was wrong—the temperature was significantly hotter than predicted. Evidently Cookie agreed. She finished rapidly and pulled him back indoors. Not that it was that much cooler inside, the air conditioner clearly no match for the sun beating down on the roof of the one-story complex.

Not sure exactly when he'd return from the track after the race, he decided to give Cookie an early dinner before he departed, rather than make her wait, hungry. He didn't like leaving her home alone for any length of time, but since his divorce from

Susan six months ago, he really had no choice. If he took her with him and left her in his car, as he often did, she'd never survive the heat today.

In the kitchen, as he poured kibble into her dish and filled her water bowl, his thoughts turned again to Rugged Landing. Any horse with seventeen lifetime wins deserved not to have to run in this weather. Fortunately the race wasn't until late afternoon, the final on the program. Maybe a breeze would develop by then.

Would the horse get claimed? Likely?—no. Possible?—yes. His age would be the main deterrent. For eight thousand plus sales tax, however, someone might want to buy his will to win.

It wouldn't be the first time he'd been claimed from Cory. Twice prior, other trainers had deposited claim forms before a race. On each occasion Cory had been heartbroken. But both times he'd eventually been able to claim him back for a lesser amount.

He reminded himself he had to be realistic about Rugged Landing. Regardless of the number of times he'd won for him. With the infirmities the horse had accumulated over the years, any race could be his last. And at nine, little improvement could be expected. Plus, as his father so adamantly stressed—never get attached to one of your horses.

As Cookie began eating, Cory decided to take a shower. A cold one. Even from the bathroom and with the shower water running, he could hear her ravenously crunching the kibble, her usual style.

Small dog, big appetite.

✦ ✦ ✦

"Any lookers?" Cory asked Carlos Souza, his longtime assistant. Carlos, Rugged Landing, and Ramon Carquinez—the horse's groom—had just joined Cory in the number-three stall of the circular Turf Paradise saddling paddock.

"No, Boss," Carlos answered. "I do not see anyone."

Cory nodded. Apparently he'd been right about the unlikeliness of Rugged Landing being claimed. If anyone were interested, Carlos probably would have spotted them while walking with Rugged Landing from the stable area to the receiving barn to here. Cory had also been right about a breeze—a slight one had sprung up, maybe tempering the stifling heat by five degrees.

Cory patted the lanky chestnut on the side of his neck. The valet for Cesar Alvarez, Rugged Landing's regular jockey, arrived with saddle, girth and stirrups. Working together, Cory and the valet began affixing the equipment to the horse. Cory really liked this part of the sport—saddling, meeting the jockey, perhaps strategizing and pre-race anticipation. He glanced quickly at the odds board and saw that Rugged Landing was five to two, lukewarm favorite in the field of ten.

"Hey guys ... Sucker's gonna win again."

Cory didn't have to look to know who had joined them. Nor that the new arrival wore the usual old beat-up tan cowboy hat and bright yellow golf shirt and shorts. This was a part of the sport Cory didn't like—dealing with Bill Donley, Rugged Landing's owner. In his mid-fifties, Donley had an enormous potbelly and a head markedly too big for his body.

"Sucker doin' good?" Donley inquired.

"Fine," Cory grunted.

"Think we'll lose him?"

"Not according to Carlos."

"Well, we do, we do. Main thing ... squeeze another win outta the sucker."

Cory winced silently. This horse could win a thousand races and Donley would have no authentic feeling for him. Once he and the valet finished the saddling, Cory rubbed his hands together, patted Rugged Landing again on the neck and motioned Ramon to walk him around the paddock. The valet left and while Carlos remained in the stall, Cory and Donley headed for the grass in the center of the paddock, where the jockeys for the race were already assembling. They had no problem finding Alvarez in Donley's bright yellow silks, almost the identical color of his shirt and shorts. Garish, no question, but at least easy to spot during a race.

"Go get 'em, jock," Donley greeted Alvarez. "Sucker's ready."

Cory winced again. He was, of course, proud of his affiliation with Rugged Landing—obviously much more than with the horse's owner. Alvarez—about forty, muscular and short, even for a jockey—shook Donley's hand, then Cory's.

"You know how to ride him," Cory said. He saw no reason for any further instruction to the jockey.

"Don't be afraid to crack him a few times," Donley chimed in, "with your stick."

Cory winced once more. Rugged Landing didn't need to be whipped. It was almost an insult. Pretty much like Cory giving the rider instructions. The horse knew exactly where he was and what he was doing at every stage of a race. Simply put, if there was any way he could beat you, he would.

A track official called for "riders up" and Ramon led Rugged Landing to a spot right in front of them. Cory boosted Alvarez aboard the horse. As the track bugler played the call to post, a spectator outside the paddock, probably inebriated, yelled something unintelligible at Alvarez. Cory watched Rugged Landing step onto the track.

"Sit with me," Donley said. "Wanna talk to you."

In truth, Cory would rather sit with Carlos and Ramon, who were moving toward a place along the outer rail of the track. Donley seemed insistent though, and at least his box seats were in the shade. On the way Cory paused to gaze at Rugged Landing, jogging past them. Beyond the horse, he couldn't help noticing the turf course and infield, the grass on both wilted into an ugly yellowish-brown. How many times had he been here, at Turf Paradise, over the years? Two, three thousand? Maybe more.

A couple of spectators approached to ask him if he liked his horse today. He merely nodded and smiled obligatorily. It didn't take long to reach Donley's box, directly above the finish line. The crowd was sparse—the heat, a weekday, final race on the program. No question Rugged Landing deserved better than this.

"Want me to get you a drink?" Donley asked as they sat down in his seats. "Or a bet?"

"Neither," Cory answered, aware that he was very much an oddity around a racetrack, in both categories. He'd never acquired a taste for alcohol and didn't care for the sweetness of soft drinks. Plain water suited him fine. And, over the years, the few times he'd bet on his own horses was like the kiss of death. They'd always lost. Nor did he have his father's acumen for betting on other people's.

"Thinking about New Mexico," Donley disclosed.

"For the summer?"

"Nah. Year round. Since they put in slots down there, purses are much better than here."

"Would you send all your horses?" Cory asked.

"Least three or four to start. Interested?"

Relocation wasn't a new topic for Cory. Actually, while driving the short distance to the track an hour ago, he reviewed his options once more. Specifically, where to go for the summer, once the Turf Paradise season ended. He'd tried New Mexico a couple of times before, with limited success. And Colorado. His favorite spot had been Yavapai Downs in Prescott, a mountain resort about a hundred miles northwest of Phoenix. The purses there were so small, though, that he didn't even cover expenses. Financially, he'd been better off sweating out that summer in Phoenix, freshening his horses. Which he'd done last year. With today's heat as a reminder, it was something he'd rather not do again.

"Have to let you know," Cory replied.

"Don't wait too long."

Donley got up and headed toward the betting windows. Cory watched Rugged Landing continue to warm up, on the opposite side of the track, near the starting gate for the six-furlong race. As his own tension mounted, Cory stood up and stretched a little. He noticed the odds changing on the board and the chestnut dipping to eight to five. Donley's money, perhaps?

✦ ✦ ✦

Almost to herald the horses beginning to enter the gate, two military jets flew noisily overhead. With his number-three post, Rugged Landing was among the first to load. Cory watched him closely. Two or three times in the past, he'd acted up. Today he stood absolutely still in the gate.

"C'mon sucker," Donley squealed as the field burst forward.

Rugged Landing broke alertly. The two horses to his inside dropped back immediately. Down the backstretch, several other horses vied for the early lead. Nearing the far turn, Rugged Landing was fifth, along the rail, waiting for a hole.

"Don't get that sucker stuck in there! Don't get that sucker stuck!"

Donley, repeatedly slapping a program against the railing of his box, as if whipping a horse, got up in front of Cory, blocking his view. Cory edged sideways enough to see Rugged Landing still waiting along the rail as the field came into the stretch. Would a hole open? Alvarez and Rugged Landing might have swung to the outside, except another horse came along then, impeding any path. Two more jets flew overhead, drowning out any crowd noise and the sounds of Donley continuing to flail his program.

And then a hole did open. Not along the rail, as Cory had anticipated. Instead, one of the leaders drifted out, creating a gap between him and the horse to his inside. Rugged Landing shot through. Cory felt the blood pounding in his temples. Seventy yards from the finish, Rugged Landing took the lead. A length. Two lengths. Near the wire, perhaps in celebration, Alvarez reached back and smacked him with his whip. The horse didn't expect it. He stumbled slightly and took a bad step. He tried to correct himself, but couldn't. He tumbled right to the track, directly in front of Cory and Donley.

Horrified, Cory leaped to his feet. Leaving the box, he scraped his left hip against the railing. The small crowd now worked in his favor because he was able to scramble downstairs unabated. He quickly glanced at the track to make sure what he was certain happened had happened. It had. Rugged Landing attempted to get up, but couldn't. Cory scurried to a little fence keeping spectators off the track. He climbed over the fence and darted under the outside rail, onto the dirt surface.

Carlos and Ramon were already there. So were the track veterinarian and Alvarez, dirty face and soiled jockey apparel the only visible indication he'd been in a spill. The other riders in the race steered clear, dismounting toward the clubhouse turn, well past their regular place near the finish line. A few spectators gathered along the little fence for a close view.

"Already sedated him for the pain," the vet, Brad Winters, told Cory. He was about fifty, stocky, balding and looking very grim.

"How bad is it?" Cory managed, both winded and scared.

"Bad. Sesamoid. Fractured right through the skin."

"Any chance to save him?"

"None," Winters reported glumly.

Cory felt like he was in shock. He looked at Rugged Landing, who appeared in shock too. Eyes open, yet glazed, he lay on his left side. His mouth was also open, and his breath seemed to come in spurts.

A green and white horse ambulance pulled up. Two men got out and went over to the chestnut. Winters whispered something to them that Cory couldn't hear, and they returned to the ambulance and extracted a large white stretcher from the rear.

"I will go with them, Boss," Carlos offered solemnly.

"No. I'll go. You and Ramon go back to the barn."

"Okay, Boss. We will go back to the barn and feed the horses."

Cory nodded. The ambulance twosome, with help from a couple of spare starting-gate crewmen, shifted Rugged Landing onto the stretcher. The four of them maneuvered the stretcher onto a hydraulic lift at the rear of the ambulance. One of the men pushed a button and the lift whirred upward. Then they conveyed the stretcher into the back of the vehicle, climbing up inside in the process.

Cory just watched, numbly. One of the ambulance crew climbed down, followed by the two gatemen, one of whom, a friend of Cory's, gently touched his shoulder while passing. The other ambulance member remained with Rugged Landing. Cory got up into the back of the ambulance, slipping slightly as he did so. He kneeled down beside the horse, quickly noticing how stifling it was inside the unventilated vehicle, much worse than outside.

"The chamber," Cory heard Winters tell someone, the ambulance driver he assumed.

The vet's words brought Cory out of his numbness, at least for the moment. "The chamber" was the one place nobody at Turf Paradise wanted to wind up. The final destination for mortally injured horses, it was where they would be euthanized and either cremated or sent to a rendering plant and ultimately sold as horse meat.

Cory heard the driver get into the ambulance and start the engine. The vehicle lurched forward. Seconds into the short trip, Cory made a decision. No way Rugged Landing would end up being "rendered" for human or animal consumption. He, Cory, would pay for the cremation himself, if Donley refused.

He patted Rugged Landing on the neck, as he'd done before the race. Except this time he didn't stop. Although relaxed and now breathing regularly, the horse was cold to the touch. His bright chestnut coloring appeared to have faded. And he didn't stir. Almost as if he recognized his fate, and had accepted it.

Cory heard a cell phone ring. He glanced at the attendant beside him, then realized it was his own. There was no one he wanted to talk to. But in case it was the vet, he removed the phone from a jeans pocket. Donley's number was on the little screen. No doubt he wanted to know the condition of his horse.

"Yeah, Bill?"

"Sucker didn't get claimed."

"No surprise."

"Photographer wants to know how many pictures you want."

"Of what?" Cory asked, having no clue what Donley was talking about.

"Of the finish line. Of that sucker crossing it. Winning the race."

In all the turmoil, Cory had forgotten that Rugged Landing had stumbled near the wire, and evidently passed under it before falling. Thus, he did win the race. A fact that seemed inconsequential now.

"I'll pass," Cory said.

"You sure? Buy you as many as you want."

"I'm sure."

"How 'bout that sucker. Doesn't go down till after the finish. Lets me cash a nice bet."

Cory didn't reply. He continued stroking Rugged Landing's neck. And looking into his glazed eyes, still open. It seemed to Cory that the horse was at peace, that he'd accomplished what he'd set out to do in this world. His last race had been a winning one.

"Sucker must've known I had big money on him," Donley bellowed.

"Congratulations," Cory muttered, then turned off the phone.

✦ ✦ ✦

"This is painless," Winters disclosed as he prepared a syringe for the euthanizing injection.

Cory didn't respond. He and the vet, plus the ambulance pair, were crowded into a small, stark, antiseptic-scented room—"the chamber"—which occupied a front corner of the veterinary hospital located in the Turf Paradise stable area. An overhead light reflected off Winters's balding head. Still on his left side, as he was on the track, Rugged Landing lay on a long gray table in the center of the room, the same stretcher still underneath him. Cory would be amazed, were he in any condition to be so, that the horse had been transported from the ambulance to here via a series of conveyor belts, the stretcher remaining beneath him at all times.

As he continued to pat the same spot on Rugged Landing's neck, Cory could feel tears in his own eyes. Since their arrival here, he'd purposely avoided speaking, fearful that if he did he'd break down. While signing cremation and euthanization forms, he'd said and questioned nothing. No doubt Winters and the ambulance crew recognized his anguish, because none of them uttered anything requiring verbal response.

Winters had already shown him the protrusion of bone through the skin. Cory knew enough equine anatomy to understand that the shattered bone was beyond repair. And even if, miraculously, surgery were initially successful, unavoidable infection would do Rugged Landing in. Furthermore, assuming the most fortuitous results throughout, the best that could be hoped for was life as a helpless cripple.

Cory *was* thankful for one thing—there was cool air coming from an air-conditioning duct in the ceiling. At least Rugged Landing could spend his final minutes in some comfort. Cory noticed a large wall clock right below the duct. As the red second hand revolved, it made a strange hissing sound that pierced the room's otherwise silence.

Winters moved Cory's hand to Rugged Landing's shoulder and spotted his syringe exactly where Cory had been stroking the horse's neck. Cory looked at the vet, then away, up at the clock again. He could feel Rugged Landing breathe. Then he felt him shudder and gasp. There was no more breathing.

"Stay as long as you want," Winters said to Cory as he placed the syringe in a receptacle nearby. He motioned to the ambulance twosome, and the three of them left the room.

Cory continued to fight back tears. He mouthed a silent good-bye. He moved his hand from Rugged Landing's shoulder to the place on his neck that he'd been stroking. Before turning to leave, he patted it one last time.

✦ ✦ ✦

It was twilight and not quite so hot when Cory got outside. He walked toward his car in the racetrack parking lot, still feeling tears in his eyes. The roadway he took passed his barn and he could have stopped to check on the other horses and update Carlos. He was in no mood for company, however.

If he felt miserable about Rugged Landing, he also couldn't help feeling sorry for himself. He'd lost a lot in the last six months. First Susan, in divorce. Then his father. Now his favorite horse. What might be next?

He was in a rut here. Maybe it was a good thing that this season would soon end, because he needed a change. New Mexico, as Donley had suggested? No, he'd already been there. He needed someplace different. Someplace he'd never been. Someplace new and fresh.

As he approached the parking lot, the security lights went on. He was able to see his old brown Chevrolet off in the distance, by itself.

✦ ✦ ✦

"California," Cory said the moment he and Carlos sat down the next morning at a table in the stable-area cafeteria.

"The north, Boss?"

"No. The south. First stop, Hollywood Park. Then Del Mar and Santa Anita."

"But, Boss, it sound like we are going not just for the summer."

"Right. Not just for the summer."

"But—our horses, they are not good for there."

"We have four or five that fit. It's a start."

The cafeteria, a large room with grayish blue walls, was half filled. Several men and a lone woman were crowded around a nearby table, and they laughed heartily at an apparent joke one of them told. Trays of breakfast sat in front of Cory and Carlos. Cory wasn't hungry and he suspected Carlos wasn't either.

They had finished training their horses about half an hour ago. Cory's contribution was minimal. He hadn't slept a wink all night, visions of Rugged Landing spinning through his mind. He kept seeing Alvarez whipping him, followed by the fall. The horse's glazed eyes. The protruding bone. Winters's syringe.

Three or four flies buzzed over their food. Cory hoped that today wouldn't turn out as hot as yesterday. Actually the prediction *was* for a couple of degrees less. Big deal.

"What will we do with Ramon, Boss? And the other men?"

"I know some trainers here looking for help."

Carlos nodded. Cory picked up a piece of toast, then set it back down. The thought of food nearly sickened him. Plus he was concerned over Carlos's obvious resistance to his plan. Something he might as well address now.

"Plenty trainers right here would love to have you too."

Carlos shrugged. One of the buzzing flies landed on Cory's eggs and he half-heartedly flicked his hand at it, chasing it away. The laughter from the nearby table started up again.

"I'm sure we can find something good for both you and the men," Cory added definitively.

"You do not want me to go with you?"

"Course I want you to go with me."

Carlos looked pensive. He used his fork to pick up a piece of bacon off his plate. Then he put both the fork and bacon back on the plate. Evidently he still wasn't hungry.

"I will go with you, Boss. We are together a long time."

Indeed, they had been. Almost fifteen years. They originally met when Cory worked as an exercise rider and Carlos as a groom in the same barn. Cory became assistant trainer for a different barn and he got Carlos hired there. When Cory decided to establish his own stable seven or eight years ago, he made Carlos his assistant. All those years, they worked practically side by side, like brothers.

Except for Carlos's much darker complexion and hair, they even looked like brothers. Practically twins. Same age, both short and slim. Each with a long aquiline nose, brown eyes and short hair. And a similar serious expression.

"Hollywood Park opens in two weeks," Cory stated. "I'd like to be there by then."

"But, we will not wait for the end of this meeting?"

"No. I want to get out of here."

"I must go visit my family, Boss."

"Go as soon as you can. I'll keep things together here till you get back."

Carlos nodded. They both grabbed a slice of toast at the same time.

PART TWO

HOLLYWOOD PARK

CHAPTER 2

THAT A DOG I SAW YOU DRIVE UP WITH?" the stout, middle-aged blonde woman inquired.

Cory grimaced as he nodded. What slight chance she'd still rent to him appeared gone. She'd already balked at his seeking short-term occupancy. Throw a dog into the mix and he might as well get into his car and drive off.

Cory and the woman—Janice—stood beside an open window offering a picturesque view of beach and the Pacific. The late-afternoon air was fresh and cool, so different from the heat he'd endured leaving Phoenix and driving across the desert to Los Angeles earlier today.

He took a deep breath. He'd always dreamed of living at the beach. In a little cottage. Exactly what he stood in now. The place was furnished, with a tiny bedroom, kitchen and bath, and rested on a bluff overlooking the ocean. Only a few miles west of Hollywood Park, it was located in an unpretentious district called Playa del Rey, about twenty miles southwest of downtown L.A.

"Where is he now?" Janice asked, obviously alluding to Cookie.

"She," Cory answered defensively.

"Where is *she*?"

"Up the street. Found a parking place in the shade."

"Looked like a cocker spaniel."

"She is."

"Can we go see her?"

"Sure," Cory shrugged.

He was tired from the day's lengthy travels and certainly didn't feel like wasting time. He still needed to find a place, or at least a motel room for the night. But he had to return to his car anyway, so what difference did it make if this woman tagged along? They left the cottage, which adjoined the side of her house, and headed to the street. As they walked, the sound of pounding surf was audible. At his car, under a big tree, he took another deep breath of ocean air.

Cookie sat in her regular seat, in front on the passenger side. He unlocked her door and opened it, attached her leash to her collar, and she jumped out. After wagging her tail and briefly allowing Janice to pet her, she pulled Cory to a nearby lawn to pee.

"I had a cocker when I was a kid," Janice recalled.

Cory didn't reply because Cookie sniffed around like she was going to do more than pee. He removed a plastic bag from a back jeans pocket. She evidently decided against, however, and returned to Janice, again wagging her tail.

"Black and white, like yours," Janice reported.

"Female?"

"Female," Janice said, as though reminiscing. "Called her Oreo. After the cookie."

"I call mine Cookie." Cory smiled. "After the Oreo."

Janice laughed. He considered telling her about Cookie's wake-up service, but what was the point? He wanted to get going. It would soon be dark, hindering opportunity to see other places. A car drove by and the driver honked and waved at Janice, who waved back.

"You must have a lot of stuff in the trunk of your car," she speculated, eyeing two tattered old suitcases in the back seat.

"Nope. Not a stitch."

"Where's the rest of your stuff?" she questioned, frowning.

"We travel light."

It was a good thing they did, too. If the old Chevy had to haul any more than Cookie, him and the two suitcases, it probably wouldn't have made it. As it was, the car overheated twice in the desert, forcing him to stop each time and pour water into the radiator. But the car, like him, seemed to revive as they neared L.A. Almost as though in crossing the desert, they'd crossed some imaginary barrier. Cory knew he felt different. Like he was beginning some great adventure. And he sensed there would be no easy return.

"How long have you owned her?" Janice queried, again patting Cookie, who hadn't stopped wagging her tail.

"Not sure I own her," Cory chuckled. "More like she owns me. Anyway, we've been together five years. Got her from one of those pet rescue places. Vet said she was about three at the time."

Janice smiled. She eyed his suitcase again. Making him feel a little self-conscious. After all, she was peering at his grand accumulation for some thirty-seven years on earth. If she explored closer, she'd find no suit or tie. No fancy shoes or slacks. No jewelry or other nonessentials. And obviously no television, computer or furniture. In other words, he'd arrived in L.A. with not much more than the shirt on his back.

"I guess," Janice said pensively, "that you and Oreo ... I mean Cookie ... don't have a place for tonight."

"If we don't find an apartment, we'll get a motel."

"Don't know any around here that'll take dogs."

Cory shrugged. Cookie kept wagging her tail and looking up at Janice. The sky was turning orange where the sun was beginning to set.

"You can only stay until the start of July?" Janice quizzed, gazing at Cookie.

"The middle," he corrected. "Then we go to Del Mar."

"Well ... I guess ... it's easier to find someone in the summer than now. Can you pay the first month today?"

He nodded and shook her hand enthusiastically. She reached down and rubbed Cookie behind the ears. In the fading light, Cory observed several seagulls flying toward them, then swooping past. Again he smelled the unmistakable scent of ocean.

No question Los Angeles had begun much better than Phoenix ended.

✦ ✦ ✦

Unfortunately, Cory didn't find the Hollywood Park stable area nearly as appealing as his new beach cottage. Walking through it from the track parking lot early the next morning, he witnessed barns constructed of ugly gray concrete. Trees, what few there were, had been clipped so short that they were more bark than foliage. Nearing their barn (he wasn't able to easily find it because of a strange numbering system), he had to dodge a large truck sprinkling water on the bumpy and dusty roadway he was using.

Actually, Hollywood Park wasn't even supposed to be open for racing anymore. An eleventh hour reprieve, however, spearheaded primarily by a horsemen's association, at least temporarily saved it from being bulldozed into other purposes. But management wasn't about to pour any money into a complex when the survival of which was currently so much in doubt.

The distant sounds of Latin music, a staple of most U.S. racetrack stable areas, cheered him slightly. As did the sight of Carlos brushing one of their horses in the horse's stall. Seeing Carlos also aroused some guilt, though—that he, Cory, really hadn't much considered his compadre in the abrupt decision to come here. And because Carlos arrived with their four horses and training equipment by van from Turf Paradise so late last night, Cory hadn't even been here to meet him.

"The trip over okay?" Cory greeted.

"It was okay."

"Hot?"

"Yes, Boss."

"We'll just walk the horses today. Let them get used to their new home."

"Okay, Boss."

"How's your new home?"

Carlos didn't reply. He'd finished brushing the horse and stepped out of the stall.

"Let's take a look at it," Cory suggested.

"It is not much to see."

That became apparent once Carlos led Cory to his room at the end of the shed row. It was tiny, barely large enough for an upper and lower bunk. Paint, the original color of which was indeterminate because of its age, was chipping off badly stained walls. There was a stale odor. An overhead light flickered on and off. Carlos had already set up a hot plate to cook most, if not all, of his meals.

"Shower and toilet?" Cory asked, a little reluctantly.

"Over there." Carlos pointed to a small concrete building beside a main roadway. Two men, carrying towels, were going inside and another was coming out of what was obviously a community facility.

"Try out the shower yet?"

"I do. The water, it is not very warm."

Cory felt more guilt pangs, even though he knew that Carlos was accustomed to this manner of accommodations. Every track they'd been to was pretty much the same. But he, Cory, had hoped for more from a major venue like Hollywood Park.

And yet, despite his disappointment, Cory was aware that this was the arrangement he and Carlos had established. Carlos always stayed in the free facilities provided by the track. There were dual purposes—he could keep a regular eye on their horses and he could save money to send home to his wife and two elementary school-aged daughters, living in Mexico, where he had recently gone to visit them.

"Do not worry, Boss," Carlos consoled, evidently perceiving Cory's concern. "In Mexico, before I come to this country, I sleep outside on the ground at one track. We use a field for a bathroom. And we take a bath in the river."

This information, variations of which Cory had already heard many times, didn't help his feelings. Especially since he and Carlos were in no position to make much money. Four mediocre horses, down from the twenty-two they'd trained in Arizona, had very little earning power. And they certainly weren't much arsenal at a major track. Thanks to Cory's decision, they'd gone from being fairly large fish in a small pond to the proverbial small fish in an ocean—who conceivably would soon drown.

Many of the eighteen horses they'd left behind weren't talented enough for Hollywood Park, and were transferred to other trainers. Or their owners preferred that they race elsewhere. Donley, for example, followed through on his intention to send horses to New Mexico.

"I have a plan," Cory said as they left Carlos's room.

"Yes, Boss?"

"You and I will do all the work around here."

"Okay, Boss."

"No grooms. No hot walkers. No exercise riders. Instead of paying them, we'll make the money ourselves."

"That is good."

"You get the horses ready every morning for the track and I'll ride them there and exercise them. Whoever has time gives them a bath afterward, and attaches them to the hot walking machine. Same with icing them and taping them."

"This remind me of Mexico again. I groom and hot walk there. I mix feed and clean the barn. I do laundry and even ride the horses."

"Good," Cory laughed, having heard excerpts of this story before too. "Maybe you don't need me. You can do all the work yourself and I can sleep late every morning."

"We need you, Boss. You must get us more horses."

✦ ✦ ✦

Before stepping into the right-hand batter's box, Perry glanced at his mother seated in the third-base bleachers. She waved to him.

About a hundred people were watching a like number of youngsters trying out for the local tee-ball league in a spacious park across the street from Santa Anita Race Track, located in the city of Arcadia, about twenty miles northeast of downtown L.A.

The early-May morning was overcast and cool. Because of the weather and because he was nervous, Perry felt cold. Trying to warm up, he took a couple of practice swings with the bat he held. A very large man—at least that's the way he appeared to Perry— placed a baseball on a black rubber tee positioned on home plate. The man, one of the league's coaches, wore a green baseball cap and a two-toned baseball undershirt, white with green sleeves. Perry addressed the ball by lightly touching his bat to it. He swung the bat. It hit nothing, not even the tee.

"No hurry, son," the man said. "Take your time."

Perry stepped out of the batter's box and looked at his mother again. Instead of waving, this time she clapped encouragingly. Perry wanted to do well in the tryout. He'd looked forward to it for the last two months, and had practiced nearly every day recently.

He went back to the tee. This time he swung harder. Again he missed. By even more than with his first swing. The other kids started laughing. He attempted to ignore them, but it wasn't easy.

"Baseball might not be your game, son."

Perry didn't reply. The other kids were still laughing. He wanted them to stop. Quickly he swung again, even harder. Another wide miss. The laughter grew louder.

"Maybe you should wait until next year, son. When you're older."

"I'm almost eight," Perry challenged, definitely not liking the large man's looks.

"Can you see the ball, son?"

"I can see it. I'm not blind."

Perry was telling the truth. On both counts. But there certainly was cause for the man's question. Perry's left eye was immobile and offered no vision. He could see the ball only with his right eye—just not well enough to hit it.

He'd already failed at both previous phases of the tryout, fielding and throwing. He'd had no luck catching balls hit to him. And his throws were erratic, since he had trouble seeing a target. Simply stated, he'd be a defensive liability. But league rules permitted a designated hitter, a player who only batted and didn't play in the field. So Perry might not have to catch or throw.

"Try one more," the man instructed, pointing to the ball still on the tee.

Again Perry swung, even harder than the previous three times. Again he missed. More laughter, louder than ever.

"Go sit over there," the man directed him, motioning toward the first-base dugout, where several players sat.

Perry looked at his mother once more, tears in his eyes. He'd rather go sit with her—away from any of the other kids and their laughter. But he knew that would be like quitting. Besides, his mother had told him that everyone trying out would make a team. And he wanted to make a team.

He dropped the bat and headed slowly for the first-base dugout.

CHAPTER 3

"WHO YOU BETTIN' ON IN HERE?" an old man asked Cory. The two of them were leaning against the white wooden railing of the outdoor Hollywood Park paddock, watching the horses in the fourth race being saddled.

"No one," Cory answered.

"Well how come you're doin' all that scribblin', then?" The old man pointed at a little blue notebook Cory had been writing in. "Seems like lotta trouble for a guy not makin' a bet."

"Case I want to claim one."

"You own horses?"

"No. I train."

"So what're you writin' down?"

"Any possible ailments I see."

That seemed to satisfy the old man, at least for the moment. He turned to look at the red odds board behind them, then back to a couple of horses being saddled nearby. He was lanky and a bit slump-shouldered. Very thick lenses on dark-green eyeglass frames suggested poor vision. He wore a threadbare black corduroy sports coat above a multicolored flannel shirt and purple suspenders holding up khaki pants. A strange outfit, particularly for a bright, very warm afternoon.

"Dumb question," he said straightforwardly. "What's a claiming horse?"

"Might be easier to answer ... what's a claiming race?"

"Okay. Shoot."

"Claiming races," Cory began, "are supposed to equalize competition because all the horses entered can be bought for the same amount. A horse in a race with too low a claiming price—like a twenty-thousand-dollar horse in a ten-thousand-dollar race—will get claimed. A horse in a race with too high a claiming price won't have much chance to win."

"What if a guy doesn't want to risk his horse getting claimed?"

"Then he puts him in a non-claiming race, like an allowance or stakes race. With even less chance to win."

But Cory could tell his last words were wasted because the old man's attention had wandered. One of the nearby horses had reared up repeatedly. His trainer directed a handler to walk him around a circular path. After five or six sprightly steps, the horse seemed to settle.

"Say I wanted to claim a horse," the old guy conjectured. "Could you help me?"

"Sure. Long as you have an owner's license. And money on deposit."

"Owner's license?"

"Simple. Cost you maybe a couple hundred. Meet with the track stewards. They'll approve you ... unless you got a criminal record."

"Do I look like a criminal?"

Cory didn't reply. It wasn't his place to comment on a man's attire. He did smile to himself, however. And observed that the fractious horse had returned to the spot nearby, and his handlers were now concluding the saddling process. Some of the jockeys for the race entered the paddock.

"How much would I need?" the old guy quizzed.

"To claim a horse? Minimum here is eight thousand. Plus sales tax."

"Got a CD coming due next week at my bank. Twenty-five grand. At my age, rather have a little fun with the dough than have it sit there."

"Can you afford to lose that much?"

"Who says I'm gonna lose it?"

"This is a risky business."

"Rent's paid up six months. So is my health care. Who says I'm gonna live that long?"

Cory laughed. The old man took a rumpled Racing Form from a jacket pocket and started to study it, holding it very close to his face. The saddling completed, the horses paraded past them, jockeys aboard, on their way to a tunnel that went under the grandstand, to the racetrack beyond. As the bugler trumpeted their arrival onto the track, Cory made another scribbling before closing his notebook.

Once it was entirely empty of both horses and people, he admired the paddock. He considered it Hollywood Park's best feature. A large grassy area enclosed by the white railing they continued to lean against—containing big shade trees, shrubbery and several kinds and colors of flowers—it offered welcome relief from the track's facilities and the surrounding neighborhoods, both of which were predominately brick and concrete.

"You just gonna stand here and wait for the next batch of horses?" the old guy inquired, interrupting Cory's brief reverie.

"Oh, no. Got more work to do."

"What kinda work?"

"Checking odds. The race. Horses pulling up after. Replay on TV."

"Pretty thorough."

"I try to be."

"Mind if I tag along while you do all this *work*?"

"Be my guest."

The old man crinkled his Racing Form shut and shoved it back into a jacket pocket. Cory saw that he was sweating. Afraid the old guy might not be able to handle the stairs up to the grandstand, Cory led him to an elevator. The weekday crowd was thin and they rode by themselves.

"Hey, what's your name?" the man asked.

"Cory. Cory Andrews."

"Never heard of you."

"No surprise. Came over from Arizona couple weeks ago. What's your name?"

"Stan. Stan Lipsky."

"Never heard of you either." Cory winked. "What's your excuse?"

Stan laughed and shook Cory's hand. The elevator stopped and Cory guided them to a vantage point directly above the finish line. As they leaned against another railing, this one separating rows of seats from the aisle they stood in, the smell of cigarette and cigar smoke was quite pungent. Cory opened his notebook again and gazed at the odds board in the track infield.

"I don't see so well," Stan admitted. "Say I get this owner's license ... Would you pick out a horse?"

"Sure. If you want me to."

"We'd be kinda like a team."

"Guess you could say that," Cory answered, scribbling another note.

"Hey, I gotta go make a bet," Stan said abruptly, pulling out his Racing Form again.

Cory watched him shuffle off toward some betting windows. With racehorse ownership being so risky, one of a trainer's biggest concerns is keeping his clients financially alive. In this case, a more immediate goal might be just keeping his prospective client *alive*.

✦ ✦ ✦

Tracy Simmons walked rapidly toward Jack Dobson's tack room in the Hollywood Park stable area. She'd left her blue jacket there after shedding it earlier, once the morning warmed. She glanced at her watch. Almost ten. She quickened her pace to a virtual trot. One thing in her favor—at least it was Saturday and the traffic shouldn't be too bad during her long drive home.

She'd just dismounted her seventh and final horse of the morning, turning him over to his groom for bathing and cooling out. Normally she rode no more than five. She worked for Dobson, southern California's perennial leading trainer, as one of the main exercise riders for his second string at Santa Anita. Today, though, a rarity, she'd agreed to come to Hollywood Park, his primary locale, because two of his top riders here were unavailable this morning.

As she stepped inside the tiny tack room, the walls shook from the rumble of a jet flying overhead. Another reason, besides the distant drive, that she disliked coming here—Hollywood Park was directly beneath the flight pattern for LAX. She picked up her jacket and started for the door. Dobson entered the room at that moment and stood in the doorway.

"On your way out?" he asked, his words spoken slowly. He was around forty and could be considered attractive, his best attributes being a carefully trimmed mustache, tall muscular build and erect posture.

"Yes," she answered. "Told my kid I'd be home by now."

"Thanks for ... comin'."

She shrugged. Earlier, maybe her third horse, she'd detected that he'd slurred his instructions to her and walked a little shakily. Now the slur was more pronounced. Everyone knew that Dobson drank. But usually he began later in the day, during or after the races.

"You ... haven't seen ... my new place," he said.

"No, I haven't."

"We could have ... little party right now."

"Thanks. But I got to go."

"Wish you'd ... come over here more. My horses ... like you. I ... like you."

"Wish I could too, Mr. Dobson," she tried humoring him. "But the drive ..."

He kept standing in the doorway of the small room, blocking her exit. Now she smelled the alcohol on his breath. Combined with the odor of old training equipment in the room, it wasn't very pleasant. She wished that someone else would come, anyone, to divert his attention, so she could get out of here.

"Think ... just 'cause you're ... good lookin'," he slurred, "get special treatment."

"I told you when you hired me, Mr. Dobson, that I could only work at Santa Anita on account of my kid. I came here today because you said you needed me."

"When I hired you ... told me you needed ... the money."

"I do."

"Well ... I got plenty money ... all you gotta do ... be nice to me."

"Mr. Dobson," she said, becoming very impatient, "if you want me for more than an exercise rider ... then I can't work for you."

"Let's leave it at that," he declared, his words more distinct.

"At what?"

"That you can't work for me."

Another plane was flying overhead and she wasn't absolutely sure she'd heard him right. But she was sure enough and impatient enough and growing angry enough to walk hastily toward the door. She didn't care if she ran him over to get out of the room. In fact she did brush against him as she bolted through the doorway to the outside.

✦ ✦ ✦

All four of Cory and Carlos's horses ran during the first month of the Hollywood Park season. Their best placing was fifth. Since trainers normally get a share (usually ten percent) of purse money only for finishes of fourth or better, they earned nothing besides the "day money" charged owners for their horses' upkeep. To make things worse, two of the horses were claimed away from them.

Cory did have some good news. Thanks to Janice, his landlady living next door, Cookie was quite content. All Cookie (or Oreo, as Janice regularly called her) had to do was scratch on their mutual wall if she wanted company or a walk or food, and Janice was quick to oblige. In fact, when Cory returned after training or after the races, he often had trouble getting Cookie back to the cottage.

He did manage to occasionally coax her away from Janice, over to the beach, where the two of them relaxed on a bright orange blanket he'd bought. Actually they spent several non-racing afternoons there. But the instant they returned home, Cookie would scratch the wall for Janice.

"So far at Hollywood Park," Cory muttered to himself one evening Cookie was next door, "I've managed to make no money ... and lose two horses and one dog."

✦ ✦ ✦

"Don't like the looks that left knee," Cory informed Stan. The two of them stood exactly where they'd first met, at the railing of the Hollywood Park outdoor paddock.

"Worse than the last time you saw him?"

"Much. Must be why they're dropping him from that twenty. See that swelling?"

Not likely. Not with Stan's eyesight. Cory realized as much when he took another look at the thickness of the old man's eyeglass lenses. This afternoon Stan wore an outfit no less outrageous than the other occasion, but at least suitable for the warm weather: purple Bermuda shorts, white tee shirt, black tennis shoes and a green baseball cap. This guy, Cory determined, besides having poor vision, was undoubtedly color-blind.

The knee in question belonged to a tall angular gray named Lasting Impression, whose handlers were just beginning to saddle him. Cory had done some research last night and liked what he found. Especially the fact that the horse had six victories in his career, reminding Cory of Rugged Landing and his strong will to win. Thus Cory made a phone call to Stan this morning, to suggest they inspect the horse now.

Cory glanced at the odds board behind them and saw that Lasting Impression was three to one, second choice in the wagering. More importantly, he also saw that there were nineteen minutes to post. The claim form, which they'd already prepared, had to be deposited within three minutes.

"I say we pass," Cory advised.

"But I've had luck with grays," Stan countered. "Always bet least two bucks on 'em."

"So bet your two bucks. Not ten thousand. Plus sales tax."

"I like the way he looks. And I'm not getting any younger."

"It's your money." Cory shrugged, unable to refute Stan's comment regarding age.

"Anyway," Stan added. "For ten grand, we're not gonna get Seabiscuit."

"For sure."

The debate concluded, Cory signaled Stan to stay there while he hustled to drop the form into the claim box, near the finish line.

✦ ✦ ✦

"How much we get if he wins?" Stan asked.

"For your two-dollar bet?" Cory replied.

"No. For my ten grand."

"Nothing. I thought you knew. The old owner gets the purse money. We get the horse."

"No matter how he does?"

"Even if he breaks his leg," Cory felt compelled to reveal, despite it causing him an immediate pang for Rugged Landing.

They stood above the finish line, in the precise spot Cory had taken Stan during their other encounter. This time Stan had stopped off along the way to bet. At least two dollars on the gray, Cory assumed. It being a Sunday, the crowd was much larger and the cigarette and cigar smoke far more insidious.

As the field for the mile-and-a-sixteenth race approached the starting gate, also directly below them, Cory felt tense, normal for him when claiming a horse. Perhaps even more so today, since this was his first claim in California. And it was for a new client, one who'd never owned a horse before. He hoped they weren't making a dreadful mistake with this particular horse.

No question Stan was game, though, and might withstand disappointment. He hadn't so much as flinched earlier when Cory enumerated various expenses pertinent to horse ownership. Things like jockey fees, vet bills and vanning.

The horses entered the gate. One of them reared, briefly delaying the start. Lasting Impression broke nicely from his number-five post and took a position in mid-pack. Cory smiled slightly at the possibility that Stan liked grays because they were easier for him to see.

Unfortunately, Cory's smile didn't last long. As the horses went from the clubhouse turn to the backstretch, Lasting Impression dropped back steadily. Sixth, seventh, eighth in the ten-horse field. By the far turn, Cory wished that the heavy cigarette and cigar smoke would obliterate the entire race. Turning into the stretch, Lasting Impression had only one horse beaten. That horse passed him too, by mid-stretch. Lasting Impression barely struggled across the finish line, dead last.

"That him back there?" Stan asked.

"'Fraid so," Cory glumly replied.

"One thing's sure."

"What?" Cory murmured, almost fearing the answer.

"We didn't miss out on any purse money. Horse didn't make any."

Cory couldn't help but laugh.

"Another thing," Stan said.

"Yeah?"

"Didn't break a leg."

"Right," Cory agreed. "He did finish the race. And long as we're looking for positives, maybe we'll have to shake."

Stan glanced at him questioningly. Cory motioned him to follow, gesturing that he would soon provide explanation.

✦ ✦ ✦

"Number one is Andrews," the claim judge declared, pointing at Cory. "Number two is Dobson."

Cory knew Jack Dobson's appearance from watching him saddle horses, and recognized that the youthful Hispanic standing next to the official wasn't him, but one of his assistants. Cory's search for a positive had materialized—they did have to shake. On their way to the claim box, next to which they now stood, Cory had informed Stan that when two or more claims are submitted for a specific horse, a dice shake determines the new owner. The judge, a rotund woman whose face appeared pushed in, dropped two numbered dice into a brown container that looked like a large mug, and shook it vigorously. She pulled out one die.

"Number one," she announced, displaying the die. "Andrews."

✦ ✦ ✦

"Want the good news first?" Cory asked Stan via phone the next morning. "Or the bad?"

"The good. Might not live long enough for the bad."

"Okay ... He should be good as new."

"When?"

"That's the bad news," Cory said, tapping a corner of the desk in Carlos and his barn office.

"What is?"

"He needs an operation."

"On the swollen knee?"

"Yep. Bone chips in there. Need to clean them out."

"How long before he races?" Stan inquired.

"All goes well," Cory speculated, "Santa Anita. Maybe ... this October."

"This October!" Stan exclaimed, raising his voice. "Might as well say this century."

But he quickly calmed down and seemed to accept the idea, which pleased Cory. A lot of owners would lobby against an operation and want to run the horse right away. Likely causing greater injury and ruining any chance to recoup their investment.

"After the operation, he'll go to a farm," Cory explained. "To convalesce."

"Out in the country?"

"Right. One of my Arizona clients used to race here. I'll call him for a recommendation. Unless you know of a place ..."

"Me?" Stan retorted. "I'm a city guy. Don't know nothin' 'bout farms."

CHAPTER 4

PERRY STOOD IN LEFT FIELD. Because of his tee-ball league's designated hitter rule, he hadn't had to play while his team, the Orioles, were on defense. Until now, that is, when the regular left fielder suddenly took sick and Perry was the only available substitute.

It was the bottom of the sixth, the last inning, and the Orioles led the Red Sox 12-10. There were two outs, with Red Sox runners on first and second. Perry tried to concentrate on the ball on the tee as the batter swung. But the sun was facing him and it was a very hot June day. Sweat was dripping into his eyes and the ball was so far away. He could hardly see it with his only one sighted eye.

The batter hit the ball and it flew down the left-field line. Perry never saw it as it landed a few feet fair and rolled all the way to the tall green fence surrounding the field. He didn't move. By the time the center fielder ran over to retrieve the ball at the fence, the two runners had scored and the batter circled the bases. The game was over, the Orioles had lost 13-12.

Perry wasn't sure what had occurred, and still didn't move. He heard the Red Sox players shouting gleefully and his own teammates yelling too. Except they were yelling at him. His coach, the same large man who'd instructed him during the tryout weeks ago, came jogging up to him.

"What happened?" he asked, towering above Perry.

The boy didn't answer. He was confused and still wasn't certain what had taken place. All he knew for sure was that there was a lot of shouting and jeering, and he seemed to be the focal point.

"I don't think you should be playing in this league," the coach declared. He raised his hand and arm to his head, as though he were going to hit Perry in frustration.

Perry started running. He headed toward center field, until the fence blocked his path. He veered toward right field. Then he saw his mother, standing near first base. He ran toward her. There was still lots of shouting and yelling. When he got to her, she put her arms around him. The coach trotted over, wiping his brow, baseball cap in hand.

"Sorry, ma'am," he said. "He can't play on this team anymore."

"Why?" she asked, arms still around Perry. "Because he didn't see the ball?"

"No, ma'am. Because he ran away from me. We can't have players running away from their coaches."

"You raised your arm. I think he thought you were going to hit him."

"Coaches don't hit players."

"I know that and you know that," she calmly asserted. "I'm not sure he does."

"He does now, ma'am."

"Maybe there's a reason he ran away from you."

"Someone hit him?" the coach guessed.

She stood there silently for a moment. The noise from the other kids, although diminished, hadn't stopped. The sun slipped behind a cloud, offering brief relief from the heat.

"I wish you'd reconsider," she said softly.

"He could hurt himself out there, ma'am."

"That's a chance we'll have to take."

Her arm was still around the boy as the two of them began to walk to her car.

✦ ✦ ✦

"Looks like you're pretty handy. Don't see too many two-man operations 'round here anymore."

Cory had just dismounted after exercising their second and final horse when the man addressed him. Cory turned the horse over to Carlos to bathe before going to their barn office to get a jacket to counteract a chilling fog. Then he walked over to near where the man was standing, against a security light pole in front of the barn.

Besides the guy's obvious arrogance, Cory didn't especially like his looks. He had the body of someone who might have been a professional football linebacker about ten years ago. Or a bouncer for a saloon now. Solid foundation for the abundant jewelry he displayed. His eyes and wavy hair were dark, and his nose was flat. The beige slacks and sweater he wore seemed far too stylish for early morning at a racetrack.

"What can I do for you?" Cory asked brusquely.

"It's what I can do for you."

"Oh?"

"Double your stable."

"Oh?"

"Right. Two new horses. A groom who also hot walks. Plus an exercise rider. All at no cost to you."

"What's the catch?" Cory questioned.

The guy shrugged.

"Let me guess," Cory proceeded. "You want me to claim two bad horses."

The guy shrugged again. Cory suspected one of the oldest racetrack scams in existence. Two trainers get together, one with horses he wants to get rid of, and the other with unsuspecting owners eager to buy. One trainer offers the other commission for claiming his bad horses.

"Why don't you work it out with the other people involved?" Cory bristled.

"Reputation."

"What about my reputation?"

"You don't have one … here," the guy answered.

"What's the point? For two horses that can't run."

"Like I said," the guy replied. "You get a groom who can hot walk. And an exercise rider. All at no cost to you."

"We already do that ourselves," Cory retorted. "Like you said … we're the last of the two-man operations."

"Plus I got a good vet," the man stated.

"I got one too."

"Mine'll get your horses to run faster."

"Meaning?"

"You figure it out."

"Drugs?" Cory asked, knowing the answer.

"You figure it out."

"Not interested."

"Not interested in your horses running faster?"

"Not interested in drugs," Cory declared.

"Must have plenty of money."

"Yeah," Cory muttered. "Plenty of money."

Cory noticed, as Carlos bathed their horse, that some of the water from the hose he was using sprayed off the horse, close to this guy. He considered suggesting they move. He also thought about alerting Carlos. In both cases, he decided against.

"You own the horses you're talking about?" he asked.

"I'm the agent."

"Who are the trainers?"

"Makes no difference."

This time it was Cory who silently shrugged. Really, what he wanted was for this conversation to end. Carlos could use his help because their horse was beginning to buck.

"Too bad about that horse you claimed," the guy said.

"What's that got to do with this?"

"Nothing. Just thought you could use a little boost."

"Getting two horses who can't run isn't my idea of a boost," Cory stated angrily. "Even if you bring us a hundred more. And the crew to go with them."

"Suit yourself." As the man turned to leave, some of his jewelry jiggled noticeably. And some of the spray from the horse's bath landed on his elegant sweater.

✦ ✦ ✦

"Congratulations," Cory told Carlos, raising his glass of wine to Carlos's glass, in toast. "Better days ahead."

The two of them had already ordered dinner in a pleasant Playa del Rey seafood restaurant not far from Cory's cottage. Although true that Cory rarely drank alcohol, this was a special occasion. Finally, earlier that day, the Fourth of July, after ten straight finishes out of the money by their horses, they hit the board. Not much of a dent—a stretch-running fourth-place finish—but enough of one for Cory to invite Carlos to celebrate.

Loud popping noises were audible in the background. When they'd asked their waiter, he told them they were from a local fireworks display. Cory recognized the irony—fireworks couldn't have been less symbolic of Carlos and his performance so far at Hollywood Park.

"I hope you are right, Boss. That we will have better days ahead."

Cory might have made light of Carlos's statement by saying it was almost mathematically impossible for them to do worse than one measly fourth-place finish from eleven opportunities. But Carlos's serious tone suggested that he tread softly. Their waiter delivering their salads served to delay any immediate response, yet Cory realized he needed to address their mutual financial plight.

"I know I dragged us over here," he began once the waiter left.

"No," Carlos disagreed. "It was time for us to take a chance."

"But we didn't have to come *here*."

"Wherever we go, Boss, we take a chance. And I do not have to come."

"Maybe we'll get lucky at Del Mar."

"We will still go to Del Mar? With only two horses?"

Cory didn't reply. A piece of crouton from his salad had lodged between two of his teeth, and he tried to poke it out with his tongue. Plus the thought ran through his mind that maybe he'd been too hasty turning down that guy about the two horses—without even talking to Carlos.

"We can go back to Arizona, Boss."

Cory grimaced—much less at the piece of crouton still stuck than the prospect of Arizona. An especially loud firecracker popped in the background.

✦ ✦ ✦

The gray, late-afternoon overcast hovering over his beach cottage was welcome relief for Cory. He and Cookie had just spent a long day in sweltering heat. They'd driven to the Santa Ynez Valley, about a hundred and forty miles northwest of L.A., to check on Stan's horse, Lasting Impression, at the farm where Cory had sent him. Even the beauty of the place and surrounding region had failed to neutralize the oppressiveness of the weather.

During their return trip, Cory had listened to a radio station that reported the local temperature at a hundred and two, which of course reminded him of Arizona—and how much he didn't want to go back. Yet he knew Carlos was right—that two horses, plus one at the farm still months away from a race, were no arsenal for a premier track like Del Mar. But he also knew that if he had any doubt about going there, today's heat had erased it.

Even Cookie seemed relieved as they drove up in front of the cottage. Of course that probably had less to do with the weather than the likelihood she'd soon be seeing Janice.

✦ ✦ ✦

"How'd he look?" Stan asked Cory the next afternoon at their regular spot alongside the Hollywood Park paddock.

"Like an allowance horse."

"Yeah?"

"Yeah. That knee is tight. No sign of swelling. And cool to the touch. Much cooler than the weather up there."

"How long before a race?"

"Let's stay with our plan. October. He's put on a little weight, but not too much. Should be able to get him in shape by then."

"No sooner?"

"'Fraid not."

The old man mumbled something under his breath. Today's outfit was slightly more restrained than on the other two occasions. It featured a navy-blue beret and red polka-dotted tie. Neither seemed appropriate for what was a warm afternoon, but Stan's attire never seemed appropriate.

"When we gonna claim another horse?" the old man asked.

"You mean our first one didn't scare you off?"

"Nah. Old horseplayer like me. What's a little adversity?"

"Don't want to run you out of money."

"Can't take it with me," Stan proclaimed. Then he crinkled up his Racing Form, nodded good-bye to Cory and shuffled off toward some betting windows.

PART THREE

DEL MAR

CHAPTER 5

DEL MAR WAS LOVE AT FIRST SIGHT for Cory. Both in terms of the racetrack complex itself and the picturesque seaside village about a mile away. Everything seemed ethereal to someone who'd never been west of Arizona until recently.

Opening day at the track was incredible. Many of the more than forty-four thousand present (the largest crowd at a California track in several years) were elegantly attired. Hats were the primary theme, with the track offering prizes for various categories. When the horses in the first race broke from the starting gate directly in front of the grandstand, a huge roar sprung up from the crowd. The Del Mar racing season was underway.

Cory loved the Spanish décor of the predominantly light-brown grandstand structure. And the view from the seats at the west end was spectacular, particularly of white surf and lavish homes perched on a bluff. Cool breezes transported the scent of fresh Pacific air.

The village, to the south, was a pedestrian's delight. Cory felt like a tourist (which he, along with legions of others, undoubtedly was) as he surveyed from the sidewalk numerous restaurants and shops. He also found himself often wandering through the lobby of an extravagant hotel near the village center.

Again, at least initially, he felt lucky about the accommodations he managed to secure—an economical bungalow behind a house. However, on further evaluation, he realized the place was no more than a converted garage. And he soon ascertained the reason for its economy—trains roared by at all hours of the day and night.

Predictably, besides the trains, he encountered one other significant problem. Cookie. She didn't want to leave L.A. He practically had to kidnap her from Janice's place—and swear to both of them that they would visit Janice sometime during the short, seven-week Del Mar season.

The first few days in the new abode, Cookie continually sulked. She even tried scratching the walls. And of course steadfastly refused to provide wake-up service.

✦ ✦ ✦

"The news isn't good, Stan."

"Fire away, Doc."

"It's spread from your lungs. If we'd caught this sooner, we could do more."

Sitting in the cancer specialist's drab office, Stan was speechless for one of the few times in his life. Eighty-three years, sick hardly a day. Good heart, low blood pressure, cholesterol fine, and he hadn't smoked in forty years. He felt so good, in fact, that he'd almost canceled his physical three weeks ago, even though he'd put off having one for five years. His doctor hadn't liked the sound of his breathing, ordered some chest x-rays and sent him to the oncologist. Today was his second visit here.

"How long I got?" Stan asked, finally breaking his silence.

"Hard to tell. Maybe a year."

Stan didn't reply. What was there to say? He hardly paid attention as the doctor briefly outlined treatment options, then handed him some printed material. His focus was out a window, at a billboard across the street, advertising Hollywood Park. That's where he wanted to be, for the Del Mar simulcast. Away from this miserable topic. He had four horses picked out in the first-race superfecta. Four juicy long shots.

When the doctor finally finished, Stan rushed out of the office. He didn't even take the printed material with him.

✦ ✦ ✦

Del Mar wasn't on Tracy Simmons's radar. Nor was Hollywood Park. And, it seemed lately, she hardly even went to Santa Anita, practically walking distance from her apartment, and where she'd worked the last five or six years as an exercise rider. Where she was now, early in the morning, going barn to barn, seeking employment—which she'd tried to do at least once a week, without much luck, during the nearly three months since her confrontation with Jack Dobson.

Oh, she'd found a sporadic horse here and there. An immature two-year-old or a rogue no one else wanted to ride. But nothing steady. Nothing she could count on.

"Got anything today, Warren?" she greeted a trainer sitting in his barn office. He had a large stable and she knew him well because she'd been one of his regular riders years ago.

"Nothing, Tracy."

"What about later? Any your people going on vacation or needing couple days off?"

"Sorry, Tracy."

"Sorry, Tracy," she muttered to herself after she'd turned to walk away.

Maybe she should go on home. Wasn't she wasting her time here? It was clear what had happened. Dobson had blacklisted her, badmouthing her to other trainers. Probably made up some stories. Not that she could prove anything. She merely sensed it from the way people looked at her.

There was one good thing out of all this—she had more time for her painting. But painting didn't pay the bills. Not with sales so infrequent and the escalating cost of art supplies.

She walked toward another barn of a trainer she knew. Maybe he needed someone for today. Or tomorrow, or the next day. Or even next week.

✦ ✦ ✦

Stan hadn't planned on going to Del Mar either. Not when he could so easily bet the Del Mar races at Hollywood Park. But when Cory had called to invite him to see Lasting Impression—a recent arrival from the farm—work out tomorrow morning, he'd jumped on the next possible train, a noon departure from downtown L.A.

At Solana Beach, the closest station to Del Mar, he transferred onto a large red English-style double-decker bus, which took train passengers to the racetrack. He had to climb up stairs to the second deck, outside in the open air, to claim the last available seat. When the bus, old and rickety, lurched forward to begin its brief trip, engine fumes caused him to cough loudly.

"Like anyone today?" he asked a young man sitting next to him, once he recovered enough to speak.

"Yeah," grumbled the man, dark-complected and gazing at a crumpled racing program. "Horse in the first. Horse in the second."

"Didn't they already run those races?"

"Yeah. And both horses won. My luck, they made me stay over and work the lunch shift. Woulda hit the double."

"Know how you feel. Can't tell you how many times I been shut outta winners."

The young guy didn't reply—which in no way discouraged Stan, even with his seatmate never looking up from his program.

"You do restaurant work?" he babbled on.

"Lousy buffet. Hardly any tips. 'Cept buncha bad ones ... on losing horses."

Stan laughed. He liked this kid. Reminded him of himself when he was young. The bus hit a bump and he had to grab the red and blue cap he was wearing, to prevent it falling off.

"Only good thing about the place," the young man stated, "is I only work the breakfast shift. Most days. Frees me up for the track."

"Hey ... you look like that golfer. What's his name?"

"Tiger Woods," the young guy answered disinterestedly. He was still gazing at his program.

"Yeah," Stan enthused. "Tiger Woods."

The young man became busy marking his program—very intently, as if not wanting to be interrupted, which of course only encouraged Stan.

"Hey ... You like anything else today?"

"Afraid I already had my two winners," the guy muttered.

"Maybe you're good for one more."

"Doubt it ... But try ... Fruit Cocktail in the fifth."

"Yeah? He wins, drinks on me."

Though his companion continued marking his program, Stan proceeded to tell him about Lasting Impression, about the workout tomorrow, and Cory. How the two of them were going to transform this ten-thousand-dollar claimer into another Seabiscuit. Or at the very least, an allowance horse. His seatmate showed absolutely no interest, and when the bus jerked to a stop near the racetrack admission gates, the kid immediately got up and, noticeably limping, walked toward the stairs.

"Hey," Stan yelled after him. "What's your name?"

"Just call me Tiger," he growled over his shoulder.

✦ ✦ ✦

Lasting Impression didn't look like an allowance horse to Stan when Stan got to the barn the following morning. No, he looked much more like a stakes horse, the top category at any track. But Stan's evaluation was undoubtedly more a reflection of his own mood than the horse's appearance. Possibly influenced by the doctor's grim diagnosis, he'd treated himself to a nice dinner last night and deluxe hotel room right across the street from the track. And the air this morning was invigoratingly fresh and cool.

Carlos now sat beside him near the top of some bleachers overlooking the backstretch of the track, adjacent to the stable area. Other owners and trainers were sitting close by. Stan noticed a stopwatch in Carlos's hand.

The track was alive with activity. Some horses, riders aboard, were racing at full speed along the inner rail. Others galloped at lesser speeds, in the center of the track. Still more were jogging slowly near the outer rail, going clockwise instead of the normal direction. When Carlos pointed to Lasting Impression as Cory rode him onto the track near them, the gray horse was snorting and kicking his hind legs in the air.

"Must not like crowds," Stan quipped. "Just like me."

"No." Carlos grinned. "He is doing that because he is happy to be here, at the track."

"Just like me," Stan laughed.

"Today is his first breeze. Cory will take him three furlongs. Very, very slow."

Stan smiled, as if he knew exactly what Carlos was saying. Cory was wearing a white shirt and Stan tried to follow it as the horse sped up. But he soon lost it. He attempted to locate a gray horse, however there was just too much traffic on the track. He did hear Carlos click his stopwatch, though, so he tried to mimic Carlos's gaze. When he heard Carlos click his watch again, he assumed the workout was over, so he nodded approvingly, as if pleased with what he had seen.

Which in this case, he hadn't.

✦ ✦ ✦

By the time Stan and Carlos had walked back to the barn, Cory was already there. With a hose in one hand and Lasting Impression's reins in the other, he was giving the gray a bath. Carlos got a sponge and soap, and went over to help. Evidently relishing the attention, Lasting Impression resumed the snorting and kicking he'd displayed on the track.

"Looks like he go good, Boss. I time him in thirty-seven and change."

"He went great." Cory winked at Stan.

"So," Stan noted, playing along, "maybe you *can* buy Seabiscuit for ten grand."

"Sure," Cory chuckled. "And the next horse we claim is … Cigar."

"Nah," Stan cracked. "Secretariat."

Cory laughed heartily. Neither Seabiscuit nor Cigar won a single triple crown race. Secretariat won all three, decades ago, one of the last horses to accomplish the feat.

✦ ✦ ✦

As the early-evening train neared Oceanside, some fifteen miles north of Del Mar, James "Tiger" Leonard finally decided to sit down. The middle seat in a row of three had been vacant since he boarded in Solana Beach, but he hadn't felt like being sandwiched between the two men already sitting in that row. Not until now, when his bad knee began to ache.

"Hey Tiger," the man next to the window greeted him once he'd sat down. Tiger turned and saw the old guy from yesterday, wearing the same thick eyeglasses and red and blue cap.

"Yeah," Tiger grumbled.

"Too bad about Fruit Cocktail."

"Right."

"Catch anything today?"

"Nah. Only winners I had all week were those two I told you about. The ones I didn't bet."

"Been playin' horses long?"

"Too long," Tiger muttered, wishing this old guy would shut up. He saw a couple of ants crawling on the back of the seat in front of him, reminding him of his tiny room, where ants seemingly were permanent residents.

"Young guy like you should be in school."

"Supposed to be. Stanford. Football scholarship."

"What happened?"

"Last game in high school, blew out my knee."

"That why you got that limp?"

"Yeah," Tiger replied, almost under his breath. He grabbed a Racing Form from a satchel he was carrying and flipped it to tomorrow's entries. Maybe this guy would take a hint and finally shut up.

"So you turned to horses," Stan persisted.

Tiger merely shrugged. So Stan proceeded to tell him about Lasting Impression's workout that morning. How he definitely would become another Seabiscuit. How the next horse they claimed would become another Secretariat. Then he invited Tiger to see Lasting Impression run at Santa Anita in October.

"Hey," he went on enthusiastically, "maybe you could do what I'm doing."

"What?" Tiger asked disinterestedly, relieved that the train was finally slowing down for his stop.

"Try owning a horse."

"With what?"

Tiger pulled out his wallet and emphatically opened it. No money. Stan immediately took out his wallet, extracted a hundred-dollar bill and handed it to Tiger.

"What's this for?"

"For reminding me of myself when I was a kid."

"You know what I'll do with it."

"Course I know what you'll do with it. Same as I did when I was your age. But I hope you'll buy yourself a nice meal first."

"Thanks," he said to Stan and put the bill in his wallet.

Tiger got up before the train came to a halt. He was the first one onto the platform outside. As he began to walk in the dark toward his room, he took a deep breath.

At least he had money to bet with at tomorrow's races.

✦ ✦ ✦

As he got into bed later that night, what amazed Stan most about his two-day jaunt to Del Mar was that, until now, he hardly even thought about the doctor's grim diagnosis.

CHAPTER 6

"I LEFT WITH FOUR HORSES," Bill Donley informed Cory one afternoon via cell phone. "Now I got six."

"Sounds like New Mexico agrees with you."

"Nah. All the quarter-horse and state-bred races these suckers got here, hardly anyplace to run. These nice purses don't do me no good."

"Too bad."

Not that Cory cared. He hadn't heard from Donley in nearly five months, since Rugged Landing's final day. Plus he had his own problems. During the last couple of weeks, Carlos and his stable had decreased by the same number Donley's had increased. Their two active runners, while finishing off the board, were both claimed from them, leaving only Lasting Impression in the barn, still several weeks from a race.

"You want my horses to train, you can have them," Donley offered.

"Here?"

"No, no. Phoenix. Four, five weeks from now. Soon as their meet begins."

"Have to let you know."

"Don't wait too long," Donley warned.

Cory mumbled a good-bye and closed his phone. Carlos had left for Mexico earlier that day and Lasting Impression needed to be fed.

✦ ✦ ✦

A particularly loud train awakened Cory late that night and he had trouble falling back asleep. No question by now, having been here more than five weeks, he'd gotten used to the sound of trains roaring by, but Donley's offer kept running through his mind. He was certainly familiar enough with Donley's impatience to know that his admonition about waiting was no idle threat.

Of course he could confer with Carlos by phone. Really, he *should* confer with Carlos by phone. Except they had a tacit understanding that Cory wouldn't bother him with business while he was visiting his family. His family was almost sacred territory. Consequently, any decision was Cory's to make.

He had to admit that, with the Del Mar season winding down, the timing of Donley's offer was good. They'd soon have to move anyway (to Santa Anita), so why not consider Turf Paradise now, instead? No doubt, despite being away all this time, he and Carlos could still assemble a decent stable there. To Donley's six horses, they could probably add eight or ten from other local former clients—and be back to being big fish in a small pond.

But that would mean giving up on California—and trading Stan, someone he liked, for Donley, someone he didn't. Plus he'd leaped over some kind of crucial imaginary line when he crossed the desert those months ago. He liked California, it was still fresh to him. He felt alive here, the staleness from all the years in Arizona had vanished.

Yet there was one unavoidable defect to his logic. He and Carlos hadn't come close to making a living here. What would they do if they couldn't? Become assistant trainers for other barns? Or exercise riders? Even grooms? All jobs they'd each done before.

But was that why they'd come here? No, they came to make a change. For the challenge. To test themselves in their profession. If they couldn't make it, shouldn't they just go back? Cross that line again, the desert, return to where they'd come from.

Cory heard another train roar by. It sounded even louder than the one that had awakened him.

✦ ✦ ✦

Everything looked the same as Carlos carried his little suitcase from the bus depot toward his house. Each home, each tree, even the pebbles on the dirt road seemed exactly how he remembered them from his youth. The long, arduous bus ride to his tiny village outside

Monterrey, Mexico—now increased from about twenty-four to over thirty hours because of the move to California—hadn't changed much either, especially below the border. Parched desert, arid farms and ranches, dusty little towns. In Mexico, only the big cities showed much progress, mostly in the form of modern buildings.

If his mood were somber, it was caused partly by the numbness in his feet and the aches in his legs and back from the lengthy journey. But mostly because he regretted sending home so little money lately. Barely enough for his family to survive.

During the past decade, he usually came home before and after the Turf Paradise meeting—in early October and late May—and over Christmas. This visit was about a month early since, with Lasting Impression not slated to run until October at Santa Anita, Cory wanted him to go now.

His mood changed when he saw the house. White with black trim below the roof and around the windows and doors, it was built originally by his grandfather more than sixty years ago. Two total rebuildings and several upgrades had been performed since, and he, Carlos, was involved in all of them.

Climbing the steps to the front porch, he imagined his wife's face. As he'd done so many times during the journey. Alicia, the only woman he'd ever known in any significant way. The only woman he'd ever really wanted to know.

Instead of simply going into the house, he knocked at the door. Something he always did the first time after being away. After all, wasn't he no more than a stranger here? Merely someone who sent home money from a distant land?

The door opened. Luisa, his ten-year-old, looked up at him. Rosa, two years her senior, came running to the door.

"Papa, Papa," they called out excitedly, in unison.

He saw Alicia standing across the living room, smiling. It would be several days before he'd have to begin the long trip back.

✦ ✦ ✦

"There anything you good at?" a red-haired boy sneered at Perry, who had been sitting off by himself near a corner of his school playground.

He didn't answer. What was the point? The three boys who'd approached him were older, bigger and stronger than he. And they were just trying to provoke him.

"Everyone laughs at you playing baseball," the redhead continued.

"Too chicken for football," another kid, wearing a brown cap, chimed in.

"Can't see to shoot baskets," the third, his appearance marred by a black eye, laughed.

"I know what he's good at," the redhead jeered. "He's good at blind man's bluff."

They all laughed. All except Perry. Who wasn't going to cry, either. Or run away as he had after the tee-ball game. Even if they looked like they were going to hit him.

It was the first day of school. Perry was starting third grade. His mother had packed him a sandwich, and he'd been eating it during lunch period when the threesome surrounded him and literally slapped the sandwich out of his mouth, all over the ground.

"Maybe he's good at running," the black-eyed boy teased. "Been doing it all his life."

The boy with the brown cap pinched Perry's cheek. Perry was afraid the tears would start. He noticed four or five other kids gathered nearby, watching them. Maybe he'd better say something or these three might bully him some more. Beat him up in front of all the other kids on the very first day of school.

"Maybe I *am* good at running," he managed.

"Sure," the redhead guffawed. "When someone's chasing you."

"Maybe I *am* good at running," Perry repeated.

"Sounds like he wants to race," the kid with the brown hat chortled.

"Give him a head start," the redhead offered. "We catch him, we kick his ass."

"No head start," Perry said, still fighting back tears. "All of us race. I win, you leave me alone. From now on."

"Why bother?" the black-eyed boy countered. "Why not kick his ass right here?"

"You guys chicken?" Perry retorted, mustering all his courage. "I win, you leave me alone."

The three boys giggled and nodded. The redhead, using his foot, marked a line in the playground dirt, their starting point. Then he gestured toward the basketball court on the other side of the playground, about a hundred yards away.

"First one there wins."

About a dozen kids were now watching. The kid with the brown cap pounded his chest so they could see. Perry moved to the starting line and the three others slowly joined him. A couple of the kids watching shouted something, but Perry couldn't understand what they said.

"On your mark," the redhead announced loudly, so the spectators could hear. "Get set ... Go!"

Perry took off like he had an engine somewhere on his anatomy. By the time the three others got serious, he was ten yards ahead. The spectators were all yelling. The redhead began to gain. Perry could feel himself tiring, his breathing becoming labored and his legs growing wobbly. As they neared the basketball court, the redhead pulled within three yards. He made one late surge. But too late, Perry had already reached the court.

He didn't stop there. He ran straight into the school, directly to his classroom.

✦ ✦ ✦

"You don't have to see well to run fast," Perry explained to his mother during dinner that evening, once he'd recounted the race.

She nodded in agreement.

"When they said go," he elaborated. "I closed my eyes and didn't open them until the race was over."

PART FOUR

SANTA ANITA

CHAPTER 7

IT WAS SLIGHTLY AFTER DAWN as Cory rode Lasting Impression from their barn toward the track, and he eagerly anticipated his first glimpse of Santa Anita. He'd heard so much about it and its picturesque setting. An overnight downpour—unusual for September, he was told by the gateman—had muddied the stable area, but also cleared the air of any haze or smog.

If yesterday were any indication, Cory sensed that his luck was about to change. After leaving Del Mar, he'd finally taken Cookie to see Janice, as he'd promised before departing L.A. seven weeks ago. The visit led to a continuation of his ease with finding accommodations when Janice referred him to a friend who selectively rented a large old trailer behind his house near Santa Anita. Not only was it inexpensive and furnished, but between its single big room and tiny bathroom, it had a little alcove that Cookie could crawl into for some privacy. They'd moved in last night.

A lovely sunrise welcomed Cory and Lasting Impression as they left the stable area and approached the track. Cory immediately got goose bumps at the scene before him. Lush green infield, splendid flowers and majestic encompassing mountains out of which the magnificent turf course seemed to extend.

Even with the early hour, the track was abuzz with activity and the horses looked elegant in the setting. Cory needed no more evidence than this to justify not going back to Arizona. Regardless of Carlos and his finances. Regardless of their failure to come close to winning a single race in California.

Lasting Impression was apparently excited to be at Santa Anita too. When Cory guided him onto the track, near the top of the stretch, he initiated his normal routine of snorting and kicking. Solely wanting to familiarize him with their new surroundings, Cory broke him off into a very light jog, clockwise along the outer rail. Two horses were breezing in tandem near the inner rail and Lasting Impression gawked at them. Then he elected to add jumping to his repertoire. A short one to begin with, followed by a longer leap.

They rounded the stretch turn in reverse of the normal direction and reached the backstretch. The sun was shining straight at them. Cory raised his right hand to shield his eyes. Lasting Impression opted to embellish upon his new stunt with a hop, then a lengthy jump. He stumbled slightly while landing, however. Cory lost his balance. He tried to regain it by grabbing the horse's mane. It was too late, though. He tumbled hard to the ground.

Lasting Impression immediately ran off in the same clockwise direction. Cory rolled over under the rail, instinctively trying to protect himself against any approaching horses. He quickly got to his feet on the other side of the rail and dusted himself off. He looked around, hoping no one had witnessed the incident. The sound of the "loose horse" buzzer blaring all over the track informed him otherwise. More bad news—his right wrist hurt. Pride mightn't be his only injury. Though he wasn't about to show pain by shaking it.

With his other arm, he waved off an oncoming ambulance crew. On his very first day at this particular track, were he bleeding to death, he'd probably decline medical attention.

Where was his horse? Shielding his eyes from the sun with his left hand, he looked up the backstretch in the direction Lasting Impression had run off. His question was answered summarily. An outrider on horseback was approaching in the center of the track, leading the gray, who was still snorting and kicking. Only the jumping aspect of his repertoire was missing.

"You okay?" the outrider called out to Cory.

"I'm okay. How 'bout him?"

"He's fine. Looks like he enjoyed himself."

Cory muttered something made inaudible by the continuing blare of the "loose horse" buzzer.

"Want me to pony him back to your barn?" the outrider asked.

"Please."

Of course Cory would have preferred simply to get on his horse and ride him back to the barn himself. But his wrist was throbbing and he knew he couldn't. He glumly gave the outrider his barn number and began to follow him on foot, trying not to show pain. Finally the "loose horse" buzzer stopped.

As he walked, Cory couldn't help pondering his conception that his luck was about to change. It *had* changed. It had gotten worse.

✦ ✦ ✦

"Your boss is a jerk," Cory told Carlos once he'd trudged back to the barn.

Carlos didn't reply and Cory realized that he, Cory, didn't have to reveal what had happened. Carlos already knew. Either the outrider had told him or the conclusion was obvious from Lasting Impression returning to the barn riderless. Whichever, Carlos had already attached the horse to the hot walking machine and the gray was now practicing the jumping component of his routine.

Although Cory still didn't want to admit to injury, even to Carlos, he continually shook his wrist. Carlos took a tub of ice intended for Lasting Impression and placed it on the desk in their little office, then motioned Cory to sit down beside it. Cory could see how swollen the wrist was. All he needed was for it to be broken.

"Better me than the horse," he grumbled, trying to console himself as he immersed his wrist in the ice.

Carlos shook his head.

"What a way to break in at a place like this," Cory lamented.

"You forgive me, Boss ... I think you make a ... *lasting impression.*"

Cory could only grimace at his compadre's sense of humor.

✦ ✦ ✦

Cory's wrist was sprained, not broken, according to their veterinarian. No treatment required, except ice. No riding for at least three weeks. Which meant Cory would have to hire someone to exercise their horse. Unless Carlos did it and they got someone to help around the barn. Either solution would add to their financial strain.

Cory chose the former because Carlos was so familiar with their barn routine. Plus Cory wouldn't feel so useless. Instead of just standing around the barn overseeing someone, at least he could follow an exercise rider to the track and watch their horse train.

✦ ✦ ✦

"Thought you might need a rider," a young woman greeted Cory the next morning when he got to the barn. "Till your wrist heals."

He didn't reply. Not because his wrist had hurt so much overnight that he was now groggy from lack of sleep. Nor because he wanted to be rude. No, he didn't reply because she was beautiful. Not showy, pretentious beauty, but more the natural unassuming kind. Sandy-blond hair, light-green eyes. Late twenties. Lean athletic figure in tan jeans, white sweatshirt and dark-brown boots.

"How you know about my wrist?" he managed.

"Not many secrets around a racetrack."

He couldn't dispute that. Anyway, he'd prefer to drop the subject. Especially if the entire local population knew the current status of his right wrist and what happened his very first morning at Santa Anita.

"Used to exercise Lasting Impression," she declared.

"He's a handful." Cory warned.

"I can handle him."

Almost on cue, Carlos led Lasting Impression, ready for the track, out of his stall. She put on a tan helmet, strode confidently over to the gray and patted him on the side of his head. Cory simply stood there, as though he had no choice in whether she worked for them. It was Carlos who helped her aboard. Probably wise, since even in peak condition Cory might've fumbled the assignment, acquiring another blemish on his Santa Anita record.

"Just a simple gallop," he spoke softly, beginning to follow her and the horse toward the track. "Once around. And be careful."

"Piece of cake." She winked back at him.

Although the morning was chilly, Cory felt himself perspiring under his shirt. The roadway was crowded with other horses and riders, yet Lasting Impression seemed on good behavior. No snorting and kicking. And absolutely no jumping. At first Cory was concerned that he wasn't feeling well, but he quickly recognized that Carlos would've alerted him to anything wrong.

He selected a vantage point on some steps leading up to the grandstand, near the top of the stretch. He watched closely as she guided the gray onto the track and soon broke him into a canter, then a full gallop. Still no shenanigans from Lasting Impression. Cory liked her riding style, head next to the horse's, as if she were whispering in his ear. She appeared to fit him perfectly, to be firmly in control, in sync with his gait while maneuvering the reins with strong hands and arms. After they'd gone around the track, she pulled him up easily, the horse still not exhibiting any of his usual antics.

"Doesn't mess with you like he does with me," Cory acknowledged, looking up at her after joining her and Lasting Impression, coming off the track.

"I reminded him of the little talks we used to have ... about his behavior."

"Yeah?"

"He remembered."

"How do you know?" Cory asked, a little amused.

"You just pretty much said so yourself."

Cory laughed. He was definitely impressed. Though much less with her apparent ability to converse with horses than her obvious riding skill.

"I could use someone tomorrow morning too," he ventured.

"And the next day?"

"Then too."

"One thing," she said as they got back to the barn. "Weekdays I drive my kid to school. Have to leave by seven thirty."

"With our one-horse stable," he chuckled, "don't think that's much problem."

She dismounted and handed the reins to Carlos, who took Lasting Impression over to begin his bath. Cory's cell phone rang, but he opted not to answer it. Once Carlos attached the horse to the hot walking machine, she went over to him and scratched the gray behind an ear.

As Cory watched her heading down the roadway, away from the barn, he realized he'd forgotten to introduce her to Carlos. Or even ask her name.

CHAPTER 8

STAN AMBLED TOWARD THE SANTA Anita outdoor walking ring, where owners, trainers, jockeys, stable personnel and horses now gathered for the upcoming race, Stan's first as an owner. He felt energized. He'd just taken a nap, something he did nearly every day now. The only difference was that he took this one on an outdoor bench at Santa Anita, where he hadn't been for several years.

Not that he had anything against Santa Anita. It just wasn't on a convenient bus route. Not like Hollywood Park, for which a bus stopped directly in front of his southwest L.A. residence and got him there in ten minutes. So no matter which track in southern California had live racing, he almost always went to Hollywood Park to wager. Of course driving would have been easier, but with his vision problems, he'd been denied a license years ago.

Stan greeted several spectators outside the walking ring. Not that he recognized anyone, he just wanted them to know his horse was running. He was pleased that the late-October Sunday was warm and sunny, and that a large crowd had come out to see his horse run. And maybe some of the other horses as well.

Tiger, whom he'd called regularly after meeting him on that train a little more than two months ago, had joined him earlier. Stan bought him lunch, if eating burgers and fries in a betting line qualifies as lunch. They'd separated soon after—Tiger to watch races and bet, Stan to nap—agreeing to meet in the walking ring for Lasting Impression's race.

Inside the ring, Stan immediately went on an introduction binge: Tiger to Cory, Tiger to Lasting Impression, Tiger to Carlos, who had to briefly stop the horse as he led him around the ring, and all the above to their jockey, Martin Pedroza, even though Cory and Carlos undoubtedly already knew him. He'd have gladly introduced them to all the other owners, trainers and jockeys there, but they seemed occupied at the moment with their own horses.

"Good luck, Martin," Stan yelled out as Cory boosted the jockey aboard Lasting Impression. "See ya in the winner's circle."

✦ ✦ ✦

"My new silks go great with my gray horse," Stan gushed when he, Cory and Tiger reached the box seats Cory had arranged for the afternoon.

"Yeah ... great," was Cory's only response as he peered at Pedroza and Lasting Impression, parading on the track in front of them. The jockey was wearing a bright orange and purple top and cap. Cory resisted comment on Stan's own outfit—a black-and-white checked shirt above canary-yellow trousers. At least no suspenders today. An outfit befitting the owner of a fifty-five-to-one shot. Odds that Cory confirmed with a quick glance at the infield board.

"Hey!" Tiger exclaimed once the three of them sat down, "you guys see who's running Thursday!" He was gazing at a sheet of entries.

"Who?" Stan bit.

"One-Eyed Bandit. Had big trouble both his races."

"Two-year-old?" Cory interjected. "Maiden. With only one eye."

"Right," Tiger affirmed, "only one eye."

"From Dobson's stable," Cory added.

"Right," Tiger repeated. "They love to bet. Got plenty of horses. Don't mind risking one now and then to try and cash."

"He in a claiming race?" Cory questioned.

"Yeah. Fifty grand. I been savin' some money to bet on him."

"You savin' money ..." Stan quipped. "Believe it when I see it."

That shut Tiger up, at least temporarily. Cory watched Lasting Impression, warming up on the backstretch. He glanced again at the odds board. No change, still fifty-five to one. Tapping nervously on the railing next to him, he wondered why he'd ever conversed with Stan about this being an allowance horse. Then feeling almost obliged to enter him in *this* allowance race, in which the board showed he had so little chance.

"Hey, maybe we should claim that horse," Stan suggested.

"Didn't know you got fifty grand," Tiger retorted.

That quieted Stan, at least momentarily. Cory looked at both of them, sitting in the row in front of him. What an odd pair. Young good-looking kid walks with a limp, and this eccentric old man.

"Your horse is now sixty to one," Tiger announced once the odds changed.

"Sixty to one," Stan echoed, probably not able to see the board. "Can't believe he's sixty to one."

"And I can't believe how well he's behaving out there," Cory said, injecting into this negative situation what little positive he could muster.

That's all Stan and Tiger had to hear. They both got up and rushed toward the betting windows, surprising Cory that either of them could move that fast.

✦ ✦ ✦

Stan felt embarrassed. Even he could see that Lasting Impression was lagging far behind. Like he might not finish the race. All this time waiting for him to finally run, and this was how he did. In front of this big crowd. He'd finished last the day he and Cory claimed him and it looked as if he'd do no better today.

Instead of watching the track as the horses entered the backstretch for the mile-and-a-sixteenth race, Stan gazed at the large matrix in the infield. Maybe that would change his luck. But no, Lasting Impression was so far behind that the orange and purple silks weren't even in the picture. Stan turned away in disgust.

He heard the track announcer utter something about the horses coming into the stretch, and the crowd roared. They certainly weren't cheering for *his* horse. And then Tiger, on his left, started to yell. Had he bet on some other horse? He, Stan, certainly wouldn't put it past him.

"C'mon gray horse, c'mon gray horse!" Tiger shouted.

What could he be yelling about? Stan hadn't noticed another gray in the race. If he had, he probably would've put a couple bucks on him himself. Tiger was now screaming, the veins in his neck sticking out. Stan looked back at the track, but could see only a blur of the horses flashing under the wire.

"I think we won! I think we won!" Tiger exclaimed, his veins still popping.

"Who won?" Stan managed, his confusion growing.

"Your horse! Didn't you see? The speed stopped and he circled the field."

Stan knew Tiger was joking. Playing him for a fool. He'd bet on some other horse. Some other gray, and he was just stringing him along. Stan looked at Cory, behind him, for any type of indication, but none was forthcoming because he seemed so tense and nervous as he watched the board. Had he bet some other horse too?

"It's a photo finish," Stan heard the announcer proclaim.

"A head-bobber," Tiger volunteered.

"We might've gotten our head down," Cory speculated, "and the other horse had his up."

Stan looked at both of them. They were talking like they'd each bet the same horse. Unless ...

"Let's edge toward the winner's circle," Cory advised. "Just in case."

Cory led them out of the box seats. Stan heard patrons in the grandstand calling out numbers, conjecturing as to which horse had won. Eight, Lasting Impression's number, and two. Eight and two. Maybe Tiger really wasn't jiving him. Maybe he, Stan, actually had won his first race as a horse owner. At odds of sixty to one.

As they walked, Stan saw the photo sign extinguished from the board. The results flashed on it. Stan couldn't make out the numbers, though. But Tiger evidently could, and he roared.

✦ ✦ ✦

Cory could feel his heart pounding. After enduring six months of utter and complete futility, he and Carlos had just gotten their first win in California. And in an allowance race, not an ordinary claimer. At odds of sixty to one. Plus this was Santa Anita, not some nondescript little track.

He tried to restrain his emotions, more or less expected of a trainer. But he couldn't help himself. He pumped his fist in the air. He shook Tiger's hand enthusiastically. He couldn't keep from vigorously hugging Stan.

When he let go of him, the old man belched loudly.

✦ ✦ ✦

Nearing the winner's circle, Stan went on a hand-shaking binge, which included two racing officials and several opposing jockeys and trainers. Once Carlos led Lasting Impression into the circle, Stan planted a kiss firmly on the horse's lips. After the track photographer snapped a picture of Stan and his horse, along with Cory, Carlos and Tiger, Stan promptly ordered three dozen prints.

"We all make a good team," he grinned.

"Told you I'd have the money," Tiger declared, disregarding Stan's comment.

"Money for what?" Stan asked.

"Money to bet on that one-eyed horse on Thursday. All the money I made bettin' your horse." Tiger pulled a handful of betting slips from his pocket.

"Yeah, long as you don't blow it between now and then. Hey, I got an idea ... Maybe we got enough money now to think about claiming that horse."

"Listen, you guys," Cory quickly interceded in a muted tone. "Don't talk here. Word'll get out and they'll scratch that horse."

Stan and Tiger both nodded and left the winner's circle with Cory. But not before Stan waved good-bye to Lasting Impression, heading off the track with Carlos. And shook hands with a couple more racing officials.

"Hey, stop politicking," Tiger scolded Stan. "We got bets to make."

"Nah," Stan replied, feeling a little weary as they walked back toward the grandstand. "Enough for today. Got a long bus ride home."

With that, the old man turned and shuffled toward the track exit gates.

✦ ✦ ✦

"Congratulations," a woman greeted Cory over his barn phone early the next morning.

"Thanks," he answered vaguely, not recognizing the voice.

"My staff at the farm tell me he was their favorite horse while he was there."

"Oh?"

"They loved his vibrant personality."

By that time Cory of course realized she was referring to Lasting Impression. He reflexively glanced at his wrist and grimaced. Probably more at the idea that someone liked the gray horse's personality than at any pain his wrist, now almost healed, still caused him.

"You own the farm?" he ventured, aware that he'd met only the farm manager—and not the proprietor—when he and Cookie traveled there that terribly hot day.

"I'm Sandra Talbot," she replied. "Yes, I own the farm. But my husband Phil ran it ... Until he ... passed away a few months ago."

"Oh," was Cory's only response.

A silence followed. For some reason, Cory felt comfortable speaking to her. Maybe because the care Lasting Impression had gotten at the farm contributed to his, Cory's, first win here. Maybe because he still felt thrilled at that initial victory.

"Wouldn't be interested in joining a partnership to claim a horse?" he risked.

"Afraid not," Sandra answered. "Unless it's a particular horse."

"Care to reveal ... ?"

"It's a one-eyed two-year-old. The breeders are old friends. Like Phil and me, they've been in the sport for decades. They hate the idea that after they sold the colt, he wound up with Jack Dobson as his trainer."

Cory couldn't believe the coincidence. That of all the horses running at Santa Anita, they were talking about the same colt. He pinched his left wrist, the one not injured, to make sure he wasn't dreaming.

Both last night and very early this morning, Cory had carefully reviewed his notes on One-Eyed Bandit. He loved what he saw. The colt broke slowly in both his races, maiden allowance sprints. He'd dropped back each time, then made a strong run before getting blocked in the final stages. Now they were stretching him out to a mile, which Cory considered positive. And Tiger was right —Dobson's stable did have plenty of horses. On several occasions Cory had observed them maneuver for good betting spots. This time they might figure that the colt's visible impediment, his blind eye, would scare off any potential claims.

"I'll call you back with some specifics," he promised before he and Sandra ended the conversation.

✦ ✦ ✦

"Let it ride!" Stan exclaimed over the phone once Cory suggested that he, Stan, could apply Lasting Impression's purse money toward the prospective claim of One-Eyed Bandit. "Plus don't forget what I made bettin'."

"Good," Cory replied. "But it probably still leaves us a little short. Even with Sandra Talbot's investment."

"What about Tiger? I'm sure he'll want a piece. Unless he blows all his money bettin' between now and then."

"We'll have to get him an owner's license."

"I'll call him," Stan volunteered.

✦ ✦ ✦

"I can not afford much, Boss," Carlos said while brushing Lasting Impression inside the horse's stall a couple of mornings later.

"Me neither," Cory replied.

"I know we need horses, Boss."

"For sure."

"But my family … they need money."

"I understand."

Of course Cory did. How could he not, working beside this man all these years? But he also understood that he wanted this colt. All his instincts told him that this was their chance to make the move to California worthwhile—even if they risked money neither of them had.

While Cory waited for Carlos to speak again, a white billy goat trundled down the roadway in front of the barn. The goat turned and doubled back. Then he turned once more and continued in his original direction. Evidently he couldn't decide which horse to hang out with next.

"I will take a thousand on the new horse, Boss."

"Good."

"Maybe I'll take some too," a female voice behind Cory said.

He turned to see their new exercise rider. Tracy. He'd managed to get her name during her second day on the job.

"Couldn't help overhearing," she apologized.

He didn't know how to respond. Initially he was concerned that word would get out about the claim. As she'd said herself—there aren't many secrets around a racetrack. He decided to trust her, though, since she looked so earnest.

"You know he's got only one eye," he cautioned.

"I know. Used to ride him for Dobson."

"Doesn't bother you?"

"I think he could run blind," she said.

"You don't mind claiming from Dobson?"

"I'd mind if we didn't."

Carlos led Lasting Impression out of the stall and Cory boosted Tracy aboard the horse. As he began to follow her to the track, Cory could only shake his head. She was full of surprises.

Conversing with horses, making unusual comments, now wanting to participate in their claim. Plus, an added bonus, she was a talented exercise rider.

"Guess you won't be needing me much longer," she called out over her shoulder.

"Meaning?"

"Your wrist. Must be much better. That was the first time you helped me up on this horse."

"You must think I'm an idiot."

"Why?" she puzzled.

"You got Lasting Impression to behave himself. So he goes out and runs a winning race."

"I didn't have much to do with it."

"I think you had plenty to do with it," he spoke emphatically. "We'd been here six months and none of our horses came even close. I'm not about to change anything. That is, if you're available."

"I'm available." She smiled down at him.

A horse started kicking frenetically on the roadway in front of them and she halted Lasting Impression. The gray was apparently eager to get to the track, though, and began pawing the dirt in front of him. Or maybe he was trying for the attention of the white billy goat, who was strolling along the roadway again, evidently seeking a new equine companion.

✦ ✦ ✦

"He look good, Boss."

Cory nodded agreement. He and Carlos watched One-Eyed Bandit walk past them into the receiving barn, where horses were brought for identification before each race. To avoid suspicion that they were there specifically to claim the colt, they observed all the other horses enter the barn and Cory wrote comments on each in his notebook. Despite the race being more than half an hour away, he was already nervous. But then he always got nervous before claims. With good reason in this case, because the fifty thousand plus tax at stake was over double the amount of any claim he'd ever made.

Cory had done the requisite paperwork much earlier and verified that all the prospective owners were properly licensed. He'd also gone to a library this morning after training, to view computerized versions of One-Eyed Bandit's two races. Sure enough, the trouble the colt had encountered was even worse than Cory's notes indicated. Horses bumping him, gliding into his path or tiring in front of him were all part of the picture. Yet in each race, he managed to show a nice run.

"Look how he carries himself," Cory said softly, almost to himself, when the colt left the receiving barn with the other horses and headed for the paddock. "Even with the eye. Like he doesn't know there's anything wrong."

Carlos's expression conveyed assent. It was the tall, light-brown colt's right eye that was stitched shut. Preferable because, while undoubtedly blind to horses on his outside, he'd have no trouble seeing those inside him or, more importantly, the rail, and wouldn't have to turn his head to handle the track's curves.

"Let's go," Cory determined. "No way I'm changing my mind."

They started immediately for the claim box, to drop in their form.

✦ ✦ ✦

Of the other prospective owners, only Tiger now sat with Cory and Carlos in the box seats that Sandra Talbot had offered them. Stan went to Hollywood Park to watch. Tracy had to pick up her son from school. Sandra rarely went to the track. In truth, Tiger was there, instead of at Del Mar, only because of the required meeting with the track stewards, held this morning, to qualify for his license.

As the horses neared the starting gate, off to their right, Cory watched the odds board intently. He was looking for any telltale betting patterns. Now nine to five, One-Eyed Bandit had been six to one when they'd sat down, some fifteen minutes ago. The drop had been steady. The horses entered the gate. Another flick of the odds—the colt fell to six to five. Plenty of money was being bet on him, definitely a good sign.

Cory wondered about the race strategy. Would Dobson try to avoid trouble by instructing One-Eyed Bandit's jockey, Alex Yanez, to take him straight to the lead? When the gates sprung open, though, it was clear that wasn't the plan. Another slow beginning. The colt got bumped sideways and he dropped back to sixth in the field of nine.

Cory was aware that, in general, two-year-old maiden fifty-thousand claiming races at one mile were not stellar contests. If One-Eyed Bandit couldn't handle this group, they were in trouble. Into the backstretch, he showed no sign of advancing. From the ache developing in the pit of his stomach, Cory could feel his own disappointment mounting. All the preparation—months of tedious note-taking and observation, then assembling the partnership group—only to have it result in another bad claim. Sure, Lasting Impression had ultimately worked out, but that certainly wasn't indicated by his performance on claim day. In fact, hadn't they wanted to lose the dice shake after the race?

Into the far turn, One-Eyed Bandit finally showed some interest. Not much, just a brief spurt. Entering the stretch, he was still fifth. Cory knew it was now or never. Definitely for this race, and likely for his own training career in California. How could he have risked so much on an unknown two-year-old? A one-eyed one at that.

Tiger stood up in front of him. So did Carlos, beside him. Cory got up too, so he could see. Barely in time for the colt's next surge. This one wasn't brief. As the crowd noise ascended, he roared past horses. In seemingly no more than ten strides, he rushed to the lead. He quickly widened. At the wire, he was fourteen or fifteen lengths in front.

"Wow!" Tiger exclaimed. "Told you he could run."

"Like a jet!" Cory concurred, very relieved. "But let's not forget … he didn't beat much."

"Too bad he's only six to five," Tiger complained.

"Let's not have to shake," Cory told Carlos.

"I have good feeling, Boss."

It turned out Carlos was right. No dice shake. When the three of them got to the claim judge near the track, she simply handed them the little white slip of paper.

One-Eyed Bandit was theirs.

CHAPTER 9

"HUNDRED THOUSAND."

A greeting uttered the instant Cory arrived at the barn the next morning, by the burly guy. The same one who'd solicited Cory to claim those ineffective horses at Hollywood Park about four months ago. Cory didn't like his dark features and obvious arrogance any better today than he did back then. Nor did he like his lavish jewelry. Ditto his gray slacks and pullover sweater. Again, he looked far too stylish for early morning at a racetrack.

Cory immediately knew the guy's intent—and with whom to confer. He went directly to Carlos, who was counting some bales of hay nearby.

"Horses okay today?"

"They are fine, Boss."

"The new horse?"

"He is fine too."

"He eat up last night?"

"Everything, Boss."

"That guy out there ... he give you the opening bid?"

"No. He only want to speak with you."

Cory went to a bag of carrots nearby and took one out. He broke it into two pieces. He stood in front of both of their horses' stalls long enough to feed each a piece. Detecting nothing unusual, he returned to the man, whose stance, hands on hips, conveyed a combination of boredom and impatience.

"Have to contact the other owners," Cory said flatly. "More money might get their attention."

"Look," the guy declared. "Didn't come here to dicker. Would've given you a much lower figure if I did."

"More money might get their attention," Cory repeated.

"You kidding? For a horse half blind?"

"Didn't seem to bother his race."

"He beat nothing," the man insisted.

"Yeah, but he beat 'em pretty good."

"Okay," the man admitted. "He ran good. But not like double your money."

"You guys must've cleaned up," Cory retorted, recalling the significant drop in odds. "How much you bet?"

"Got nothin' to do with it."

"Probably *made* a hundred thousand. Even after you pay us."

"Got nothin' to do with it," the man repeated.

"Anyway, can't transfer ownership for at least thirty days."

"We can get around that."

"You guys try to get around a lot of things," Cory accused.

"What's that supposed to mean?"

Cory shrugged. No sense bringing up the incident of four months ago.

"Need a better reason to call the other owners," he said.

"How much better?"

"Up to you. You're the one with all the money."

The guy glared at him, then brusquely turned to walk off. Like during their other encounter, his jewelry jiggled conspicuously. Cory headed back to the bag of carrots, to offer both of their horses another piece.

✦ ✦ ✦

Tracy Simmons was running a little late this morning and she walked quickly along the roadway to Cory and Carlos's barn. She'd been delayed by several teams of horses and riders on the bridle path leading to the stables, blocking her entrance to the parking lot. While waiting in her car for them to pass, she hadn't minded, though. The early-morning shadowy silhouettes had presented a remarkable scene, reminding her to one day bring her drawing pad and sit nearby before work to sketch horses and riders going by in the faint light.

"Thought I'd get your opinion," Cory greeted her once she reached the barn.

"About what?"

"About whether to speak to the others."

"About what?"

He told her of the offer for One-Eyed Bandit. She liked the sound of it, at least initially. A nice quick profit certainly wouldn't hurt her finances—which had been virtually depleted by her not working much the past few months, and by her impulsive investment.

She still couldn't believe she'd done it—withdrawn so much money practically on a whim. She'd never considered racehorse ownership before, didn't even have an owner's license a few days ago. What had come over her? And yet, looking at Cory now, she sensed there was more at stake here than a quick profit.

"We need horses, don't we?" she said softly.

"Just thought I'd ask," he replied. "My conservative nature."

"You're not conservative."

"How do you know?"

"You'd never taken the risk coming to California."

She glanced over at Carlos, who was leading Lasting Impression out of his stall. A horse whinnied loudly from a neighboring barn. She went over to One-Eyed Bandit's stall and greeted him, calling him Bandit and patting him on the forehead, directly above his missing eye. Then she put on her helmet and walked to Carlos, who helped her aboard Lasting Impression.

As she began the short ride to the track, she could feel Cory's gaze upon her.

✦ ✦ ✦

That morning's training routine was simple enough. One-Eyed Bandit, overseen by Carlos, merely ambled around while attached to the hot walker. Lasting Impression galloped once around the track. He was now being ridden back to the barn by Tracy, Cory walking slightly behind them.

"Looks like he's still behaving himself," he said.

"Not entirely," she replied.

"Oh?"

"Had to have another talk with him."

"He listen?"

"Reluctantly ... He's got a little stubborn streak."

"Don't most males?" he chuckled.

She didn't answer. Not that he minded. He would have preferred a different dialogue. Like a return to their earlier conversation, when she showed loyalty to the barn by mentioning their need for horses, then commenting that he wasn't conservative. Her level of involvement with their barn and, possibly, with him had been surprising. Could it be that there might be more between them than just trainer and exercise rider?

They got to the barn. He considered inviting her to the stable cafeteria for breakfast or coffee. But then he recalled her edict about having to leave early on weekdays to take her son to school. The rapid way she dismounted Lasting Impression and handed Carlos his reins indicated that today would be no exception.

✦ ✦ ✦

"Loose horse! Loose horse! Loose horse!"

Tracy heard these shouts from unknown sources while she walked along a roadway toward her car, after leaving the barn that same morning. Then she saw the reason for the warnings—a jet-black riderless horse speeding in her direction. Instinctively she stepped into his path and waved her arms, hoping to slow him. If anything, he sped up, heading right for her. She could see his eyes glazed with fear. She froze, almost feeling the impending collision. Fortunately, at the last instant, he veered off slightly, missing her by inches.

The air fanned by his passing brought her back to motion. She turned and ran after him, hoping to somehow stop him, or at least alert others. The horse turned left onto another roadway. She got to the intersection just in time to see him suddenly skid to a stop, his path blocked by a team of five or six horses and riders heading toward the track. One of the riders grabbed the horse's loose reins. Just like that, the crisis was over, a fact confirmed by one of the other riders signaling her that they had the wayward horse under control.

Convinced that she could do no more, she turned and headed toward her car again. The combination of the run and her fear reduced her breath to short bursts. Despite the early morning warming up nicely, she suddenly felt cold and clammy, and zipped up the blue down jacket she had on.

She wondered why she'd become so cavalier lately—buy a piece of a horse, then decline a fast profit. She with a son to raise without a stitch of outside help. What if that horse had run her over? What if she got hurt riding and could neither ride nor paint? She really needed look no further than Cory, with his sprained wrist, to see what could happen.

If she were confused about her recent brashness, she was at least certain of one thing—that even though they'd owned Bandit less than twenty-four hours, she was already attached to him, to his tall athletic appearance, his light-brown coloring and to the notion he had only one eye. She looked forward to seeing him again tomorrow morning.

CHAPTER 10

"GOOD TRAINER CAN ALWAYS INFLUENCE his owners," the burly man told Cory a few mornings later at the barn.

"Who says I'm a good trainer?"

"My people will pay another twenty-five."

"Thousand?"

"Thousand."

Tracy arrived for work. Lasting Impression would be their first horse for the morning, and Carlos already had him outside. Tracy walked over to One-Eyed Bandit's stall and greeted him by name. Because Carlos had a slight cold, Cory went over to boost her aboard Lasting Impression.

"Breeze him a half," he told her. "Nice and easy. And gallop him another eighth."

"You want him to finish strong?"

"Long as you don't push him."

She started riding toward the track and Cory began to follow, only to be intercepted by the burly guy. His outfit today featured a dark-blue lightweight pullover jacket with white trim. And of course ample jewelry.

"Wouldn't go getting any ideas about that little exercise girl," he advised once Tracy was out of earshot. "Straight as they come. Married to that kid of hers."

"You seem to know everyone's business."

"That's my business. Knowing everyone's business."

"Guess I better get back to mine, then," Cory replied, turning to follow Tracy again toward the track. "That is ... if I'm ever to become a good trainer."

He laughed at his own words. The man didn't. In fact, he scowled.

"I'd keep a close eye on things," he called after Cory.

"What's that supposed to mean?"

"You're the wise guy," he answered angrily. "You figure it out."

✦ ✦ ✦

"Know that guy I was talking to?" Cory asked Tracy as she rode Lasting Impression back to the barn after breezing him in forty-nine and change.

"Kosko? Sure. Big-shot agent. Always got a horse to sell."

"This case, he wants to buy."

"Bandit," she presumed.

"Yep. A while back, tried to get me to claim a couple bad horses."

"Sounds like him."

"He work only for Dobson?"

"Mainly," she answered. "But I'm not sure he works for Dobson or Dobson works for him."

A big black crow screeched at Lasting Impression from the side of the roadway, but the horse paid no attention. He seemed more interested in a little rabbit scampering into some shrubbery on ahead.

"Not the most congenial guy I ever met," Cory frowned.

"He's miserable. Don't know anyone who likes him. Except maybe Dobson. They're two of a kind."

"Evidently you don't like Dobson either."

"Putting it mildly."

He laughed at her candor. Then he mentioned the new offer. She didn't respond.

"The money's getting serious," he said. "Guess I'd better contact the others. Unless you think I'm being too conservative."

"You're not conservative," was her only comment.

✦ ✦ ✦

"Let it ride."

Stan's telephone response didn't surprise Cory once he'd disclosed the latest offer.

"But we'd be more than doubling our money," Cory contended, wanting to make sure the old man under-stood. "Practically overnight."

"Let it ride."

"You might be making a mistake. It's not like we can't claim other horses."

"Not like him," Stan rebutted. "Two-year-old. Whole life ahead. They must want him back pretty bad."

"Maybe they don't want to risk being embarrassed. With what they made betting, probably a luxury they can afford."

"Me too," Stan retorted. "Whatever money we got for him ... can't take it with me."

Cory smiled at Stan's words, which of course wasn't the first time he'd heard them.

✦ ✦ ✦

"Good horses don't grow on trees," was Sandra Talbot's way of concurring with Stan, while making it clear she was quoting Phil, her recently deceased husband.

Carlos and Tiger agreed with Stan too, though much less adamantly. Like Cory, they could use the cash. Carlos of course, to send to his family, Tiger presumably to bet with. And like Cory, both knew things could change overnight in this business. A horse could be worth a hundred twenty-five thousand today and nothing tomorrow.

Nearly seven months had passed since Rugged Landing's tragic ending. To Cory, it seemed like yesterday.

✦ ✦ ✦

"Go a nice easy five-eighths," Cory told Tracy. "Maybe a minute, three seconds. Remember, nice and easy."

She nodded and rode One-Eyed Bandit onto the track. Cory stopped at the trackside clocker's booth to report their horse's name and workout distance. Then he headed toward his regular vantage point, on the steps leading up to the grandstand, near the top of the stretch.

The early-November morning was brisk and he pulled his green coat tight around his neck. He felt a little weak and suspected he was catching Carlos's cold. Or maybe it was just nerves before an important workout. He was watching a hundred twenty-five thousand dollars out there on the track, by far the most valuable horse he'd ever trained.

He pressed the button on his stopwatch when Tracy broke Bandit from the five-eighths pole, across the track. They seemed to be going easily, as he intended. He liked how she fit the colt, in sync with his long, effortless stride. But then he liked how she fit everything in their barn. All two horses. When they passed by him at the top of the stretch, he felt a chill rush through him. And he was certain it wasn't from catching a cold. No, this was another reason to stay in California—to maybe train a really good horse.

He watched them flash under the wire, and flicked off his stopwatch. Then he began to walk briskly toward the path leading under the grandstand, where they'd be coming off the track.

✦ ✦ ✦

"Well?" he asked Tracy, aware that Bandit wasn't even breathing hard.

"He's all business," she answered from atop the colt. "Never guess he's only a two-year-old."

"Talent?"

"Worlds."

"What about his eye?"

"Doesn't know it's missing."

They stopped for a horse edging sideways on the bridle path, in front of them. Briefly, he looked like he might hit the railing. Once they started moving again, nearing the entrance to the stable area, Cory took out his stopwatch from a coat pocket. His expression grew serious.

"Thought I told you nice and easy," he said sternly.

"That's how we went," she answered a bit defensively. "You said a minute, three seconds."

"Right," he replied, holding up his watch for her to see. "Not fifty-nine and change."

She shrugged and appeared ready to apologize. Until he smiled. A smile that became a grin. They both patted Bandit on the shoulder at the same time, simultaneously acknowledging that he just might be something special.

✦ ✦ ✦

"Lasting Impression's an allowance horse," Stan told Cory over the phone from his apartment one morning.

"There are claiming races he fits better."

"He's an allowance horse."

"Next category's much tougher."

"He's an allowance horse," Stan repeated emphatically.

Stan hung up, knowing he'd made his point. Why risk the first horse he ever owned getting claimed? Especially after he'd won his first race so nicely. At odds of sixty to one.

The thought of going to Hollywood Park this afternoon wasn't appealing. Particularly the idea of taking his afternoon nap on that hard bench. Why not stay right here for the day? Maybe call Tiger and send out a bet or two with him. And then watch the race replays tonight on TV.

◆ ◆ ◆

Sandra sat down at Phil's black desk in the office of the farm in the Santa Ynez Valley. She immediately encountered an old photograph of the two of them before they were married, from about thirty-five years ago. She was amazed at how young they looked. He wore a leisure suit, popular at that time. She had on a dark sweater and short skirt. She smiled at his long brown hair and hers, much shorter than his. How could so much time have passed?

She'd driven by the farm entrance about ten minutes ago. Recalling her last visit here, with Phil back in early spring, she'd quickly observed that everything looked exactly the same. The large gray iron gate and adjacent bronze statue of horse and rider. The trees and foliage decorating the sides of the roadway. Likewise the horses languishing in the distance. Did she think things would look different just because her own life had changed so much?

"Hi, Mrs. Talbot."

Luke Ridley, the farm manager Phil hired about fifteen years ago, had entered the office, and she put down the photograph. She got up from the desk and shook his hand. He was a large man, overweight, late forties, wearing standard farm attire of jeans, denim shirt, cowboy hat and boots. He'd attended both Phil's sixtieth birthday party and funeral, and kept in touch with Sandra daily by phone since.

"Sorry to keep you waiting," he apologized. "Had to finish with the vet. Little training accident this morning."

"One of ours, Luke?"

"No, no. A boarder."

"Was it serious?"

"Could've been. Horse took a tumble. But it turned out minor. Just a few scrapes and bruises. Same for the rider."

She sighed, relieved. At her suggestion, they stepped outside, stopping at a tree near the office. Because the terrain sloped downward, they had a wonderful view of virtually the entire farm. Several broodmares grazed in a pasture close by. Beyond that, weanlings frolicked in a circular field. The racetrack and training center, where she and Phil had watched their young horses develop, lay further out. The whole scene was enhanced by background mountains, seemingly surrounding the property.

"I hate to do it, Luke," she said resolutely, "but I've got to downsize. I've decided to sell the farm and a lot of the horses."

"Thought you might, Mrs. Talbot."

"I'd like your help, Luke."

"Sure, Mrs. Talbot."

"First with the sales."

"Yes, ma'am."

"Then as manager ... of my racing and breeding interests."

"So you intend to keep racing."

"Phil would want me to. If only to keep our dream alive—of raising that one championship horse ... He'd also want me to keep the farm, but it's too much for me."

"Could I ask a question, Mrs. Talbot?"

"Sure, Luke."

"This manager ... of your racing and breeding interests. Where would he work?"

"Phil set up an office in our house."

"In L.A.?"

"Yes."

"Let's not forget something," he said almost apologetically. "I'm a country boy. I could help you sell the farm, but beyond that ..."

She nodded. He went on to disclose that he'd received an offer from another farm, here in the Santa Ynez Valley. A beautiful modern spread, everything first class. He'd consented to talk with them only because he anticipated she'd make changes.

"Do they want to make you farm manager, Luke?"

"Yes, Mrs. Talbot."

"Have you already accepted?"

"No. They know I had to speak to you first."

"You go ahead and take it, Luke."

He shrugged. As they shook hands good-bye, she could see sadness in his eyes. During his fifteen-year tenure, he'd never masked his admiration for Phil. Walking back to the office, she took one last look at the scene below them, especially the broodmares grazing in the pasture.

Back inside, she sat down at Phil's desk again and gazed at the old photograph once more. She picked it up and held it close, smiling at his long hair. Before getting up to leave, she carefully placed the photograph in her purse.

CHAPTER 11

"WHY DIDN'T YOU CALL ME when it happened?" Cory exclaimed when he got to the barn early one morning.

"The vet, he take good care of me, Boss."

"You still should've called. How bad is it?"

"It is not as bad as it look."

That wasn't much consolation because, indeed, Carlos did look bad. Especially his face. Black eye, cut lip, gash along one cheek—all on the left side. Plus his left wrist was taped heavily.

"My wrist. It is the worse."

"Broken?"

"No. Sprain. Like you."

Cory recognized the irony—just as his wrist heals, Carlos's is injured. The only difference was that Cory had hurt his right one.

"How'd it happen?"

"Two men. Late last night. I am sleeping. They tape my mouth so I cannot call for help."

"You know them?"

"No, Boss. I do not know them."

"I have a pretty good idea who sent them," Cory mused.

Undoubtedly so did Carlos. But neither of them speculated further. Cory felt awful. California hadn't been Carlos's idea. He'd come out of loyalty. And until their recent success, had benefited little, financially or otherwise. Now this.

"We'll trade jobs till you're better," Cory said.

"No. I am okay."

"I don't want you trying to handle horses with that wrist. I'll do the horses. You do the training."

"That mean I do nothing, Boss."

"Thanks a lot," Cory replied, smiling faintly.

✦ ✦ ✦

"Whatever you do," Tracy told Cory later that morning, "don't give in to them."

"Yeah, but who knows who'll be next?"

"Your career here's at stake. You let them bully you, word'll get out. Anytime you claim a good horse, same thing'll happen. You'll have no choice but to leave. Maybe go back to Arizona."

"So you don't want to sell Bandit."

"If I did, I don't now."

They stood outside their barn office, having just finished training. Cory had prepared both horses for the track, given them baths after their workouts, then attached them to the hot walker to cool out. Carlos had followed Tracy as she rode each horse to the track, to watch them train. Cory thought it strange that Tracy lingered now, since she normally rushed off right after riding her last horse. Then he remembered it was Saturday and she wouldn't have to take her son to school.

"What if I try to meet with the stewards?" he asked her. "Let them know what happened."

"Beats selling."

"It's risky. Word gets out, they might retaliate."

"The more people that know, the better."

"Doesn't scare you?" he frowned.

"No. We do nothing, they won't stop. Least we'll be telling them we won't be bullied."

"We?" he asked, a little surprised at her use of that pronoun.

"I own a share of the horse."

"That mean you'd go with me to the stewards?"

"Sure. Long as it doesn't interfere with my kid's school."

"No school on Sunday," he responded. "I'll see if I can arrange a meeting for tomorrow, right after training."

Carlos, standing near the hot walker, pointed to Bandit, still cooling out. Cory realized that he was late disconnecting the colt and leading him back to his stall.

"Wouldn't have time for breakfast, would you?" Cory asked Tracy shyly. "Soon as I finish up."

"Sorry. My kid's waiting at home. Promised to make him pancakes this morning."

She turned and headed toward the parking lot. He watched her, admiring her taut jeans cloaking the lower half of her slender figure. Once she'd gone from his sight, he walked over to disengage Bandit.

"If you will do my job, Boss," Carlos smiled, "you must do better to keep track of the time."

"Like to do better with other things too," Cory muttered.

✦ ✦ ✦

"Hundred fifty thousand," Kosko snarled the next morning, as he stood right outside Bandit's stall.

"Price is rising," Cory noted. He was inside the stall, brushing Bandit for his workout. Tracy and Carlos hadn't come back from the track yet, with Lasting Impression.

"My people saw him breeze the other day. Fell right into your trap."

"What trap?"

"Work him fast as you can. Coax the price up. Personally, don't think he's worth what you paid."

"You see him breeze?"

"Got better things to do."

"Like what?" Cory bristled. "Having people beat up?"

"Oh? Something happen?" An exaggerated innocent look crossed Kosko's face.

"You know very well what happened."

"Course you got proof. Otherwise you wouldn't make accusations."

Cory didn't answer. He stepped out of Bandit's stall, nudging Kosko lightly while doing so. The burly man didn't budge. His stance seemed rock solid, and Cory immediately felt the inadequacy of his own slight build. Because the morning was cold, Cory went to the little office nearby and put a jacket on over the sweater he wore. He returned to Bandit's stall, this time carefully avoiding any physical contact with Kosko. He began brushing the colt again.

"Hundred fifty thousand," Kosko repeated. "Probably afford a groom with that kind of money."

Cory didn't reply.

"Your owners know their trainer grooms their horses?"

Again no reply.

"If I were you, I'd talk to them," Kosko snapped. "I'd talk to them real soon."

✦ ✦ ✦

Along with Tracy, Cory did talk real soon—less than an hour later, to one of the track stewards. They sat in the official's office and detailed Carlos's beating, Kosko's repeated appearances at the barn and his threatening manner. Plus his escalating monetary offers.

"Nothing unusual about someone trying to buy a horse," the steward—a refined-looking older man in a gray suit—informed them. "Happens around here every day."

"Yes," Cory replied, "but with physical force, sir? Beating people up."

"Do you have proof Kosko or his affiliates were involved?"

"Not at this time." Cory shrugged.

"I will admit," the official stated, "yours isn't the first complaint we've gotten about them. And I'm sure it won't be the last. I'd be willing to write them a letter, let them know we're watching."

Cory and Tracy both thanked him and shook his hand. On their way out of the office, Cory noticed on the wall several pictures of horses, all former winners of the Santa Anita Handicap. Outside, the morning had warmed only slightly.

"Think we did any good?" Cory asked her.

"I think we did what we could."

They stopped for some horses and riders on the bridle path leading to the stable area. Evidently Tracy knew one of the riders, because she waved at her.

"I suppose ..." Cory said once they resumed walking, "that you promised to make your son waffles this morning."

"How'd you know?"

"Anyone who likes pancakes likes waffles."

She grinned.

"You know," he said, "they do serve waffles in restaurants. And save you the trouble of cooking."

"It's no trouble. I like to cook."

They walked on in silence. He opted not to press her further. Apparently she would limit his company to racing matters.

"Thanks for coming with me to the steward," he said as they neared the parking lot.

She smiled acknowledgment. Then, for the second consecutive day, he watched her walk away from him. His only consolation was the view offered by the pleasing taper of her tight jeans.

✦ ✦ ✦

Cory felt very nervous. Which only made sense. If he were nervous the day they claimed One-Eyed Bandit and for the colt's workout, how else could he be for his first race for them?

All the owners were there, in Sandra's box seats. All except Tracy, that is. It being a Friday, she'd gone to pick up her son at school, which let out shortly before the race. Rather than disturb the others by arriving late, she informed Cory that she'd watch the race from the grandstand, with her son. Now, as the horses approached the starting gate for the mile-and-a-sixteenth race, Cory found himself peering toward the grandstand seats, hoping to spot her in the crowd.

He'd also glanced occasionally at Sandra. He was seeing her for the first time, and he liked what he saw, especially considering her age. Appealing smile, tall and stately. Dark hair, dark eyes and neatly dressed in a fitted beige pantsuit.

"How you like our silks?" Stan asked everyone.

"Very nice," Sandra praised.

Indeed, they were nice. Emerald green with white trim. A fine contrast with Bandit's light-brown coloring. And they were a nice reflection of his elegance on the track.

"Picked them out myself."

Stan's statement brought a slight smile to Cory's face. It was only partially true. Because Stan was the senior member of the partnership, Cory had given him the honor of selecting their silks. But, based on what he'd seen of Stan's wardrobe—today highlighted by a black cap, pink vest and orange trousers—he had restricted him to three very restrained choices. To his credit, however, Stan had picked Cory's favorite among them.

"Much tougher race today," Tiger noted, gazing at the odds board.

"Much," Cory agreed.

"Legitimate allowance race," Tiger appraised. "No maiden claimers in here."

"The reason he's six to one," Cory said. "Not six to five."

"The reason I'm not puttin' more money on him. That plus the rider switch. Couldn't get Yanez?"

"Didn't want him," Cory advised. "Victor Espinoza's real patient. And a good finisher."

"Maybe. But Yanez rode him great last time."

"You're right. I wanted no connection to that other stable, though. Trainer or jockey."

That seemed to satisfy Tiger. Or maybe he just wanted to concentrate on the odds board. Regardless, Cory glanced at Stan, sitting in the row in front of him, and was aware that the old man hadn't spoken as much as he normally did. Like Cory, could he also be feeling nervous and worried?

"Buena suerte, Boss."

These words, spoken as the horses entered the gate, were Carlos's standard means of wishing Cory luck before any big race of theirs. In response, Cory managed only a weak smile at his compadre, sitting next to him. Cory had been much more enthusiastic this morning, when Carlos showed him how improved his wrist was. Actually, for the first time since the incident, Carlos had been able to help prepare their horses for the track. And with saddling Bandit minutes ago, for the race. His face had healed nicely too, with only a couple of minor bruises still visible.

Bandit stood patiently in the gate. When it sprang open, Cory was relieved that he got off to the best start of his career. Breaking from the rail post, he actually led before Espinoza eased him back. Going into the clubhouse turn, he was fifth in the ten-horse field. Two more horses passed him on the outside at the beginning of the backstretch. Another ran by him while Bandit remained stuck on the rail, apparently with no place to go.

Cory was even more worried now than he'd been before. What if the reason Bandit had no place to go was because he just wasn't good enough? Or because of his, Cory's, training methods? Maybe he'd been too soft, protective. As he'd instructed Tracy, "nice and easy." Perhaps Bandit's talent was compromised by his trainer's inexperience with valuable horses.

Was Cory now watching a hundred fifty thousand dollars go down the drain? He who hadn't bothered to even contact the other owners after the latest offer. Not being influential, as Kosko had accused. Were his deficiencies about to cost them? He quickly glanced at the others and saw disappointment etched on their faces.

A hole opened up for Bandit as the field entered the stretch, the horse in front of him tiring and drifting out. Bandit quickly sped up. He was fifth in mid-stretch and gaining on the leaders. But, as Tiger pointed out, this wasn't the easy bunch of maiden claimers he beat last time—these were legitimate allowance horses. Would his speed be effective against this type of colt?

The answer became apparent in the next instant. Bandit burst through the seam near the rail. His sudden velocity transported him rapidly to the lead. At the wire he was two lengths in front.

✦ ✦ ✦

"Easy game," Stan shouted from the winner's circle.

The old man folded his hands together above his head, in triumph. Sandra, Carlos and Tiger, next to him, all laughed. Cory, on the track with Bandit and Espinoza, still aboard, beamed while shaking his head. At least Stan hadn't unleashed the handshaking binge Cory recalled from the old man's other visit to the winner's circle.

Cory purposely circled Bandit on the track, hoping to give Tracy and her son time to join them. He glanced up into the grandstand, but saw no sign of her. Had they missed the race entirely?

"Never had a horse stick to the rail like that," Espinoza told Cory from atop the colt.

"I think he's comfortable there," Cory replied, patting Bandit on the left shoulder. "His eye ..."

"Yeah, but he makes up for any handicap ... with his *heart*."

Cory grinned at the jockey's words. A racing official impatiently motioned Cory toward the winner's circle. Reluctantly he led Bandit there. Several spectators nearby, with Stan as their cheerleader, applauded loudly for the colt.

When the track photographer snapped their picture, Cory caught himself gazing up into the grandstand again, looking for Tracy.

CHAPTER 12

COOKIE HAD A BOYFRIEND—a big brown Irish setter from the neighborhood. She looked for him whenever Cory walked her. Every time they met, she'd lick his face and want to follow him—which would have been embarrassing if the dog's owner, a middle-aged man usually dressed in business clothes, wasn't so cordial.

Cory began noticing her barking sooner than the twenty minutes she normally allotted between waking him and expecting to start her walk. Also, another change, she didn't seem to mind him giving her a bath. Nor coat brushings and teeth cleanings.

There was only one logical explanation—Cookie was in love.

✦ ✦ ✦

Lasting Impression ran during the final days of the current Santa Anita meeting—before the southern California racing scene switched to Hollywood Park—and finished a fast-closing second. Thus, for three Santa Anita races, Cory and Carlos had two wins and a second. Plus, based on Kosko's most recent offer, One-Eyed Bandit, their only claim for the meeting, had tripled in value.

Evidently the decision to stay in California after the Del Mar season was a sound one.

✦ ✦ ✦

"Trouble!" Tracy greeted Cory in the barn office immediately after she arrived for work one morning.

"What!"

"Got a call last night," she replied tensely. "My kid answered. A man said one word—kill."

"Kill?"

"I took the phone. He had a strange voice. Like a computer. With an echo."

"Yeah?"

"Sounded far away. He said one word ..."

"Kill?" he guessed.

"Kill."

"We'll have a meeting," he said. "All of Bandit's owners. Now go on home."

"I came to do my job."

"I can exercise the horses today."

"I came to do my job," she insisted.

Clearly he wasn't going to win the debate. They walked out of the office. Carlos was waiting with Lasting Impression, just outside his stall. Cory assisted her aboard the horse.

"Just jog him today," he told her. "Easy. Once around."

She began riding toward the track. He shook his head at her determination.

✦ ✦ ✦

"Think they're nuts ... they're offering two hundred thousand."

Same man, same place. The only difference was today Kosko didn't come until after they'd trained both horses and gotten them back into their stalls. Well after Tracy had left.

"Didn't want to chance running into my exercise rider," Cory accused.

"She got nothing to do with this. We deal with you."

"And not her kid," Cory said emphatically.

"Don't know what you're talking about."

"First my assistant. Then my exercise rider and her kid. How low you guys gonna go!"

"Look ... Didn't come here for insults. Came here to offer lot more than that horse's worth."

Cory didn't answer. He saw a horseshoer approaching on the roadway in front of the barn. Today was the day Lasting Impression was to get new shoes. Cory started toward his stall, to make sure he was ready.

"Suggest you call your owners," Kosko continued. "Convince them take the money. Before something happens to their prize possession."

"Oh," Cory exclaimed, close to shouting, "now you're threatening the horse!"

"Look pal, this is racing. Anytime a horse steps on that track, something can happen."

Kosko turned and began walking away. Cory almost yelled after him, but realized it wouldn't do any good. He tried to calm himself by going the rest of the way to Lasting Impression's stall, where the horseshoer would soon start work.

✦ ✦ ✦

"If we take the offer," Cory pointed out, "I figure we'll all make more than four times what we put up. Counting Bandit's purse the other day."

He glanced at Stan, at Tiger, at Sandra, Carlos and Tracy. They all sat in Sandra's spacious, opulently furnished living room, which had several paintings of her horses on the walls. The home was magnificent, a Victorian-style mansion located in Hancock Park, a stately historic district two or three miles west of downtown L.A.

Cory had called Sandra about having a meeting. Despite his protest, she'd insisted that they use her house and that dinner be included. Prepared and served by her housekeeper, it had been a splendid meal—principally of roast pheasant, boiled potatoes and turnip greens—which they'd consumed in the dining room.

Here in the living room, over dessert—caramel pie and vanilla ice cream—Cory had already disclosed to everyone what happened to Carlos and the current threat to Tracy and her son, prompting Sandra to shake her head then and again now.

"Can't believe them threatening children," she said. "I didn't invest to have this kind of trouble."

"Me neither," Stan chimed in. "With what we make we can get a dozen horses. Run one every day of the week."

"Yeah," Tiger concurred. "With plenty money to bet on 'em."

"I will be able to send money to my family," Carlos said softly.

"So it's unanimous," Cory summarized. "We sell."

Silence ensued. Cory looked around the room again. Stan nodded. Tiger, no doubt anticipating improved cash flow, smiled. Sandra appeared resolute. No reaction from Carlos. Or Tracy. Meanwhile, Sandra's housekeeper had entered the room, and was noiselessly gathering dessert dishes.

"No," Tracy said softly.

"What, dear?" Sandra asked.

"It's not unanimous," Tracy answered, a little louder.

There was another silence. Cory glanced around the room once more. Except for Tracy, everyone looked surprised. The same as he felt. He'd assumed this meeting was primarily to protect her and her son. That she'd be the first to want to sell. Apparently he'd been wrong.

"I don't like bullies," she said, breaking the silence.

"But we'll be getting four times our money," Tiger disputed.

"I don't care if we'll be getting forty times our money. I don't like giving in to bullies. There must be another way."

More silence. Cory looked at Stan, Tiger, Sandra and Carlos once again. Next at Tracy. No question everyone except her wanted to sell. He was sure he could persuade her, too. But he didn't want to be influential here, not when it wasn't unanimous, not when there was so much potentially at stake, and not when no one knew how really good this colt might be. When it was conceivable that he could be worth, to use Tracy's figures, forty times what they'd paid for him.

"Hate to admit it," Sandra reflected, finally breaking the silence, "but Phil and I once had a horse with Dobson. And Kosko was involved."

"Oh?" Cory said.

"And I've got something on them. Something I'm sure they don't want becoming public."

"We do not want trouble for you," Carlos declared.

"Don't worry. I know exactly who and what I'm dealing with."

"Please be sure," Cory insisted. "Before you get involved."

"I'm sure. And I'm with Tracy ... I don't like bullies either."

"What will you do?" Stan asked.

"Contact them. Be sure that they know that I know what I know."

Cory glanced around the room one more time. The discussion appeared over. By the expressions he saw, the decision now seemed unanimous. They'd retain ownership of Bandit. Even if, quoting Tracy again, they were offered forty times their money.

✦ ✦ ✦

Tracy drove past the downtown skyscrapers, on her way from Sandra's house to pick up her son at the home of a friend, with whom she had a reciprocal child-care arrangement. She wondered whether she hadn't made a terrible mistake, continuing to jeopardize the boy and herself. Not to mention the other owners.

Besides the recent threat, Carlos had already been hurt. Who or what might be next?

Then there was the money. Cavalierly turning down a sizable profit as if she had no responsibilities. As if she were a rich woman, like Sandra for example. Speaking of Sandra, Tracy had noticed the paintings of Sandra's horses on the living room wall and thought about letting her know that she did similar paintings. She actually considered giving her a business card, but had scrapped the idea because she didn't know her well enough. Plus the meeting obviously had another purpose.

Leaving downtown, she decided to take the Pasadena Freeway. Despite it being the shortest route to her friend's, she didn't like its frequent dangerous curves. But didn't they reflect her recent decisions—risk over safety? Passing the off-ramp to Dodger Stadium, she reminded herself to take her son to a ball game next season. Something she'd intended to do in the past, yet hadn't quite found time.

Her thoughts returned to the meeting. Even with all her concerns, she knew she'd done the right thing. As she'd said, she didn't like bullies and she didn't like giving in to them. While negotiating one of the difficult curves, she made a vow. Not only would she not give in to bullies, but she'd refuse to alter her life in any way. Her time with the boy, their routine, her painting, the racetrack.

Nothing would change, because if it did, that would be like allowing herself to be bullied.

✦ ✦ ✦

"I think they'll leave us alone now," Sandra told Cory by phone a few days later. "Dobson knows I mean business."

"That's great. You didn't put yourself in any jeopardy?"

"No. Nor anyone else. My attorney has all the details. Dobson knows any more trouble, he contacts the authorities."

"Thank you ... from all of us. And thanks for having us over for that terrific dinner."

"Thank *you*," she replied. "For the chance to be part of this."

CHAPTER 13

"I CAN SEE WHY YOU WANNA go the track every day," Tiger told Stan. "Nothin' but buncha old people 'round here."

"What d'ya expect?" Stan answered. "This *is* a *senior* residence."

No question about that from what Cory had seen so far this afternoon. He, Carlos, Stan and Tiger were in Stan's tiny seventh-floor efficiency. They had just finished having Thanksgiving dinner in the complex's "restaurant," at Stan's invitation. Not a very sumptuous meal, especially when compared to the recent one at Sandra's house. Bland turkey, watery cranberry sauce, lumpy mashed potatoes, coarse string beans. And the rolls and small slice of pumpkin pie tasted stale.

Nor had the atmosphere been the least bit appetizing. The large dining room, adjacent to the complex's lobby on the first floor, had accommodated over a hundred people, many of whom used walkers or canes. They sat on metal chairs at folding card tables, surrounded by sickening brownish-yellow bare walls. Two waiters, both wearing plain white aprons splattered with food stains, served the meals. Accompanying entertainment was provided by one of the residents, who played old standards on a badly tuned piano.

Stan's unit was no improvement over the "restaurant" décor. Another card table and folding chairs, on which the four of them now sat. One large room and a tiny bathroom—toilet visible and constantly running. Bare white walls embellished only by a single framed winner's circle picture of Lasting Impression. Near the bed was a large pile of Racing Forms, yellowing with age.

"What d'ya do for chicks 'round here?" Tiger asked Stan.

"Not much."

"Don't blame you."

"Yeah." Stan shrugged. "Little old even for an old guy like me."

"Maybe I can dig you up some young stuff," Tiger teased. "Someone under a hundred."

Stan muttered something beneath his breath. It was getting dark outside and the room had become cold. Cory began to wonder whether this place had heat. He glanced at Carlos, and he looked cold too. Almost immediately Cory heard what sounded like a furnace groaning somewhere, and felt air coming through a vent on the wall near the bathroom.

"You have family?" he asked Stan.

"No more. Had a wife. Elizabeth. Married forty-eight years. Died twelve years ago. Before I moved out here from Chicago."

"Kids?"

"No."

"What did you do for a living?"

"Manufacturer's rep. Menswear."

"How'd you get into horses?"

"What is this?" Tiger quipped. "Twenty questions?"

"My father," Stan answered Cory, ignoring Tiger. "First took me to Arlington Park when I was a kid. Day after my bar mitzvah. Broke me in real good."

"Mine did too," Cory said.

"Funny," Stan sighed. "After all these years ... think of my father a lot."

Cory shook his head. He tried not to reminisce, but he couldn't help himself. At least in his thoughts. His mind dwelled on last Thanksgiving and how he and his own father had spent the day together, part of their final holiday season before his death.

It would've been nice to fly his father over for this weekend. To Cory's knowledge, he had never been to California. They could have rehashed their days at the track. And Cory was sure his father would've loved Santa Anita and coming out early in the morning for training.

"Long as you guys are gettin' sentimental," Tiger interjected. "Tell you what I think of a lot."

"What?" Cory bit.

"My knee. The one I blew out playin' football. Happened last minutes of my high school career. Cost me my scholarship to Stanford."

"Ever exercise or work out?" Cory asked.

"Nah. Too busy doin' what I'm doin'."

"Maybe you should."

"You be my trainer?" Tiger laughed.

"Sure. If you need one."

"What I need more from you is a good tip on a horse once in a while. Haven't cashed a bet since they moved to Hollywood Park."

Cory didn't reply. He heard what he thought was the furnace groaning again. This time the air stopped coming in from the vent near the bathroom.

"You got a family, Carlos?" Stan quizzed.

"Yes, I do. My wife and two girls, they live in Mexico."

"They ever visit?"

"No. It cost too much money. I go there three time a year."

"We keep doin' good with our horses ... maybe they could come here."

"That would be nice." Carlos grinned.

"Hey, any you guys bring tomorrow's Form?" Tiger interrupted.

"Loaned mine to a guy down the hall," Stan answered. "Tryin' to get him interested in bein' an owner. All I gotta do is call him and he'll bring it back."

"Please," Tiger said impatiently. "Got a horse I wanna check."

Stan moved toward his phone, on a little stand below the vent near the bathroom.

✦ ✦ ✦

"Where's Tracy today?" Stan asked. "I like that girl. She's got ... chutzpah."

"Picking up her son at school," Cory responded, refraining from any comment on Tracy's "chutzpah," since he had only a vague idea what the word meant. "They'll watch on TV at Santa Anita. Says she doesn't like Hollywood Park."

"Neither does Tiger," Stan reported. "Claims he has nothing but bad luck here."

It was nearly post time for One-Eyed Bandit's next race, at one mile on the grass. Carlos had just joined Cory, Stan and Sandra at Sandra's box seats. Since the Hollywood Park meeting—now in its third week—would only last a month and a half, Cory had opted to continue training the horses at Santa Anita and van them over on the day of their races. This decision seemed logical since: 1) he didn't want to move from his trailer, 2) didn't want to face a daily one-way commute to Hollywood Park of nearly thirty miles, 3) possibly lose Tracy as his exercise rider in the process and 4) the next Santa Anita season, which began the day after Christmas, would be a full four months.

Lasting Impression had run earlier on the program, in an allowance race. He'd disappointed them, making only a brief move at the top of the stretch. He finished last, the same as the day they claimed him. Cory speculated it was the tougher competition this time, however, rather than his knee acting up.

"Hope we're doing the right thing running Bandit on grass," Cory mused.

"Is he bred for it?" Sandra asked.

"Not exactly. But there's no other race for him. And nothing coming up. Unless we tried a stake ..."

"You could wait."

"You're right. And maybe we should have. This race came up tough. But if he takes to grass, it gives us more options."

"Phil always liked this turf course."

"He was right," Cory agreed. "According to everyone I've checked with."

"Buena suerte, Boss."

Cory nodded at Carlos. The horses were in the gate. As usual, Cory was nervous. All the more because of Bandit's lack of grass breeding and the risk in running him on it. Plus the colt was eleven to one in the five-horse field, demonstrating how difficult this race really was. At least he'd drawn the rail again, which Cory considered a positive.

Bandit's start was fine, except for a slight jostle from the horse beside him. After recovering, he breezed into the first turn in third place. Entering the backstretch, jockey Espinoza maintained their position on the rail. A spectator, yelling loudly from a couple of rows behind, both diverted and annoyed Cory, all the more when he couldn't tell who the guy was rooting for.

As the field reached the far turn, the inside horse, of the two in front of Bandit, drifted out, opening a hole on the rail. Espinoza had a decision to make—whether to wait and chance that the hole would close and another wouldn't materialize, or to try sending Bandit through now, possibly prematurely. He chose the latter. With a sudden burst, Bandit shot to the lead and, entering the stretch, quickly opened up two lengths.

The crowd noise elevated, drowning out the loudmouth behind them. Or maybe it was Cory himself, on his feet, cheering for

Bandit, rendering that voice inaudible. Nearing the wire, two horses menaced the colt from the outside. Another, even farther out, threatened to pass the other two. Bandit was running hard, but the threesome were gaining. All four flashed across the line simultaneously.

Although the photo sign appeared on the board, Cory suspected Bandit hadn't won. Nor, he feared, had he placed second or third. With the crowd noise diminished, he could hear the guy behind them again. Loud and clear. Cory still couldn't determine who the guy was rooting for. Or against, for that matter.

The photo sign came down. The numbers went up. Cory's suppositions were accurate. One-Eyed Bandit had finished fourth.

✦ ✦ ✦

"My fault," Espinoza acknowledged. "Should have waited."

"You might not have gotten through," Cory replied.

The rider nodded. He was muscular, with wavy black hair. He'd already weighed out, and Cory now walked with him toward the jockeys' room under the grandstand.

"I'm sure he would have won," Espinoza contended, "if he'd seen those other horses. They snuck up on him."

The rider disappeared into the jockeys' room. Although Cory's own perceptions of the race coincided with Espinoza's, he welcomed the rider's confirmation. But he certainly didn't welcome the afternoon's results. Their two horses had recorded a sort of exacta in reverse. Last and next to last.

✦ ✦ ✦

Like Tracy and Tiger, Cory felt that Hollywood Park wasn't exactly congenial to Carlos and him either. Back during the spring-summer season there, not one of their horses finished first, second or third. His own good fortune had seemed limited only to his association with Janice and the beach cottage he rented. And now their racing luck appeared headed in the same bleak direction.

Cory made a decision. He, Carlos and their two horses would avoid Hollywood Park and wait until the beginning of Santa Anita, less than a month away, to race again. The closest he'd come to Hollywood Park would be to take Cookie to visit Janice, and buy Janice dinner, long overdue.

✦ ✦ ✦

"I'm having a little party on Christmas Eve," Tracy told Cory and Carlos one brisk morning at the barn. "You're both invited."

"That is nice," Carlos said. "But I will be in Mexico with my family."

"When do you leave?" she asked.

"One week."

"Come over before you go. How about Sunday night?"

"That is good."

"I'll make us dinner. You can both meet my son."

"You mean the famous pancake kid?" Cory grinned. "Or is it the well-known waffle dude?"

✦ ✦ ✦

"I got a problem," Tiger informed Stan while standing beside him near some betting windows under the grandstand at Hollywood Park.

"Yeah? Me too."

"Age before beauty," Tiger cracked.

"Well ... Cory wants to put Lasting Impression in a claiming race."

"Because it'll be easier."

"That's what he says."

"His last race an allowance race?" Tiger asked, fully aware of the answer.

"Yeah."

"How'd he finish?" Again Tiger knew.

"Last."

"I know what you can tell Cory."

"What?"

"Tell him," Tiger snickered, "you like finishing last."

That shut Stan up. Or maybe it was the cigarette smoke wafting in their direction. Regardless, the old man started to wheeze, like he was very uncomfortable. Tiger thought he might be suffering some type of attack and spotted a first aid station nearby, just in case.

"Want to hear my problem?" Tiger asked, once Stan began breathing easier.

"Yeah."

"Well ... all my money's tied up in Bandit. And I got none left to bet."

"You want a loan," Stan guessed.

"No. I want to sell my share."

"Of the horse you picked out for us? Who we wouldn't have without you."

"Right."

"You got no sentiment."

"I got no money." Tiger shrugged.

The cigarette smoke was still wafting in their direction. Stan started wheezing again, and took out a handkerchief from a coat pocket and coughed into it. Tiger considered suggesting they go outside into the open air, but the old man put the handkerchief back in his pocket and appeared more comfortable. Besides, Tiger didn't want to lose any momentum established in their dialogue.

"Thought about saying more that night all of us met at Sandra's place," he continued. "I wanted to take that guy's offer. But that chick Tracy seemed so intent. And I didn't want to cheat you and Cory and Carlos outta a nice horse."

"But you'd cheat yourself."

"Rent's due tomorrow."

"You're making a mistake," Stan declared. "And I won't let you do it."

Tiger felt disappointed. No, angry. He'd come all this way, only to get turned down. He hated Hollywood Park even more. He'd never come here again. Ever.

"Tell you what," he said, trying to stay calm. "What that guy offered makes my share of Bandit worth more than ten grand. I'll settle for eight."

"Won't let you do it. Without you, we'd never had this horse."

"If you won't buy my share, least loan me the money."

"No. No buyout. No loan."

Tiger stood there, simmering. He couldn't believe this. The old guy praising him for finding Bandit, yet refusing to help. The smoke wafted again, worse than before, and Stan began wheezing once more. Tiger ignored it. The old guy could choke to death for all he cared.

"I'll give you the money," Stan offered hoarsely.

"What?" Tiger asked, sure he'd heard wrong.

"I'll give you the money. We'll go the ATM right now."

"With my share of Bandit as collateral?"

"No. No collateral."

"But why?"

"I've got my reasons," Stan wheezed. "I've got my reasons."

CHAPTER 14

"WHERE'S THE PANCAKE KID?" Cory asked Tracy. She had just opened her apartment door and welcomed Carlos and him inside her living room.

"Playing in his room." She smiled. "I'll get him in a few minutes."

Cory nodded. He couldn't help staring at her. At her sandy-blond hair tied behind her head with a yellow ribbon. At her gleaming light-green eyes. At the turquoise earrings she had on. For the first time in his presence, she wore a dress—ankle length, also yellow. Though the dress cloaked her figure, the turquoise belt around her waist showed how slender she was.

"I baked a turkey," she said. "Are either of you good at carving?"

"I will do it," Carlos volunteered. "Cory, he will just make a mess."

No question. Especially in his current state. Even under normal circumstances, the turkey would be splattered all over. An outcome he'd certainly rather avoid here, now.

Tracy and Carlos went into the kitchen, while Cory remained in the living room. The aroma of turkey was prominent, something he hadn't perceived before. He looked around. The room was small. There was a tiny adjoining dining room with a plain brown table set for dinner. He assumed that the rest of the apartment was small, too. The living room furniture was simple, mostly beige, the color of the carpeting. Several paintings of horses adorned the walls.

"Taking beverage orders," she addressed him from behind, startling him briefly.

"Water's fine."

"You sure? I've got several choices."

"I'm sure," he answered, glancing from her to the paintings. "You do these?"

"I did."

"They're remarkable. You're very talented."

"Thanks," she replied softly.

He looked closely at the paintings, done in watercolor. He could tell they were portraits of former great racing stars, by the names etched on the saddlecloth of each horse. Native Dancer, Kelso, Cigar, Nashua and Secretariat were all depicted. Although his knowledge of their appearances was limited to old photographs, he sensed each painting was a perfect replica.

"These are good enough to be in museums," he praised.

"In my dreams ... But a restaurant and gallery around here *do* let me hang my work."

"For sale?"

"Yes. But buyers are rare. I do much better on my commissioned stuff."

"Commissioned stuff?" he questioned.

"I have some steady clients who own horses and want paintings of them."

"Like the ones Sandra has in her living room?"

"Very observant," she commended.

"You didn't paint hers?"

"I wish ... Maybe some day."

She turned and left the room again. This time she went down a short hallway. He considered joining Carlos in the kitchen, but knew he would only be in the way. She returned to the room, this time a small boy following her.

"Cory," she said, "this is Perry."

Cory shook hands with the boy. He suddenly understood a lot. Tracy's protectiveness of Perry. Avoiding the other partners whenever Bandit raced. Rejecting his, Cory's, breakfast invitations where Perry might be involved. It all now made sense, for it was apparent that Perry could see from solely his right eye, his left was immobile and offered no vision.

Cory took Perry's hand again and shook it once more.

✦ ✦ ✦

"Perry and I have never been to Mexico," Tracy told Carlos soon after the four of them sat down at the dining room table and started the meal. "We'd like to go someday."

"You would be welcome to stay at my house," Carlos replied.

"Thank you. That's very nice."

"You can go anytime. Let me know when you would like to."

Cory didn't mind being omitted from their dialogue. On the contrary, it gave him the chance to gaze at the boy and then at his mother, both sitting across the table from him. Plus he could admire the food in front of them all. In addition to turkey—beets, peas and corn on the cob. And everything tasted even better to him than it had at Sandra's elegant dinner.

"Perry likes baseball," Tracy informed them, obviously trying to involve the youngster in the conversation.

"Really," Cory enthused. "I like baseball too."

"He played in a league last summer."

"Oh?"

"Tee ball."

"Great." Cory grinned. "Maybe we could work out sometime."

Perry smiled. He had a very nice smile, his entire face lighting up and his blue eyes twinkling. He had brown hair and, like his mother, a slender frame.

"Do you follow the major leagues?" Cory asked him.

"Yes."

"Me too."

"Who's your favorite team?" Perry inquired.

"In Arizona I followed the Diamondbacks."

"You mean the D-Backs," Perry corrected, proving himself a knowledgeable baseball enthusiast, since that's how one would refer to the team.

"Right. But before the D-Backs, I liked the Dodgers. When I was a teenager, we could get their games on radio. I loved hearing Vin Scully. Now I can listen to him here."

"Maybe you also like the Dodgers," Carlos said to Perry.

"No. I like the American League. Because they have the designated hitter."

More information that made sense to Cory. For if Perry had trouble seeing, then he'd have trouble fielding. Thus he would favor teams for which a player might not have to field.

At that moment, Cory felt like reaching across the table and shaking Perry's hand again. This time he managed to restrain himself.

✦ ✦ ✦

"We have brought you gifts," Carlos announced after returning from Cory's car with two wrapped packages.

He handed one to Perry and the other to Tracy. Next he sat down in a chair across from them and Cory, who were sitting on a large couch that seemingly took up most of the space in the living room. They'd already done the dishes—Carlos clearing the table, Tracy washing and Cory and Perry drying. Cory felt uncomfortable, not because of any concern over whether they'd like the gifts, but because he'd badly overeaten.

"Thank you," Tracy said, "but there was no need."

"There was no need for you to make us this nice dinner," Carlos retorted.

"Can we wait until Christmas to open them?" She looked a little shy, or possibly it was embarrassment.

"I will not be back until after Christmas from Mexico."

"Okay, let's let Perry open his now. I'll wait until you get back."

That's all Perry needed to hear. He literally tore his present open, even with Tracy admonishing him to slow down. Cory and Carlos both laughed. Perry immediately held up the contents—a dark-brown cowboy hat—and his face lighted up again.

This time he initiated the handshakes, first with Carlos, then with Cory.

✦ ✦ ✦

Cory was even more impressed with Sandra's house this time. It was a few days before Christmas and her place was decorated resplendently for the season. That wasn't the reason, however. No, on the other occasion, after the threat to Tracy about a month ago, it was evening. This afternoon, in broad daylight, Sandra had just given him the complete tour of her estate, not possible the other time in the dark.

He'd been amazed by her backyard. Back acreage would be better terminology. He couldn't see where her property ended and someone else's began. What he could see were numerous trees, thick foliage, two flower gardens and a huge swimming pool.

Once they sat down in her living room, a large picture window presenting a terrific view of what they'd just surveyed, he wondered why she'd invited him here. Something he'd done regularly since her phone call yesterday. He was certain it hadn't been solely to provide a magnificent tour. Nor to offer holiday greetings. Or to brief him on any recent exchange she'd had with Dobson. No, she must have something fresh in mind.

"Phil and I lived here thirty-two years," she informed him, supplying no clue. "Originally I sold him the house. I was working in real estate back then."

"Interesting," Cory replied, able to think of no other response.

"I helped him furnish it and decorate. I even helped him find a housekeeper and gardener. Eventually he proposed tying everything together into a package deal. With me being part of the package ... as his wife."

Cory listened without saying anything, not sure what response was expected, yet fairly certain she hadn't brought him here solely to chronicle the details of her courtship. He observed that a gardener had come and was beginning to mow some grass off in the distance.

"We had a good life together," she sighed. "Horses always part of it. I don't want that to change ... just because I've lost him."

"If I can help ..." Cory ventured, still unsure.

"You can," she quickly answered. "I'm looking for just the right person. Someone I can trust."

She paused there. Maybe she expected a reaction, but he offered none. The gardener came closer, so that Cory could now hear the mower.

"I'm looking for someone to manage my racing and breeding operations," she continued. "Someone who can help me downsize and streamline. The right person would earn a nice income. I'm pretty sure *you're* the right person."

He realized he should have had some idea this was coming. Certainly he knew that she had plenty to deal with. And that it would be a lot for anyone, even someone as competent as she appeared, to manage everything without able assistance. Yet he'd been so busy trying to eke out a living with their little two-horse stable that he hadn't given her situation any thought. And never even dreamed she might call upon him.

"Wow," was all he could muster.

"I'm sure you'll need some time to think things over."

Really, he'd already started thinking things over. Without doubt he trusted her. And wasn't concerned about their ability to work together. Plus he definitely could use the income. Still, there were immediate questions.

"Would I be able to keep my stable?"

"I've given that plenty of consideration ... I'm afraid not. I'd want you to be exclusive. Phil never liked any possibility of divided allegiance."

"What about Carlos? Could he assist me?"

"I'm sure we could find something for him. With one of my other trainers."

"But he and I have worked together many years. Side by side."

Her shrug indicated unwillingness to compromise. Presumably she'd have the same attitude toward Tracy. Why even bring her up? He thought about their horses, too. He definitely didn't like the idea of Bandit and Lasting Impression winding up in the hands of other trainers.

"I'm honored you'd consider me," he said softly. "Very honored. But I'm afraid I'm *not* the right person."

"Why? Because I want you and only you ... working for me?"

"There's more to it."

"Business reasons?" she guessed.

"Hardly. Not with just two horses in our stable."

"With me you might have at least ten times that many to oversee."

"I know ... But you said manage your horses ... not train them."

"Right."

"You told me about your marriage, Sandra. Time for me to tell you a little about mine."

"Okay."

"Susan used to say that I was married to the horses I trained ... much more than I ever was married to her. It still bothers me a lot because I'm afraid she was right. I'm a trainer, Sandra. No more, no less."

"Even if a better offer comes along?"

"I'm a trainer, Sandra. No more, no less."

"I see ..."

"I came to California for a fresh outlook. Maybe get the chance to train a really good horse or two. Which, at least partly thanks to you, seems to have happened."

She didn't reply. Not that he'd have heard her anyway. The gardener was working on a section nearby, and the mower was noisy.

"Maybe I could help you, though," he practically shouted.

"How?" she spoke loudly back.

"Maybe I could help you find someone."

"Do you have someone in mind?"

"Let me think about it ... Oh ... and thanks for considering me."

"Happy holidays."

He wished her the same. Before getting up to leave, he took one last look through the picture window, at the splendid view outside.

✦ ✦ ✦

"This is not a good life for any of us," Alicia told Carlos.

They sat in the living room. Rosa and Luisa were in their bedroom, wrapping Christmas gifts. It was early evening and the weather had turned cold, an icy wind whistling through nearby shrubbery. They had their furnace on high, yet the room still felt chilly. Carlos had arrived this morning and although he had napped earlier, he remained tired from the lengthy bus ride home.

He sat in his favorite chair, reserved only for him. It was an heirloom his grandfather constructed as a young man. Ordinarily Alicia spoke Spanish to him. Except when she had something serious to say. Then, for some reason, she spoke English.

"The girls, they are getting older," she continued. "They will soon be in high school. And they hardly know their father."

He remained silent. Really, what was there to say? Alicia spoke the truth. They'd had this conversation previously, but he recognized that this time she was more determined. He wouldn't be able to brush her off easily, like he'd done before. Instead of replying, he merely gazed at her. At her dark hair, brown eyes, cherubic face and ample figure, much fuller than his own slim one.

"I speak the other day with Orozco," she went on. "He say he is growing old and needs help. He say you can work for him."

"I do not want to work for Orozco," Carlos declared impatiently. "I do not want to ranch. As a boy, that is all I do."

"What do you do now? What is the difference?"

"You think a cow is a racehorse?" he answered sharply, as the wind outside lashed some window shutters. "You think a pig is a racehorse? Do not ask me what is the difference."

"Cows. Pigs. Horses. I think they are all the same ... if they allow a man to live with his family."

He knew this was very serious. She had never before disparaged his profession. He felt his anger mount. Then he remembered her original point. His daughters were getting older. And doing so mostly without their father.

He didn't reply right away. He was thinking. He was thinking of the two horses in California, Cory and his. In all the years they'd been together, they'd never had horses this good. Horses that had each won a race at Santa Anita. Allowance races, no less.

"I would like six months," he said softly. "Until June. Until school is over for the summer."

She didn't respond. He sensed they'd struck a bargain. That's what he liked most about her—she was reasonable. She'd given him time before and now evidently she'd done it again. He got up from the chair and kissed her cheek.

He started inside to see Rosa and Luisa. He wanted to spend all the time he could with them. Before he had to make the long trip back to California.

✦ ✦ ✦

Standing on the sidewalk in front of her apartment, Cory knew he was making a mistake. Christmas simply wasn't a day to drop in on someone, uninvited. Even bearing a gift for the boy. Or bringing Cookie along. Or having something to discuss. None of these could atone for the intrusion.

He led Cookie back toward his car, parked nearby on the street. The morning was so cold he could see their breath in front of them. When he got to the car, he turned around and looked at her apartment door, as if the sight of it could help him with his indecision. Then he remembered that this was the first morning in almost three months that he hadn't seen her.

He'd insisted she take the morning off, and exercised the horses himself. No easy task with both her and Carlos not there. He'd hired a groom temporarily though, who helped him get the horses ready for the track, so he managed. Anyway it was a good excuse to ride, something he liked doing once in a while, if only to keep in shape.

He edged back toward her apartment. He held the long, narrow, poorly wrapped gift in one hand, Cookie's leash in the other. He knew he should have called ahead. That was the least he could do on a day as special as Christmas. But then that would've spoiled the surprise.

He heard a kid shout from up the street, and thought it might be the boy. No, no such luck, this youngster, breezing by on a bicycle, was much older. This time Cory made it all the way to the door.

He knocked. No immediate answer. Maybe she and the boy had gone out to visit friends, or to church, or to Christmas brunch somewhere. Then he remembered she'd mentioned having a little party on Christmas Eve. Mightn't that have something to do with her not answering?

He knocked again. Still no sign of anyone home. It appeared that he was lucky—she'd never know of his indiscretion. He turned away, leading Cookie. Then he heard something from inside. The door opened. He turned around and saw Tracy standing there.

"Hi," she greeted.

"Wanted to talk to you," he mumbled, his voice wavering.

"Come in."

"Maybe we'd better stay outside. Because of Cookie."

"Don't be silly. She can come in too."

She reached down and patted Cookie behind her left ear. Cory observed that Tracy's breath wasn't visible like his and Cookie's. She wore an outfit he'd seen on her before—tan jeans and a light-brown fitted top under a sleeveless green down jacket.

"Perry and I decorated since you and Carlos were here," she said as he and Cookie followed her into her living room. "We've had time since he's been out of school for the holidays."

Cory was treated to a roomful of bright Christmas ornaments. Although not so abundant as what he'd witnessed at Sandra's, they were more colorful. Unfortunately they only made him more aware of his intrusion, and he silently chided himself.

"Where's Perry?" he asked, awkwardly shifting the gift from one hand to the other.

"Putting on his jacket and shoes. We were just going out for a walk."

"Sorry. I've intruded."

"No you haven't. You can come too. Perry loves dogs."

Right on cue, Perry entered the room. He was wearing the dark-brown cowboy hat Cory and Carlos had given him. When Tracy pointed to one of his shoes being untied, he merely shrugged, without allowing her admonition to alter his direct course to Cookie.

"Once you tie your shoes," Cory coaxed, elevating the wrapped gift.

"You already gave him something," Tracy objected.

"That was from Carlos."

"You had no part in it?"

"That was from Carlos," he repeated.

She smiled. Kneeling beside Cookie, Perry quickly tied his shoe. Then he reached out to Cory and shook his hand, obviously recalling their handshakes during their other encounter. Cory gave him the present and he eagerly unwrapped it.

"Oh boy." He beamed at a shiny brown wooden baseball bat.

"There's a card," Cory said.

"Could you read it, Mom?"

Perry handed it to her. She silently mouthed the message. First she smiled. Then she broke into laughter.

"It shows every team in the American League, Perry. All chasing a pennant. And all searching for a designated hitter who will help them. Guess who?"

"Who, Mom?"

"The owner of the bat."

Perry laughed and shook Cory's hand again. "Could I take the bat with me on our walk, Mom?"

"Okay. Provided you go put on a heavier jacket."

That didn't take long. They all went outside, Cory on Tracy's right, leading Cookie, Perry on Tracy's left, holding his new bat. Ironically, the same kid Cory had seen earlier whizzed by on his bicycle again. This time, though, he was headed the opposite way.

"How about a trade, Perry?" Cory suggested. "I'll take the bat, you take Cookie?"

After hesitating briefly, Perry reached for the leash. Following the exchange, he led Cookie on ahead. Or, more accurately, she led him. Cory noticed that Tracy's breath, unlike his, Perry's or Cookie's, still wasn't visible in the cold air.

"Can you use some extra money?" he asked, once Perry was out of earshot.

"Who can't?"

"Wanted to talk to you first. Before I brought up your name."

"To who?"

"To Sandra Talbot."

"About what?"

"She's looking for someone to help manage her horses. Racing and breeding."

"Could I still ride?"

"Don't think so. But I'm sure she'll pay well. Lots more than me."

"What about hours?"

"Don't know," he admitted.

"Shall I call her?"

"No. I'll do it."

"Thanks. But what's in it for you?"

"Just trying to keep one of my owners happy." He smiled.

"Which one?" she asked, a gleam in her eye. "Sandra or me?"

"Sandra, of course," he winked.

✦ ✦ ✦

"Want to come in?" Tracy asked Cory once they all got back to her doorstep. "I'll make some hot chocolate. Warm us up a little."

Of course he would. Except that he didn't want to acknowledge any purpose to his visit other than delivering Perry's gift and discussing the job opportunity. Nor did he want to admit missing being with her at the track this morning. Besides, Cookie hadn't seen her boyfriend, the Irish setter, yet today and she might start barking. Something he'd feared she'd do when the four of them stopped at a park a little while ago so Perry could take a few swings with the new bat.

"We've imposed enough," he replied.

"You didn't impose."

"Merry Christmas."

"Merry Christmas," Tracy and Perry responded, in unison.

And, of course, Perry, for the third time this morning, shook Cory's hand.

CHAPTER 15

LIKE THE FIRST TIME HE SAW Santa Anita some three months ago, Cory got goose bumps. This time it was from watching Lasting Impression, whom he had just finished saddling, heading toward the track, jockey Pedroza aboard, for the very first race of the new meeting.

It was the day after Christmas, regular opening day for the Santa Anita winter season. Cory had been told that this particular day had the most tradition of any in California racing, however it took experiencing it himself to understand. Though it was still early, before noon, it had warmed up nicely and a huge crowd was already present. A vibrant mariachi band was performing outside the grandstand. People seemed much friendlier, smiles everywhere, than on a typical day at the track. Even the horses had looked different—more stately and refined—while parading around the walking ring for the race, a twenty-five-thousand-dollar claimer.

As he headed toward Sandra's box seats to join Stan and Tiger, Cory heard the bugler play the call to the post, signaling the initial horse's arrival onto the track. He felt his goose bumps grow even more pronounced. The fact that their horse was running in the very first race today, and that he, Cory, was actually a participant in the festivities, only heightened his exhilaration.

✦ ✦ ✦

Besides being big, the opening-day crowd was loud. As the field in the first race sprinted into the stretch, Stan got to his feet and yelled along with everyone. Lasting Impression was fifth, but spurting. Yet even Stan, with his limited sight, could tell that his horse's move was too little, too late. Yes, he passed one horse, then another at the wire, however he managed to finish only a distant third.

"Sorry," Cory, standing next to Stan, apologized.

"Don't be," Stan replied. "Nothin' wrong with third."

"Not that," Cory explained. "It's the red tag in the jockey valet's pocket."

"You mean they claimed him?"

"'Fraid so."

As a horseplayer, Stan had lost thousands of bets. As a horse owner, he'd never lost a horse, and he didn't know exactly how to react. Waves of anger and grief passed through him.

"Told you we should've stuck to allowance races," he accused.

"And he'd probably finish last again," Tiger retorted from the row in front.

"I liked that horse," Stan grumbled.

"I'd liked him better if he'd won," Tiger complained.

"He was good to us," Cory interjected. "A win, a second and a third. Plus the profit on the claim."

"Not talking profit here," Stan disputed. "Talking sentiment."

"Maybe you'd like a hankie," Tiger laughed, pulling a white one from a pants pocket and handing it to Stan.

✦ ✦ ✦

"I think they're now playing by the rules," Cory told Sandra the next morning over his barn phone. "Thanks to you."

"You mean Dobson?" she inquired.

"And Kosko. They claimed Lasting Impression yesterday."

"Is that good?"

"It's not bad. The horse was beginning to tail off."

"Oh," was all she said.

"Anyway, the good news is this may be their way of retaliating for Bandit. Instead of that other stuff."

"What if they claim all your horses?" she queried, sounding concerned.

"All one of them," he snickered. "Bandit. He won't be in a claiming race."

"Told you I had something good on them."

"Glad you don't have something good on me."

"Wish I did," she teased. "I'd make you accept my offer."

He didn't answer. He spotted jockey Espinoza's agent passing in front of the barn, and he made a mental note to discuss with him possible races for Bandit.

"Sure you won't reconsider?" she asked.

"I'm sure. But I do have someone to recommend."

✦ ✦ ✦

"Cory speaks highly of you," Sandra told Tracy above the sound of raindrops beating hard against the Santa Anita grandstand roof. "Do you think you can handle the job?"

"I'd like to try," Tracy answered earnestly.

The two of them sat in Sandra's box. One of her horses would be running in an hour and Sandra had invited Tracy to meet here forty-five minutes ago, and had already gone over the basics of the new position. Things like maintaining inventory of the horses, progress reports on each horse, sales dates and regular estimates on the value of every horse. Plus Tracy's schedule and prospective salary. Fortunately they'd both arrived before the deluge began, so neither was wet. Cold was another matter, as a wintry wind sliced through the grandstand.

"Any questions?" Sandra asked.

"Can't think of anything."

"Any concerns?"

"Just one," Tracy answered.

"What?"

"Not what," she clarified. "Who."

"Who?"

"My son, Perry. He's always priority in my life. In fact, I've got to leave soon to pick him up at school."

"How old is he?"

"Eight."

"You're forgetting something," Sandra said.

"What?"

"I'm a mother myself."

✦ ✦ ✦

Cookie had lost interest in her boyfriend. Lately, she walked right by him, not even stopping. No more following him. In fact if anyone followed anyone, it was him following her. Cory accused her of being fickle. But he really couldn't blame her. Not with Perry, who adored her, now so firmly in her life.

With Tracy's permission, Cory had given Perry his cell phone number. Regularly, normally late in the afternoon, Perry called. Cory would leave Santa Anita or wherever he was, go by his place to pick up Cookie and drive to Perry's apartment. The three of them, plus Tracy sometimes, would head off on a walk.

✦ ✦ ✦

"We've never talked about your father," Cory said one afternoon Tracy wasn't along.

"We never talk about him," Perry replied.

"Did you know him?"

"We never talk about him," he repeated sadly.

"Then let's talk about something else."

In reality, they'd already talked about several other things so far during their walk. A movie Perry had seen. A football game they'd both watched on TV last weekend, separately. How Cookie had given Cory a scare when she was much younger, after developing a bad case of mange.

Like on Christmas day, Perry held Cookie's leash and Cory held Perry's bat. They'd stopped at a park a few blocks from Perry's and let Cookie roam. While Cory watched closely, Perry took several swings with the bat. Afterward, the day being sunny and warm, they'd visited a grocery store for cold drinks, and some water for Cookie.

"How's school?" Cory asked, fulfilling the requisite change of subjects.

"Fine. The other kids don't bother me anymore."

"Did they bother you before?"

"Yes. Till I got them to stop."

"How'd you do that?"

"Running," Perry answered.

"You ran away from them?"

"Sort of. We had a race. I won. So they leave me alone now."

Cory wasn't sure of the logic behind all this, but he opted not to question it. Besides, at that moment his attention was diverted by the same kid he'd seen Christmas morning, whizzing by them on his bicycle.

✦ ✦ ✦

"Would you trade me for two new horses?" Tracy asked right after arriving at the barn one foggy January morning.

"No way," Cory answered. "You're worth at least a dozen."

"Sorry." She smiled. "Not according to my new boss."

"Sandra?"

"Sandra."

"She won't let you keep riding for me?"

"Nope. Claims it shows favoritism. Can't have me working for you when most her horses are with other trainers. Anyway, I wouldn't have time. She wants me inspecting all her horses at the track and updating her every morning."

He wasn't happy. Of course he knew this might happen. If Sandra required his exclusivity, why wouldn't she ask the same of Tracy? Especially since an arsenal like Sandra's was far more significant than their measly one-horse stable.

Maybe he should have conferred with Sandra about whether they'd be losing their exercise rider, before so cavalierly recommending her. Yet how could he complain? Tracy was bettering herself. Instead of the pittance he could barely afford to pay her, now she'd likely make a living at the track.

"Don't look so sad," she teased. "Have only yourself to blame."

Were his thoughts that transparent? Or did she have mind-reading abilities, along with all her other skills? Maybe she simply liked to rub it in. Regardless, his theorizing was interrupted by a trainer he'd recently met, who walked past in the fog and waved.

"Tried to get her to send you more horses," she disclosed. "At first she wasn't going to give you any … as your penalty for turning her down, I think. Got her to compromise … at two."

"Guess I should thank you," he muttered.

"Guess so." She grinned. Then her expression turned serious. "Why didn't we talk *before* you rejected her offer? We could've discussed it from your side too."

"Lot we haven't discussed," he snapped.

"Like what?"

"Like Perry's father."

"What's that have to do with this?" she reacted curtly.

"You riding for us today?" he summarily changed the subject as Carlos led Bandit from his stall. "Or do I have to go find someone else?"

"I'm riding today," she confirmed softly. "I guess for the last time."

"I *guess* you better get to work, then. Gallop him once around."

"One thing I did get her to promise," she said. "I can spend as much time with Bandit as I want. That is, if it's okay with you."

"Can't stop an owner seeing their horse," he grunted.

He watched Carlos boost her aboard Bandit. As she and the colt headed for the track, Cory trailed far behind. He realized that, once they got there, he'd have a hard time seeing her gallop him in the fog. But then he could always draw upon all his past images of her riding, and how well she fit the colt. Like he'd no doubt be doing after today.

CHAPTER 16

"THIS MONEY'S BURNING A HOLE IN my pocket," Stan told Cory, who was watching Bandit warm up on the track for his next race, just minutes away. Besides the two of them, Tracy, Carlos and Tiger were seated in Sandra's box.

"Money burnin'!" Tiger enthused. "Let's go bet it."

"It's not bettin' money," Stan explained. "It's claimin' money. Want Cory to hurry up, claim another horse."

"Looking every day," Cory responded. "Thought I had one couple days ago. Talked myself out of it."

"Don't be so choosy," Stan chided. "Remember, I'm not getting any younger."

"That's for sure," Tiger laughed. "Anyway, let's quit this small talk and go make some bets ... while you're still *living.*"

He got up and practically dragged the old man out of his seat, toward the betting windows. Tracy and Carlos both chuckled at their antics, but Cory didn't. Plain and simple, as usual, he was nervous before a big race. Especially since this was a stakes, and a hundred-thousand-dollar one at that—by far the biggest purse for which he and Carlos had ever competed.

Because all racehorses, for simplification purposes, had a mythical birthday of January 1, Bandit was now three. Cory didn't relish the idea of a stakes race, with its difficult opposition, but the colt had been training well and an allowance race he would have preferred failed to draw enough entrants. Thus today's Sham Stakes, restricted to three-year-olds, at one mile.

"Thought you had money burning?" Tiger chastised as he and Stan returned. "Fifty lousy bucks."

"Figure of speech," the old man rebutted.

"*Figure of speech,*" Tiger mimicked. "What kinda horse think you can claim for fifty bucks? An amputee?"

"Yeah, an amputee. Kinda horse you like to bet on."

"Drags me all the way up there," Tiger complained, "for fifty lousy bucks."

Cory did achieve a smile at this exchange. Particularly when he recalled that Tiger had dragged Stan, not the reverse as Tiger had accused. A quick glance at the board, however, wiped the smile off Cory's face. He was reminded that Bandit was the longest shot in the race, at odds of twenty-seven to one.

"Hey," Stan said, turning toward Tracy while the first of the nine horses entered the starting gate. "Where's Sandra today?"

"One of her grandchildren's in a school play," she answered. " 'One Potato, Two Potato'. I think he's playing Potato Number Two."

"And where's Perry?" Cory asked her.

"Not feeling well."

"Oh?"

"Just the sniffles. I decided to splurge and get him a sitter for the afternoon. Now that I'm on salary ..."

"Don't rub it in," Cory grinned.

None of this repartee, though, relieved Cory's tension. Nor did Carlos wishing him "buena suerte." The odds had climbed to twenty-nine to one. The colt was obviously over his head and they should have waited for an allowance race, no matter how long it took.

The start didn't help Cory's nerves. Although Bandit appeared to break well, jockey Espinoza eased him back. When a horse bore out in front of them, they were forced farther back. Into the first turn, they hadn't a single horse beaten and were nearly twenty lengths behind the leader.

Cory felt some anger. Though he'd given Espinoza no instructions, this certainly wasn't a strategy. The colt had shown a little useful early speed in his other races. Why not deploy some of it today?

Nothing changed around the turn or through the backstretch. By the time the field reached the far turn, Cory's anger had won out over his nerves. Bandit was even farther back, perhaps twenty-five lengths, with no sign of making the slightest impact. As the noise from the large Saturday crowd began swelling, Cory wished he could disappear. Their first "hundred grander," something he'd only dreamed about before, was rapidly becoming a nightmare.

A definite possibility crossed his mind. The colt had gone wrong and Espinoza was simply protecting him. A minor injury could become major if he were forced to extend himself. What other reason could there be for this strategy?

The field entered the stretch. Still last. Espinoza swung Bandit to the far outside. The colt began to show some life. A horse in front of him was making a solid move and he followed, flashing sudden acceleration. "Flight" might be a better term. The crowd noise reached new crescendo, as if accompaniment for Bandit's furious climax. Still on the far outside, he passed horse after horse, including the one he had followed. His only problem—the wire came too soon. Three or four strides past it, he took the lead. Two horses had crossed the finish line in front of him, however.

One-Eyed Bandit had placed third in the one-hundred-thousand-dollar Sham Stakes.

✦ ✦ ✦

"Maybe you want to fire me," Espinoza told Cory after dismounting Bandit and patting his neck once.

"Why?"

"Moved too late this time. Wanted him sneaking up on *them* ... not them on him like last time."

Cory didn't reply. He was a little out of breath from rushing with Carlos to the track from Sandra's seats. He watched Carlos lead Bandit off toward the barn. Espinoza went over to the scales to weigh out, then returned to Cory.

"Even with me screwing up," the rider said, "he almost made up for it. Got lots of heart and loves to run."

The two of them walked through the tunnel under the grandstand, leading toward the path to the jockeys' room. A spectator yelled at Espinoza, complaining that he'd just cost him thousands of dollars.

"Another thing," the rider continued, ignoring the spectator. "Wanted an idea how far he'd run."

"How far?" Cory bit.

"Far as they run."

"You're not thinking Santa Anita Derby?"

"And maybe Kentucky," Espinoza winked.

✦ ✦ ✦

To say Cory was ecstatic about Bandit's performance would be understatement. Ditto, to an even greater extent, for his feelings about Espinoza's comments regarding the colt. Here was a jockey who had participated frequently in the Kentucky Derby, unquestionably the most famous and consequential race in America, introducing the possibility of riding Bandit in this year's edition. (He'd even won the race twice, in 2002 and in 2014.) Granted, Cory recognized this was no commitment from the jockey, and that jockeys and their agents were notoriously fickle, yet the concept was certainly appealing.

Cory knew better than to allow his euphoria to last, however. Not with him understanding how quickly things could change in this game. Not with the reality of Carlos and him having to return to their daily grind. With Tracy no longer available to them, and their stable, thanks to Sandra, now up to three, they resumed their former method of training. Basically, Carlos prepared each horse every morning and Cory exercised them. They split the other chores according to who had time. As Kosko accused during his very first visit, theirs was one of the last of the two-man stables.

The two new horses Sandra sent them couldn't have been more opposite. A green unraced, unnamed two-year-old filly fresh off the farm, and a seven-year-old pro with no fewer than twelve wins on his resumé. The latter had a record reminiscent of Rugged Landing's. He even looked like Rugged Landing—lanky and chestnut. Plus he had a similar name—Turbulent Flight. All this of course reminded Cory of those final days in Arizona nine months ago, and at times he even caught himself gazing at the new horse in his stall, for no apparent reason.

The new filly wouldn't run for at least a couple of months, hopefully in one of a series of two-furlong races Cory learned were carded for two-year-olds late in the Santa Anita meeting. Turbulent Flight, on the other hand, would likely run next week in an upper-level claimer.

Judging from his recent form, he'd have an excellent chance to win. A welcome prospect, because it had been nearly three months since Cory and Carlos's last victory.

✦　✦　✦

"You're trusting me more," Cory told Tracy one cool afternoon. They were walking almost a hundred feet behind Perry and Cookie.

"Meaning?" she asked.

"Perry ... Letting me take him without you."

"Trust has nothing to do with it. Sandra's been keeping me busy. Afternoon's the only time I can paint."

"So you don't trust me."

"I didn't say that." She grinned.

Cory was right. If not about trust, then about taking Perry out alone more often. In fact this was the first time in two weeks Tracy went along.

"How's the job?" he asked.

"Not easy. She's got a lot of horses to keep up with."

"How many?"

"Right now at the track ... eighteen."

"Didn't know she had that many."

"She's been shuffling some in from her farm. The number changes almost daily."

"Good thing you're a math whiz," he winked.

"But I'm not. And working with some of these people isn't easy."

"Her trainers?" he quizzed.

"Yes. Some of them are real jerks."

"Present company included?"

"Remains to be seen." She smiled.

On ahead, Cookie stopped on some grass to pee. When she and Perry continued walking once she finished, Cory noticed that she was limping on her left front leg. He was about to speed up and call out to alert Perry, but the boy observed the problem himself. He kneeled down and apparently extracted something from Cookie's foot. Problem solved—Cookie resumed her normal walk.

"Your son, the doctor?" Cory kidded.

"I'll settle for him becoming a vet," she laughed.

"Probably make as much money."

"Around a racetrack," she opined, "probably make more."

"His eyesight ..." he ventured cautiously after pausing, aware he was entering unexplored territory. "Is it a problem in school?"

"Not really. Most of the work's up close. His trouble's depth and distance."

"Will it get better?"

"His sight?" she answered. "No, it won't get better. It's his optic nerve. Can't be repaired."

He considered asking how it happened. Whether Perry was born this way, or suffered some type of accident or disease. But something, likely her reflective melancholy expression, discouraged him. He chose a more oblique approach.

"You like his playing baseball?"

"Up to him."

"If it's up to him, I think he'll keep playing."

She shrugged without replying, then zipped the gray jacket she was wearing.

"Why's baseball so important?" he pressed on.

Another shrug.

"Anything to do with his father?" he guessed.

"We try not to talk about his father."

"You don't trust me to know."

"Trust has nothing to do with it."

"Maybe I can help," he offered.

"You are."

"How?"

"By doing exactly what you're doing."

"What am I doing?"

"Being a friend."

"To who? Perry, or you?"

"He's crazy about you."

"Looks like he likes Cookie better," he joked, gesturing toward the two of them, strolling on well ahead.

"I like you too," she said, ignoring his comment, a diffident look in her eyes.

This quieted him a moment. She'd never, in the slightest way, mentioned affection before. Not to him, anyway. Yet he wanted to forge on, try to achieve some understanding of her past. Perry's past.

"His father play baseball?"

"I'd rather not talk about it."

"I'd like to know."

"If I tell you, will you stop there?"

"Yes."

"Yes," she said following a pause. "His father played baseball. Took Perry to his games. I'm sure it's an identity thing now. A way for Perry to hold on."

"But he doesn't want to talk about him either," Cory replied, a little confused.

"You said you'd stop if I answered your question."

She was right, he had. Besides, he'd probably probed enough for one afternoon. Almost reflexively, they both began walking faster. Perry and Cookie had gotten too far ahead.

✦ ✦ ✦

"Within a month," Sandra told Tracy, "I'd like us to decide which horses we keep to race and which ones we sell."

"How many will we keep?" Tracy asked.

"No more than ten."

It was mid-morning and they sat virtually alone in a little coffeehouse near Santa Anita. Tracy had recommended it because she liked the old Victorian building housing it and the dark-brown woodcuts embellishing the walls. Sandra had come to Santa Anita during training hours this morning for only the second time since Tracy began working for her, picking today because one of her horses was running this afternoon, in the first race on the program. From a vantage point on the steps leading up to the grandstand, near where Cory usually stood at the top of the stretch, they'd watched most of her horses train.

"I've asked Luke Ridley to help us decide about my broodmares on the farm," Sandra said as a couple of people entered the coffeehouse. "Which to keep and which to sell."

"How many will we keep?"

"Five at the most. He starts a new position for another farm the first of the month. At the beginning of breeding season. He promised me he'd make his recommendations by then."

"What will you do with your farm?"

"Put it up for sale."

"Where will the broodmares go?" Tracy asked.

"Luke will take them with him to the other farm. As boarders. He'll keep the babies there too. Until we can sort everything out."

Tracy nodded. She could see that working for Sandra would be even more complicated than she thought. Momentarily, her attention was diverted by the loud whirring of a blender in the background. She liked the pungent coffee aroma it produced.

"The main thing, though ..." Sandra said once the noise subsided, "is to keep the dream alive. Phil and mine ... To develop a champion."

Tracy nodded again. She sensed Sandra's sadness, however, so she tried to think of a way to graciously change the subject. Sandra, after taking a bite of sweet roll they'd bought earlier, beat her to it.

"Enough about this. I want to hear about you. How'd you get into racing?"

"It's nothing unusual," Tracy replied, fingering a napkin on the table in front of her.

"Tell me."

"Grew up in Half Moon Bay, near San Francisco. They had stables there. I used to sneak off to ride. Someone knew someone who knew someone at Bay Meadows, close by. When I was in high school, I'd walk hots on weekends. Someone else there gave me a chance to ride."

"Do you have family?"

"Not a pretty picture. My mother died when I was six and my father remarried. The wicked stepmother thing. I probably used horses as an escape."

"You must miss riding now," Sandra speculated.

"Yes."

"I could feel it earlier, when we were watching the horses train."

Tracy was sure Sandra wasn't happy about this. Ditto her childhood history. So she didn't say any more. Besides, the blender noise started up again. And she could tell Sandra was getting edgy. As if she didn't like this place she, Tracy, had suggested.

Plus one of Sandra's horses would be running soon.

CHAPTER 17

CORY TOSSED A PITCH OVER THE middle of home plate. Perry swung and missed. For the sixth consecutive time. He was using his new bat. No danger he'd break it, though. A bat wouldn't break hitting only air.

"You're getting closer," Cory encouraged.

It was true. Whereas Perry was missing by several feet when they started two or three minutes ago, he now missed by only several inches. Of course it helped that Cory had moved much closer, to less than twenty feet away from him. And slowed his pitches to a lob.

Cory had an idea. Perry had been batting with a closed stance, as if peering around a corner at the pitcher. Likely making it hard to follow the ball, with vision solely from his right eye. Cory went over and moved Perry's left leg, opening his stance considerably. Now he faced the pitcher more, hopefully enabling him to better see the ball.

Cory had gone to a local library recently and scanned several computer articles about persons with only one sighted eye, and their depth perception. Or lack of it. One particular article presented a technique for enhancing depth perception by cocking the head slightly when watching a moving object. He demonstrated for Perry.

Satisfied that the boy understood, Cory moved back to where he'd been pitching. He tossed another ball. Swing and a miss, even with Perry using the new technique. Fortunately Cory had bought about a dozen old balls from a sporting goods shop, so they didn't have to retrieve after every pitch. Cory tossed another. Same result. A couple of kids watching off to one side broke into laughter. Next pitch. Another miss.

The afternoon was warm and Cory removed the cap he was wearing and wiped some perspiration off his forehead with a sleeve from his shirt. Time for another plan. Maybe the problem wasn't entirely physical, but at least partly mental. The swing-and-miss routine must be broken. If they accomplished that, Perry might make consistent contact.

Cory moved even closer to him. Of course he could simply place the ball on a tee and let him hit it. But Perry had already experienced that in his league last summer and it would be like admitting defeat. No, Cory wanted him hitting a moving pitch. If Perry could make solid contact just once, it might alter his outlook.

Cory tossed a slow underhand delivery. Swing and a miss. The two kids were pointing at Perry and laughing. Another lob, even slower, right over the plate. Perry swung and managed a foul tip.

"Way to go, Perry. Next one's out of the park."

The boy smiled and resumed his batting stance. But the next one didn't go out of the park. It barely trickled onto the field. They were making progress, though. That is, until the next pitch. Despite still using the techniques Cory showed him, Perry swung and missed.

They took a little break by shagging all the balls. Cory saw the two kids awkwardly swinging imaginary bats toward Perry and laughing. When Cory tossed the next pitch, he wished Perry could shut them up by belting it into the outfield. A wish unfulfilled by the ensuing swing and miss.

"Don't give up, Perry."

No chance of that occurring. It looked like Perry would play all afternoon. And into the evening, provided the park had lights. If anyone gave up, it would be Cory, now getting a little tired in addition to being hot.

Another slow pitch, underhand. Cory didn't have to see what happened—the sharp crack of bat meeting ball informed him. Actually he never witnessed the end result, he was too busy ducking out of the way of the liner headed right toward him. Perry laughed. Not at Cory's distress, but because he'd finally connected.

Had it been only a fluke? Cory was eager to find out. He got another ball and faced Perry. The sun seemed much warmer than when they began. He tossed another underhand lob. Perry swung and lofted a long fly to left field. Was it possible that the plan was working, that the boy was developing confidence? That the pattern of swing-and-miss had finally been broken?

Cory was determined to force the issue. He moved back from Perry, to about thirty feet away. He observed that the two kids had shut up and were watching the drama, no doubt keen to resume their laughter and mimicry. Cory threw another pitch, this one overhand, much harder, off the plate and difficult to hit. Perry swung. The crisp sound of the bat followed. The ball flew into right center field.

"Way to go, Perry. Adrian Gonzalez of the Dodgers!"

"No," Perry corrected, laughing again. "Big Papi, David Ortiz of the Red Sox!"

Cory clapped at Perry's response. Instead of someone who regularly played a defensive position, he had named probably the best designated hitter of the last decade or two.

✦ ✦ ✦

"Your pocket's not burning anymore," Cory greeted Stan by cell phone late one afternoon in early February.

"We finally do something!" the old man responded excitedly, obviously comprehending Cory's meaning.

"We did. And I think we did pretty good."

"He win?"

"By six lengths."

"Wow!" Stan exclaimed.

Cory beamed at the old guy's exuberance. And at their new horse circling in front of Carlos and him on the hot walker. They had claimed him from a race less than an hour ago. Jet black and muscularly compact, he was apparently eager to resume running, because he kept tugging determinedly at the machine.

"What's his name?" Stan asked.

"Tall Order."

"We have to shake for him?"

"Nine-way. We got lucky."

"We gonna make another allowance horse outta him?"

"Can't," Cory answered. "He's out of conditions. Why he was in a claiming race."

"What about a stakes horse, then?"

"We could." Cory smiled again at Stan's exuberance. "Long as you don't mind having no shot to win."

The conversation ended on that note. Cory ambled over to the hot walker. He reached out, intending to pat Tall Order's shoulder. The horse reached out too, intending to bite Cory's arm. Fortunately, Cory pulled back his outstretched extremity barely in time.

Cory contemplated how lucky he'd been in everything to do with their new horse. Lucky to submit a claim for him. Lucky he'd run so well. Lucky to win the nine-party shake. Lucky to avoid getting his arm bitten off.

Too bad the rest of the day hadn't been so fortuitous. Earlier in the program, before they claimed Tall Order, Turbulent Flight had raced. After being bumped off stride in the stretch, he finished second, a nose behind the winner. The bump had cost him the victory. And of course Cory and Carlos got nothing for Tall Order's easy triumph (other than the horse), since the former stable, not the new one, is credited with the win and all purse money.

Consequently, what was nearly a three-month losing streak about three weeks ago, was now heading for four.

✦ ✦ ✦

"How about breezing Sandra's little filly?" Tracy asked Cory early one cool morning at the barn. "To see what we got."

"Not ready for a breeze."

"She's in the Pomona sale next month. We'd like an idea what she's worth. Or if we should even sell her."

"Not ready for a breeze," Cory repeated after coughing from a cold he was trying to get over. "Still too green. Today we gallop."

"You're awfully patient."

"Didn't someone once call that a virtue?"

"Not when we need to know if she's any good. How about an eighth of a mile?"

"Not an eighth of an inch," he snapped. "Call me stubborn, but what good do I do you if I break her down?"

She didn't answer. Coughing again and tightening his jacket around his throat, he walked toward the filly's stall to check whether Carlos had her ready for the track.

"Maybe take her to one of Sandra's other trainers," he called back to Tracy. "I'm probably much too much a jerk to do what you want."

"My, we're touchy this morning."

No question about that. His cold was bugging him. So was their losing streak. As time went on and they didn't win a race, he kept thinking about when they first came to California and it taking six months to finally win one. No doubt Tracy had become the target of his frustration.

"Look, I'm sorry," he apologized softly.

"Don't be," she replied, sounding a little apologetic herself. "You know what's best."

Carlos handed the filly's reins to him and Cory led her out of her stall. He checked her saddle for tightness, then patted her forehead. Carlos boosted him aboard. Tracy began to follow on foot as Cory and the filly started for the track.

"A little role reversal," he said to her over his shoulder.

"Meaning?"

"I ride ... you watch."

She didn't answer.

"I don't imagine," he winked, "you'll enjoy watching me as much as I enjoyed watching you."

"Some people have all the fun."

He laughed. Clearly he was feeling better. Undoubtedly because what they were now doing seemed so familiar. No matter which of them was on horseback.

✦ ✦ ✦

Riding off the track on the filly, Cory felt very foolish. During her long steady gallop, she had behaved perfectly, not displaying the slightest sign of immaturity. Even a loose horse zigzagging in front of her on the track hadn't bothered her. Tracy joined them as they headed back to the barn, walking beside them.

"Doesn't look too green to me," she remarked pointedly.

"For good reason," he quickly replied, trying to conceal his embarrassment.

"Why?"

"Horses always act better when you're around."

Her doubting look conveyed that she wasn't buying his explanation. Someone was shouting in Spanish ahead of them. When the noise abated, he hoped for a change in subject, which she soon provided.

"Told Sandra a couple of weeks ago how much I missed riding."

"Oh?"

"I'm grouchy all the time."

"Like me earlier?"

"Not that bad." She grinned.

"How long since you've been on a horse?"

"Since I rode Bandit ... that last time for you."

"Can always have your old job back."

She smiled up at him. She was wearing a low-cut navy-blue top and he caught a glimpse of undergarment beneath it. They approached the barn and he wondered if she'd rush off the instant they got there.

"Speaking of Bandit," he said. "I think I know why they were so eager to get him back."

"Why?"

"Before we claimed him, they nominated him to all the big three-year-old races. All over the country, according to the racing office."

"Then why run him in a claiming race?" she asked.

"Near as I can figure ... wanted their cake and eat it too. Win a race, cash a bet. Didn't think they'd lose him. But if they did, buy him back with some the money they made."

"Guess they didn't count on us being so stubborn."

He nodded. They reached the barn and he dismounted the filly, reluctantly abandoning his strategic vantage point of Tracy's low-cut top. Carlos was preparing Bandit for the track. Cory considered attempting to entice Tracy into staying by suggesting she exercise Bandit this morning. Another coughing spell spoiled the mood, though.

"Do me a favor," he managed.

"What?"

"Talk to our horses. Like you did with Lasting Impression."

"And tell them what?"

"That it's time they won a race."

"Okay. If you think it'll help."

"It can't hurt." He smiled, achieving one more glimpse of her top.

He went to the barn office for some paper towels with which to blow his nose. His cell phone started ringing, but he decided not to answer. After going back outside, he silently congratulated himself. She had lingered, after all. If only to stand outside Bandit's stall and pat him while Carlos continued getting him ready.

CHAPTER 18

"YOU BETTER GO SEE, BOSS," Carlos greeted Cory grimly one drizzly morning not quite four weeks after One-Eyed Bandit's fine performance in the Sham Stakes. After training, Cory planned to enter the colt in the Robert B. Lewis Stakes, a two-hundred-thousand-dollar race at a mile and a sixteenth.

"What is it?" Cory asked, alarmed by Carlos's demeanor.

"You better go see, Boss."

Carlos led Cory toward Bandit's stall. The colt was drinking water when they got there. Carlos pointed to Bandit's left front ankle. Cory was horrified. The ankle was swollen twice its normal size. Like it might have been broken or, at the very least, causing great pain.

Cory entered the stall. He kneeled and probed the ankle. Oddly, he felt no heat. Incongruous with what seemed an obvious injury. Plus, no matter how hard he pressed on it, Bandit didn't so much as flinch.

Cory scanned the colt's other legs and the rest of his body, searching for additional possible problems. He found nothing. Shaking his head, he stepped out of the stall.

"What could have happened?"

"I do not know."

"All we did was walk him yesterday. And he was fine before and after."

"It is a mystery, Boss."

Carlos was right, it was a mystery. Cory shook his head again. He'd breezed Bandit five furlongs two days ago. Of course he knew there was no precise timetable for when an injury might reveal itself. And yet, had the colt hurt himself in the workout, there should have been at least some indication yesterday.

"Let's have the vet take x-rays," Cory said.

"Okay, Boss."

"Of both ankles."

"Both?"

"Both," Cory answered emphatically. "I have a hunch."

✦ ✦ ✦

By the time Cory got back to his trailer half an hour later, the drizzle had turned into a steady rain. Inside, he found that Cookie wasn't feeling well and had vomited in her little alcove near the bathroom—which certainly fit the theme for the morning thus far.

Cory wasn't feeling so hot himself. He still hadn't gotten over his cold. And their losing streak wasn't over. Plus now the news of a possible injury to Bandit.

He'd left the barn soon after examining the colt. Instead of galloping Turbulent Flight and Tall Order as planned, he'd hired someone to pony them once around the training track. And asked Carlos to simply walk both their other horses.

He got some paper towels to clean up the vomit. Before starting, he got down on his hands and knees next to Cookie and gently rubbed her coat. A small mouse scampered through the single large room and disappeared into a tiny crack near the bathroom door. This was Cory's first rodent sighting in the five months they'd lived in the trailer, and he wondered if Cookie had somehow consumed its droppings, making her sick.

He also wondered what other unpleasant discoveries were in store for him this morning, to add to the growing list.

✦ ✦ ✦

"Both ankles are identical," the veterinarian, a large youthful-looking man, reported early that afternoon, laying the x-rays out on the desk of the barn office. "No injury to either."

"Really," Cory replied guardedly. "How do you explain the swelling?"

"Can't."

"Any chance this could be a spider or insect bite?" Cory spoke reflectively, then thought of their rodent intruder this morning. "Or a mouse..? Or a rat?"

"Doubtful."

"What about running some other types of tests?" Cory queried, choking back a cough. "Help us find out what happened."

"We could. Might not learn anything, though. And even if we did, can't see much point."

"I didn't enter him in that stakes race I was considering," Cory divulged.

"Wise."

"When can I start training him again?"

"Soon," the vet answered. "Unless you want to play it safe. Nice colt like him."

Cory nodded. The vet left. Just in time, it turned out, because Cory wasn't able to suppress his next cough, which quickly became several, plus a couple of sneezes thrown in. Fortunately there were plenty of paper towels nearby.

Following the attack, he went to the office door and gazed outside. The rain had stopped. The afternoon was looking much better than this morning and he decided to head over to the races. There were a couple of horses he wanted to look at, in case Stan suggested they claim another.

✦ ✦ ✦

"I've had an offer for the little filly," Sandra informed Cory via phone that evening. "I'm glad we didn't name her, because the new people said they wanted to."

"You're not going to wait for the sale?"

"Only if you tell me to."

"Green. But getting more mature. Some talent ... That's all I can say for now."

"Tracy says you're very patient with the filly."

"Stubborn might describe me better," he admitted.

"Stubborn doesn't tell me what I need to know."

"It doesn't cause injuries either."

"I'll turn down the offer," she stated.

"I'll try to be less stubborn."

"Patient," she corrected.

✦ ✦ ✦

"Two hundred fifty thousand," was Kosko's greeting the next morning at the barn. "Quarter million."

Cory scratched his head in response.

"My people liked his race the other day," Kosko added.

"See where you guys nominated him for all the big three-year-old races."

"We do that with most our young horses. Case one of them gets good."

"Oh," Cory answered, not believing a word.

"Quarter million. Not exactly pocket change."

"Do I call my owners before or after your vet inspection?" Cory questioned.

"No vet. No inspection."

"Quarter million," Cory reflected. "And they don't even want a look?"

"They trust my judgment."

"They must," Cory replied, scratching his head again.

✦ ✦ ✦

"Strange," Cory told Carlos later that morning.

"What, Boss?"

"Almost like the whole thing was planned."

"What, Boss?"

"An injury ... We're alarmed ... They up the offer ... No vet inspection."

Carlos looked at him questioningly.

"Except how could they know he was injured?" Cory puzzled, scratching his head once more. "Unless ... ?"

"I do not know, Boss. I do know the other night I hear something. Maybe from Bandit's stall."

"The night before we discovered his problem?"

"Yes, Boss."

"What did you hear?" Cory asked intently.

"I do not know ... A noise. I wake up. I go to the stall. But I see nothing."

This time it was Cory who looked at Carlos questioningly. He didn't like what he was thinking.

✦ ✦ ✦

Cory lay inside an old sleeping bag on the floor beside the closed door of their barn office. This was his third consecutive night here and by far the coldest, an icy wind blowing incessantly. Although he had brought his warmest coat and a borrowed electric blanket, neither was much defense against the chill outside. Fortunately he was over his cold.

He got here each night around ten, after walking Cookie and leading her back to the trailer. He could have taken her with him, except he was afraid she might bark at a crucial moment. He'd parked his car inconspicuously in the stable lot, then taken a circuitous route to the barn, using fence and foliage to shield himself from view. By tonight he'd actually broken into laughter along the way. Wasn't he playing the role of third-rate detective in a sixth-rate movie?

He knew, though, that hiring a night watchman, more affordable for larger stables, was expensive. Besides, if someone was tampering with Bandit, he'd rather catch the person himself. Each night he'd knocked lightly on Carlos's door down the shed row, to let him know he'd arrived. Then, before settling into the sleeping bag, he quietly checked each of their horses to make sure they were all right.

He'd considered notifying Sandra of the latest development with Bandit. To suggest that Dobson and Kosko had stopped playing by the rules. But what proof did he have that they might be involved? Or, for that matter, that a person, not some freak occurrence, had caused Bandit's condition. Anyway, he liked the idea of handling things himself. Wasn't he the one ultimately responsible for the horse? And, aside from the cold, he could just as easily sleep here as in his trailer.

He felt himself begin to nod off. He heard a noise outside. Getting up out of the sleeping bag, he stood poised beside the closed door, listening intently. Carefully he edged the door open. The wind gusted against his face and against the door. He feared it would blow the door wide open, so he held it tightly. Even then, the door started shimmying.

No sounds were audible, he concluded, except those caused by the wind. Still he remained by the door, holding it slightly ajar. From the minimal illumination of a nearby security light, he could see that paint had chipped off the door in several places. For some reason, he stared at the damaged spots.

Satisfied that whatever he originally heard was also created by the wind, he began to close the door. What little warmth the sleeping bag offered would be welcome. Another noise. He slid the door open a bit wider than a moment ago. He could feel himself shivering, although he couldn't tell whether it was from the cold or from nerves. Now he could see outside. Another noise from up the shed row. Yes, he could discern two men approaching in the dark, moving toward Bandit's stall, close to the office.

They each carried something, but in the limited light he couldn't tell what. He had come to the part of his overall plan that, unfortunately, he had yet to develop. Should he yell to Carlos for help? No, that would only prompt them to flee. His best chance for preventing their escape was to let them go inside Bandit's stall, if that was their objective. Though he certainly didn't want them doing whatever they were there to do, it was the only way to catch them in the act.

Standing there stiffly, he could feel the short bursts of his own breath. Sure enough, the two men entered Bandit's stall. He waited until he could no longer see them before opening the door wider and slipping quietly outside, closing the door gently behind him so that it wouldn't be slammed shut by the wind.

He edged toward a post near the stall. With the wind, he couldn't even hear his own footsteps. He stopped behind the post, where he had both some cover and a perfect vantage point into the stall. Bandit was facing away. The men, also facing away, were bent over near Bandit's left front leg, the one with the swollen ankle.

"Don't move!" Cory yelled loudly. "'Less you want to get shot."

He was afraid they couldn't hear him in the wind, that he'd have to get closer and yell louder. One of them flinched, however, indicating he'd heard.

"You don't believe me ... another inch and you're dead."

The man froze and Cory went closer, within a few feet of them. What if they had guns? Or knives? They could shoot or stab the colt. Or him. He knew he'd have to have them turn toward him, to protect Bandit. What if they saw he had no gun and was only pretending?

Clenching his right fist in his coat pocket, he raised it next to his chest. In the dark they might believe his fist was a gun. Or they might not risk that it wasn't.

"Now get up and turn around real slow," he ordered emphatically. "Hands up high ... Move too quick and I shoot." For an instant he again felt like a third-rate detective in a sixth-rate movie.

Carlos appeared in the doorway of his room. A security guard drove up in a motorized cart. The two men in the stall, one tall and one short, now stood facing Cory, their hands up. Cory's fist remained clenched in his coat pocket. With Carlos and the security guard nearby, he felt safer. Unless the two men had weapons.

"Were you guys here the other night?" he shouted at them.

They didn't answer. Carlos and the security guard approached from different directions. The guard had his gun drawn, pointed toward the ground.

"Were you guys here the other night?" Cory repeated, even louder. "Tell me or I shoot."

"No shoot, no shoot," the tall one answered excitedly in broken English. "We here, we here."

"You work for Dobson?"

"No shoot. No shoot ... We work for Kosko."

"Were you the guys roughed him up?" Cory yelled, pointing toward Carlos.

"No, no. We not do that."

"Who did?"

"We not know. Maybe Kosko know."

The security guard directed the men out of the stall. Two other guards arrived in a patrol car, undoubtedly summoned by the first one when he got there. While the guards were frisking and handcuffing the two men, uncovering no weapons, Cory and Carlos entered the stall. Cory finally took his clenched fist from his pocket and reached down to pick up two syringes off the ground.

"You use these?" he shouted at the tall guy.

"No, we not use," he replied, clearly still scared.

"What about last time?"

"Yes. We use last time."

"What's in here?"

"We not know. We not know. Maybe Kosko know."

Cory handed the syringes to one of the guards after the guard reached for them. He considered asking permission to keep one of them for the vet to test, but realized the futility. They'd want both for evidence, since each could contain a different substance. The two other guards led the men toward the patrol car parked in front of the barn, their footsteps audible because the wind gusts had diminished.

"You call security?" Cory asked Carlos while kneeling down to check Bandit.

"Yes, Boss, I call. I am sorry. You look like you are in trouble ... I am sorry."

"Don't be silly," Cory asserted, rising and patting Carlos on the back. "You saved me. And Bandit too."

Carlos shrugged. Cory went back to his inspection, which revealed nothing more than the colt's left front ankle still swollen.

Though not nearly so bad as a few days ago, when they first discovered it.

✦ ✦ ✦

"Unauthorized firearms are illegal in the stable area," the steward informed Cory and Carlos.

"We didn't have any," Cory replied.

"I know. I want to make certain you both understand."

Cory and Carlos nodded. It was the afternoon following the incident. They sat in the office of the same older, refined-looking steward who had met with Cory and Tracy after Carlos's beating. This time the stewards were clearly more involved, Cory having learned from a security guard that they had already questioned the two suspects. And they'd obviously wasted little time summoning Carlos and him to the office.

"There will be a full investigation," the steward stated officiously. "We've scheduled individual hearings for both Mr. Kosko and Mr. Dobson."

"Were you able to determine what was in the syringes?" Cory asked.

"The substance is at the lab now. Preliminary indications are it's a combination of chemicals. Injected into a horse's joints, it causes extreme swelling. Otherwise it's harmless."

Cory didn't respond, although he felt relieved, especially since Bandit's symptoms and progress seemed to fit the hypothesis. Yet he also felt angry. How could a character like Kosko be operating at a place like Santa Anita?

"Are you the one who was roughed up?" the steward inquired, gazing at Carlos.

"Yes, sir," Carlos answered, appearing embarrassed.

"Are you okay now?"

"I am okay, sir."

"One final comment," the steward said, shifting his gaze to Cory. "I know you were simply protecting your horse ..."

"Right, sir."

"But you're not to threaten to shoot anyone ... with or without a gun."

"Right, sir," Cory assented, recognizing debate as pointless. Getting up to leave, Cory noticed on the wall the same pictures he'd seen after the other meeting with the steward, of horses that had won past Santa Anita Handicaps.

CHAPTER 19

"IT'S ALL HE TALKS ABOUT," Tracy said, sitting down next to Cory on her living room couch. She handed him one of the two glasses of cold water she'd gotten from the kitchen.

"What is?" he asked.

"Batting. Now I see why."

"He works hard."

"So do you," she smiled.

In the last hour, she'd witnessed firsthand the latter two points about working hard. She had accompanied Cory, Perry and Cookie on their latest walk. They stopped at the nearby park for batting practice. Cory pitched to Perry while Tracy and Cookie served as fielders, Tracy using an old glove Cory brought her, Cookie using her mouth. Perry continued his progress, slugging balls into the outfield.

Afterward, Tracy had invited Cory and Cookie into the apartment. Arousing his curiosity because she hadn't done so since Christmas Day. She'd immediately told Perry to go straighten his room and, yes, he could take Cookie with him— which made Cory even more curious.

"It's all over the track," she continued after drinking some water. "About what happened the other night."

"Oh?"

"You're kind of a folk hero ... The man without a gun."

"Never had a horse like this," he explained a little sheepishly. Actually he felt uncomfortable about the entire incident. "In case you didn't know, Carlos saved us both."

She didn't respond. He sensed something else was on her mind, though he could only guess what. All he knew for sure was she smelled good, fresh, despite running everywhere on the field, chasing Perry's hits. And it felt good to sit so close to her, her leg brushing against his a time or two. Plus her hair looked nice, tied up behind her head with a green bow. He imagined reaching up and touching her bare neck.

"I never thanked you," she spoke softly, ending a brief silence.

"For what?"

"For letting me invest in Bandit."

"We should thank *you*," he countered. "We might not have had the money."

"And I never thanked you for recommending me to Sandra."

He nodded acknowledgment. Another silence. She lay back and rested her head against the back of the couch, so that it was just an inch or two from his shoulder. Her light-green eyes gazed at the ceiling. He sensed she'd been fencing with him, that she was leading up to something more significant. Though he still had no clue. He could hear Perry jabbering to Cookie inside and wondered what they were doing, but he hadn't the slightest inclination to go find out.

"You're not going to hurt him?" she asked, finally.

"Who?"

"Perry."

"No way ... I adore him."

"So did his father," she blurted.

"What happened?"

"You see what happened," she answered firmly, yet softly, like she was ashamed.

"He did that!" he exclaimed, incredulous.

"A moment of anger ... and a little kid's life changes forever."

He could only shake his head.

"I won't let that happen again," she declared.

Once more he didn't answer.

"Funny thing," she sighed. "I'm the one he was angry at."

Cory didn't know what to say. He saw tears in her eyes. He wanted to do something to comfort her. To make her pain go away. He reached out and touched her neck, then guided her head toward his. He kissed her forehead. Then he kissed her lips, putting both arms around her.

She turned away, easing herself from his grasp. Cookie, leash in her mouth, had entered the room, followed by Perry. Cory couldn't tell whether Tracy had reacted to them, or to him and what he'd done.

"I think she has to go to the bathroom," Perry announced.

Cory stood up and attached Cookie's leash to her collar. Certainly he would laugh at the intrusion later, but he didn't now because the conversation had become so serious. As he led Cookie toward the door, he tried to catch Tracy's eye for some inkling of her feelings about what had happened, however she seemed focused on Perry and betrayed none.

"Mind if Perry comes outside with me?" he asked her. "You're welcome, too."

"We'd better not. It's getting late."

Cory realized, more by her expression than her words, that she wanted him to leave. He opened the door. Before he and Cookie departed, though, of course Perry came over to shake his hand good-bye.

✦ ✦ ✦

"Hot as a firecracker!" Tiger exclaimed when he met Stan on a bench at Santa Anita. "Hit the exacta first two races and the tri in the third. Got a nice super picked out next race."

"Great," Stan answered. "Hope some that luck rubs off on Tall Order later today."

"No sweat. He'll crush that field. Singled him in the pick six ... Hey, you don't look so good."

"Long bus ride out here ... Always tires me out."

Tiger nodded. But Stan knew it was more than the bus ride compromising his appearance. He'd been to the cancer specialist again and the news wasn't good. It was awful, really. The disease had progressed to where the doctor recommended that Stan look into hospice care. Or at the very least, assisted living. Stan had done neither so far, nor did he intend to soon. Not with so much happening with his horses.

"Go bet your super," Stan said. "Think I'll take little nap."

"Hey, want a piece?"

"Nah. Meet you back here after the fifth. Now go ahead."

"Right," Tiger replied, definitely not needing anyone to twist his arm to get him to go make a bet.

✦ ✦ ✦

When Tiger returned after the fifth, he found Stan sitting on the bench, head down, asleep. So sound asleep, in fact, that it looked like he could sleep right through Tall Order's race, the seventh.

Tiger shook him gently. The old man didn't stir. He tried again. Same result. Tiger was beginning to get scared. Maybe there was something wrong. His next shake was more vigorous. Finally Stan opened his eyes. But he closed them again. Tiger shook him once more. This time, after opening his eyes, Stan picked his head up.

"Hit the super?" he asked.

"Nah. Neither race. Photoed out in one. Jockey fell off in the other."

"So you're not hot as a firecracker no more."

"Right," Tiger acknowledged. "But I still made plenty money. Enough to start paying you back."

"Paying me back for what?"

"For that money you gave me. That day at Hollywood Park."

"I *gave* you that money."

"I never felt right about that," Tiger admitted. "I want to start paying you back right now."

"Don't want you paying me back."

"Ever?"

"Ever," Stan emphasized.

"I don't get it."

"I've got my reasons," Stan answered, providing the same explanation he'd given Tiger almost three months ago at Hollywood Park.

A couple of kids nearby were tossing a football around. One of them missed the ball and it rolled over and hit Stan in the leg. Either because he was angry it hit Stan or because he'd had to give up playing football due to his bad knee, Tiger picked up the ball and kicked it far over the kids' heads.

"Hey," Tiger said to Stan while eyeing the flight of the ball, "how 'bout goin' halves on another super?"

"No thanks."

"Split somethin' else?"

"No thanks."

"I'll be right back."

"Before you go," Stan said. "Like a few words with you."

"Sure ..."

Stan sat up straight on the bench. The two kids, after giving Tiger a dirty look and retrieving the football, were playing catch again. The track bugler trumpeted the arrival of the horses into the walking ring from the paddock, for the next race. Tiger, standing next to Stan, put one foot up on the bench.

"You're a young guy," Stan began.

"Yeah?"

"Whole life ahead ..."

"Yeah?"

"I'm not much of a role model ... Been coming to the track seventy years ..."

"Yeah?" Tiger questioned once more, wondering where this was headed.

"There's more to life than betting horses ..."

"Yeah?"

"That's all. Now go bet your super."

Tiger removed his foot from the bench, pivoted and left immediately. Again, nobody needed to twist his arm to get him to go make a bet.

✦ ✦ ✦

"I'm almost sure we're going to lose him," Cory informed Stan and Tiger when they joined him in Sandra's box before Tall Order's race.

"He'll crush this field," Tiger repeated his earlier notion. "I don't blame anyone for claiming him."

"Well," Stan said resignedly, "if we lose him, we lose him. Sure can't take him with me."

"How come you don't care all of a sudden?" Tiger asked. "Used to cry about losing your horse."

Stan muttered an explanation so incoherent that even he couldn't understand it. This was certainly no time for revelation. No time to bring up the doctor's warning.

"Anyway, you're right about not taking him with you," Tiger teased. "Not where you're going. No way they allow horses there."

Stan didn't laugh. Or even smile. Maybe the thought of no horses where he was going was even more depressing than where he was going.

✦ ✦ ✦

Cory felt happy the next morning as he and Carlos sat in the barn office munching on some donuts Cory bought, a celebration of sorts. Tiger had been right about the race—Tall Order did crush the field, winning by eight lengths. Their first victory in about four months.

Unfortunately, Cory had been right too. Tall Order did get claimed. By Dobson again, in a six-way shake. Cory didn't want to lose the horse, but at least they'd won and Stan turned a nice profit.

The biggest reason for Cory's good humor, however, was that Bandit was training so nicely and the ankle swelling had completely disappeared. Although the incident occurred over two weeks ago, and the vet cleared Bandit to begin training again soon after, Cory had decided to wait until this week to start serious workouts.

The barn phone interrupted the munchies. Carlos moved to answer it, but Cory beat him to it. He immediately recognized the voice of the refined-looking steward.

"We've completed the investigation."

"Yes, sir."

"We've denied Kosko access to all California tracks for two years."

"Only two years, sir?"

"A longer penalty would invite legal ramifications."

"What about Dobson?" Cory asked.

"Kosko confessed. We suspect to spare Dobson any connection. We can't prove anything against him."

"So he gets off free."

"We reprimanded him," the steward reported.

"What about the substance they injected into our horse?"

"As we conjectured, it's a combination of chemicals, basically harmless, used to induce swelling."

"Dobson keeps claiming our horses," Cory remarked.

"Can't prevent a licensed trainer claiming a horse."

After hanging up, Cory found the donuts less appetizing. He wasn't thrilled with the rulings. His only consolation was that Bandit had recovered and the episode finally seemed behind them.

CHAPTER 20

"YOUR TALK DID SOME GOOD," Cory told Tracy in front of Bandit's stall, shortly after he'd dismounted Turbulent Flight.

She looked at him questioningly, without replying. She was rubbing Bandit behind his right ear and the colt appeared to enjoy it, his mouth wide open like he was smiling. The morning was cold and Tracy had on a turquoise scarf—Cory had never seen her wear one before—which nicely complemented her light-green eyes.

"I assume you spoke with our horses," he clarified. "We finally won a race."

"So I heard. Congratulations."

Her voice conveyed little enthusiasm, though. And her attention never strayed from Bandit. Cory hadn't seen her in more than a week, not since the afternoon in her apartment. If she came by the barn to check on Sandra's horses, or talk to their horses or visit with Bandit, she did so when he wasn't there. Nor had Perry phoned to see Cookie or play baseball. Cory could only conclude that she and the boy were avoiding him.

"I like to see him every day," she sighed, continuing to rub Bandit behind the ear.

"I'm sure he feels the same about you."

"Do you think it would be a bad idea for me to bring Perry here to meet him?" she queried pensively.

"I think it would be a bad idea if you didn't."

"You know," she mused. "Bandit's first race for us ... I purposely kept Perry at a distance ... so he wouldn't see Bandit had only one eye."

"I remember you didn't come to the winner's circle."

"I didn't know how Perry would react."

"Maybe it's a mistake to avoid it," he suggested. "It might be a positive thing ... if he sees that Bandit's dealing with it."

She looked at him reflectively. There was a scent of someone cooking meat nearby, probably on a hot plate. He was aware it was Sunday and she wouldn't have to rush back to her place to take Perry to school. Maybe he should invite her to breakfast again, so they could further discuss Perry meeting Bandit—and touch on what happened that afternoon in her apartment. But she had turned back to Bandit and seemed focused on him, as if she preferred his company to further conversation.

Instead of pressing her right then, Cory decided to head off for the racing office and enter Turbulent Flight in an upcoming race. Maybe she'd still be there when he got back.

✦ ✦ ✦

Tracy was about to leave Bandit when Carlos came over from the hot walker, where he'd been watching Turbulent Flight circle. He was wearing a navy-blue sweatshirt displaying Santa Anita insignia, no doubt acquired at one of the track promotion days. Actually she recalled a sweatshirt giveaway last weekend and had considered bringing Perry, but her painting, and a play date of his, had interfered. Clearly Carlos's sweatshirt was warm because, even in the cold weather, he was perspiring.

"How is Perry?" he asked.

"Fine. Sleeping late this morning."

"He is a nice boy."

"Thanks." She smiled. "He's always wearing the cowboy hat you got him for Christmas."

"Cory, he say he like the baseball bat too."

"Yes ... And I like the house plant you both brought me."

"That is good."

"How's your family, Carlos?"

"They are fine."

"When will you go see them again?"

"I do not know. We are so busy now."

Tracy nodded. A fly landed on Bandit's shoulder and she brushed it away. She resumed rubbing behind his right ear and Bandit resumed his open-mouthed "smile."

"I have a dream ..." Carlos stated.

"Tell me."

"I have a dream ... that some day my family, I can bring them here to live."

"Sounds nice."

"Bandit, he is part of the dream. Maybe he will become so good ... and worth so much money ... that I can bring them here to live."

"Sounds like you've been thinking about this a lot," she speculated.

"Yes, I have been thinking about this a lot."

"Sounds like more of a plan than a dream."

Carlos shrugged. He gazed at Turbulent Flight, still circling on the hot walker. Or maybe he was looking off in the distance, thinking that his dream had now become a plan. Tracy couldn't tell which.

"Do you want me to talk to Bandit about your plan?" she asked, patting the colt's chin with her other hand.

"Yes, I would like you to talk to Bandit ... if you do not mind."

"I will," she confirmed.

She spotted Cory walking on the roadway, toward the barn, no doubt returning from wherever he'd gone. Time for her to leave. She patted Bandit twice on the shoulder, touched Carlos's hand and started for her car in the parking lot.

"Off to see some of Sandra's other horses?" Cory called out to her.

"No ... Perry."

"Pancakes this morning?"

"No, waffles," she replied, unable to fight off a smile.

"Hope you'll bring him here soon."

She nodded while picking up her pace.

✦ ✦ ✦

Several hours later, Carlos sat by himself in the stable cafeteria, finishing his lunch. As he'd anticipated, the regular noon-time crowd had gone long ago. Thus he could sit quietly without having to converse or be disturbed by idle chatter.

He was feeling good after talking with Tracy. Their dialogue, plus the horses he and Cory currently had in their stable, provided optimism. True, after losing Tall Order, they were back to only three. But they were talented horses, not simply cheap claimers. Horses capable of earning nice purses.

"This is not a good life for any of us."

Now, as he'd done so often lately, he recalled Alicia's words spoken during his Christmas visit.

"The girls ... they are getting older. They will soon be in high school. And they hardly know their father."

Of course she was right. And he hardly knew them either. Not after all his years away, trying to eke out a living. They'd be seeing boys soon and he wasn't there to offer guidance. At their age, girls needed their father.

Again, he thought about his dream. No, his plan, as Tracy had corrected. He was certain Alicia would listen, provided he presented a sound financial concept. She'd always been reasonable. No question she'd be getting what she most wanted— the family together, permanently. And undoubtedly California offered a better life than Mexico. Plus he'd no longer have to make the difficult journeys to see them.

Alicia, Rosa and Luisa could become U.S. citizens, as he'd done many years ago during an amnesty period. No, they could become U.S. citizens *because* he'd become one. A wife can qualify easily. Children can apply.

His being able to afford their living here was another matter. He knew how high expenses were. They had hardly any savings, and little equity in the house because they'd had to take out loans. Plus very few other possessions.

Bandit was the key. That is, his small share in Bandit. Based on the offer they'd already received, it was worth several thousand now. If the colt continued to develop, several thousand might grow to tens of thousands—to possibly enough for a stake in a new life here for his family.

He glanced at the clock on the cafeteria wall. It was time to go back to the barn. The horses would be looking for their dinner before long. And he still had to prepare it.

He hoped Tracy would talk to Bandit soon.

✦ ✦ ✦

"One more horse to train," Cory told Perry. "Want to go with me to the track?"

"No thanks. I want to stay here with him."

No surprise. To say that Perry was utterly transfixed with One-Eyed Bandit from the moment Tracy dropped him at the barn early this cool Saturday morning was no exaggeration. Cory hiring an exercise rider for the day, so he could be with Perry, proved almost irrelevant. All Perry wanted was to remain with Bandit.

While Cory had gone to the track earlier to watch the rider exercise Turbulent Flight, Perry waited with Carlos as he brushed and saddled Bandit. When Bandit headed to the track, Perry had walked right beside him with Cory. As the colt galloped once around the oval, Perry watched him exclusively, despite the presence of dozens of other horses. Now that Bandit had returned to the barn following his workout, and was attached to the hot walker, Perry stood right outside his circular path.

"Can I ask a question?" the boy queried Cory, standing next to him. "Before you go to the track."

"Sure."

"Does it bother him to race with only one eye?"

"I don't think he knows he has only one."

Perry, seemingly deep in thought, didn't reply right away. Cory watched Carlos lead Sandra's little filly from her stall and boost the rider aboard.

"Can I ask another question?" Perry inquired.

"Go ahead."

"Does he ever close his good eye ... so he can run faster?"

"I don't know for sure ... but I don't think so."

"Oh."

Cory sensed that Perry wasn't quite satisfied with that answer. He knew he should be following Sandra's filly and the rider to the track, but he lingered with Perry.

"A little while ago, when we were at the track," the boy said, "I saw how fast he can run."

"And that wasn't even full speed."

"So ... you don't have to see well to run fast," Perry sighed, almost to himself.

✦ ✦ ✦

Cory probably wasn't quite as convinced as Carlos that Tracy's conversations with their horses actually inspired them. But when Turbulent Flight easily won his next race, his conviction grew. The fact that it was a contentious allowance race convinced him further.

✦ ✦ ✦

"I'm afraid I've been replaced as a role model," Tracy smiled. "By a horse."

Laughter ensued, although no one commented on the obvious connection between Perry and Bandit. All of Bandit's owners, plus Perry, were present in Sandra's box. The occasion was Bandit's next race, the San Felipe Stakes at a mile and a sixteenth, which had attracted most of the best three-year-olds in the west. The purse was three hundred thousand dollars, another milestone for Cory and Carlos.

The large purse and significance of the race as the final prep for the Santa Anita Derby, four weeks away, had drawn a big crowd for the early-March Saturday program. When the announcer introduced the race participants, Cory had noticed that Bandit received a nice applause. Evidently spectators were growing aware of his handicap and it was earning him popularity.

"Buena suerte, Boss."

Cory nodded to Carlos as the horses neared the starting gate. Cory had observed that, aside from Tracy's witticism, the group seemed subdued today, which he hoped wasn't portent of Bandit's performance. Sure, Stan and Tiger had made their usual betting soirees. But Stan appeared lethargic and even his apparel—plain brown pants and shirt—looked muted. And Tiger, likely in another losing streak at the windows, didn't bother hurling his customary verbal daggers at the old man. The mood certainly hadn't been helped by Sandra revealing that one of her grandchildren, the boy in "One Potato, Two Potato," apparently needed surgery to correct an elbow deformity. Nor did Tracy improve things by her continued coolness and distance, at least toward Cory.

As Bandit entered the number-five gate, right in the middle of the nine-horse pack, Cory as usual grew anxious. Was he doing the right thing running him here? Granted, Bandit had trained well recently and the ankle swelling hadn't returned. And he was among the betting favorites, at nine to two. But could these positives outweigh the major negative of missing a couple weeks' training at a key time? Especially with this race being against the best horses he had ever faced.

Bandit broke sharply. To little avail, however, as he got pinballed between the number-four horse, bearing out, and the six, coming in. Espinoza had to drop him back to seventh as the field passed in front of Sandra's box. No change as they began the first turn. Midway around the curve, two horses clipped heels, one of them stumbling and losing his jockey. Another, behind Bandit, leaped the supine rider, simultaneously tossing his own jockey. Down the backstretch, Bandit lolled along in sixth, Espinoza seemingly in no hurry to move.

Into the far turn, Espinoza asked Bandit the question, churning his strong arms and shoulders. No immediate response. The missed training taking its toll? Or maybe the colt simply wasn't good enough for this type of competition.

Bandit made a brief surge as the field entered the stretch, moving up to fifth. He had a clear path on the outside. But where was the potent burst they had become so accustomed to? The eighth pole came and went. The crowd noise ascended. None of it came from Sandra's box. A horse on the outside passed Bandit. Another passed him on his inside.

When the pack flashed under the wire, Cory realized Bandit had beaten only two horses—the ones who'd lost their jockeys.

✦ ✦ ✦

On the train home after the race, Tiger sat perfectly still. Unfortunately, so did the train. Although he had a window seat, he had no interest in looking outside. Instead he gazed straight ahead, at the back of the seat in front of him. The guy next to him had on apple-scented cologne that smelled stale, but Tiger hardly noticed.

The train had broken down just outside Oceanside, his destination. Tiger would have been angry had he had someplace to go other than his room. So small and dingy. Pretty much like his life. Incessant train rides to and from the track. Working the sordid buffet every morning. No real social life. No real future.

Bandit wasn't his only loser today. In fact, he hadn't cashed a single ticket. Yesterday either. Nor the day before. Actually, this particular losing streak was now in its second week.

"There's more to life than betting horses."

Stan's words, spoken at Santa Anita the day Tall Order won, came to Tiger as he sat there waiting for the train to start. Maybe there was some truth in those words. The way things were right now, there certainly could be *more* to *his* life.

The train finally groaned to a start. Tiger almost wished that it hadn't.

CHAPTER 21

"IT WASN'T *BANDIT'S* FAULT IN YESTERDAY'S race," Cory said. "It was *mine*."

Tracy didn't answer. Possibly because she was still being cool toward him. More likely because the room was noisy from numerous conversations and she didn't feel like competing. They stood in Sandra's living room, two of many people invited to a party at Sandra's home. Trainers, jockeys, breeders, owners and racing officials were present—all associated with Sandra's horses. Among Bandit's owners, Stan and Carlos were there too. Sandra had also invited Tiger and Perry, but Tiger declined, owing to the distance, and Tracy didn't feel right bringing Perry to a party attended almost exclusively by adults.

"Plain and simple," Cory continued above the chatter. "I didn't train him enough once he got that swelling. I talked to Espinoza after the race and he said Bandit wanted to run in the stretch, but he was just too tired."

Tracy shrugged. To their side, someone dropped a plate of hors d'oeuvres on the floor. Tracy looked uneasy. Probably less from the accident than from the snug fit of the elegant tan pantsuit she was wearing. She rotated her head and neck two or three times, seemingly to slide her jacket into a more comfortable position.

"I think Sandra expects me to mingle," she said, edging away from him.

"Right. I forgot you're working."

"Not exactly," she corrected before walking off.

Feeling uneasy himself, Cory looked around for Stan and Carlos—who had carpooled with him—hoping to entice them into an early departure.

✦ ✦ ✦

"Should we call a tow truck?" Tracy asked.

"Don't feel like messing with it tonight," Cory grumbled. "I'll call a taxi."

They stood together near his disabled old brown Chevy. Tracy held an umbrella up, protecting them both against a steady drizzle. Cory had already gotten wet, however, from several umbrella-less trips between the party and his car.

Stan and Carlos were in his back seat, where they'd been for the past fifteen minutes, ever since he did manage to persuade them to leave the party. Except his car hadn't started. When he'd returned to Sandra's, seeking help, Tracy volunteered. But the jumper cables she kept in her small white Toyota didn't start the car either. A fitting ending to what had been so far—Bandit's dismal performance setting the tone—a dismal weekend.

"I'll take you home," she offered. "In my car."

"No, no. We'll take a taxi."

"I'll take you," she insisted.

"Thought you had to stay at the party ... and mingle."

"I've mingled enough. I'll go tell Sandra I'm leaving. She knows I can't stay late. Because of Perry."

"We need to drop Stan at his place. And Carlos."

"No problem."

"Thanks," he said.

They returned her jumper cables to her car. He watched her head back toward Sandra's before he got into his car, out of the drizzle. He tried starting his engine once more. No luck.

✦ ✦ ✦

"Where's Perry tonight?" Cory asked her after they had dropped Stan at his residence and Carlos at Santa Anita.

"With a friend. Haven't I mentioned? ... I've got this reciprocal child-care deal. Sunday is my night out."

"Then you could've stayed longer at Sandra's ... and mingled some more," he noted sarcastically.

"I guess ..."

He proceeded to give her directions for the five-minute drive from Santa Anita to his place. She simply nodded at each instruction, continuing to be distant. And his mood certainly wasn't helped by his car being disabled. Or by the prospect of having to walk to the barn tomorrow morning, then negotiate a way back to Sandra's to tend to his car. Nor by the fact he was still a little wet and cold from being out in the drizzle earlier.

"How's Cookie?" she asked, breaking her brief silence as she stopped on the street in front of his trailer. "Haven't seen her since that day we played ball with Perry."

"She's fine."

"Mind if I visit her?"

"Don't you have to get Perry?"

"Not for another hour," she replied, glancing at her watch. "My friend took him and her kids to the movies. No school tomorrow. Spring break."

"I'll go get Cookie."

"I'll come too. I've never seen your place."

"Believe me," he shrugged, "it's not much to see."

They each got out of the car. The drizzle had turned into steady rain. She held her umbrella for them both as they walked past the main house, toward his trailer beyond. Remembering he hadn't tidied up before leaving for Sandra's, he became uncomfortable.

"You don't really want to come in," he said, not certain he was asking or telling.

"Well I sure don't want to stand out here in the rain. And I doubt Cookie does either."

He couldn't dispute her logic. Reluctantly, he unlocked the door. He couldn't remember how messy he'd left the place and wasn't especially eager to find out. He was pleasantly surprised, though, when he turned on the overhead light inside. Yes, a few clothes were strewn around, a couple of dishes sat unwashed and there were slices of tomato and avocado that he'd forgotten to put back in the little refrigerator, but things could have been a lot worse.

Tracy went right over to Cookie, asleep in her little alcove. She immediately woke up, greeting Tracy with a tail wagging. Meanwhile, Cory went to his closet, removed a jacket and put it on over his damp clothing. Next he returned the tomato and avocado to the fridge and canvassed it for any sign of refreshments. A carton of lemonade was his only option. He found two clean glasses near the sink and poured some lemonade into each. He handed a glass to Tracy, kneeling beside Cookie, and she took a sip before placing it on the floor.

Cookie was now fully awake and wanting to play. She barked several times and began running around the single big room. Tracy sipped more lemonade, then got up to chase Cookie. They both circled the room. Cory considered joining in, but couldn't decide which one to chase. Finally, Tracy cornered Cookie near the alcove. Cookie kept barking. Tracy grabbed her and wrestled her to the floor. Cory spotted a puddle near Cookie and assumed one of them knocked over Tracy's lemonade. Then he remembered Cookie needed a walk.

Fancy pantsuit and all, Tracy mounted Cookie, who continued barking. They rolled over twice, taking turns being on top. Cory decided to jump in. Avoiding Tracy's lemonade and Cookie's puddle, he knelt down and tried to maneuver between them. It didn't work. For some reason, they both wound up on top of him.

Cookie was still barking. Tracy was laughing. Together they'd pinned him—face up—to the floor. Tracy began to tickle him. Softly at first, then more vigorously. Next she kissed him. Inexplicably, Cookie stopped barking and got off him, wandering back to her alcove. Tracy kissed him again, far more passionately this time.

Still pinning him to the ground, her legs around his midsection, she took off her jacket. He recalled her earlier discomfort with its snug fit, at Sandra's party, and was sure that's why she removed it. His conclusion was refuted, though, when she unbuttoned her tan blouse. Unless it was the source of her unease. When she took it off, he could only think of that morning a couple of months ago, when he glimpsed undergarment beneath her top. Now he was seeing it, frilly and pink, unobstructed by concealing apparel.

What should he do now? The one time he tried something she'd pretty much withdrawn until ... Actually she was still pretty much withdrawn ... except for this ... whatever this was.

There was a large black spider crawling on his ceiling. He noticed it take one or two steps, then stop. One or two more in a different direction, before another stop. If Cory were looking for some type of symbolic guidance, the spider certainly wasn't offering any.

He compromised. He reached up with both hands and touched her shoulders. His fingers traced a path to her neck. Her skin was soft and pliant. She kissed him again. He deeply wanted to touch the softness hidden by the pink undergarment, but he didn't dare.

Then she removed the undergarment. She kissed him once more, holding him close, her bare chest nestling against the jacket he had put on minutes ago. He knew he wanted her in every way a man could want a woman.

"I love you," he heard himself whisper in her ear.

✦ ✦ ✦

"I think we passed the test," he smiled.

"What test?" she questioned, her head nuzzled against his naked chest. He had wrapped his jacket around her to keep her warm.

"Cookie approves."

"How can you tell?"

"If she didn't, she'd be barking her head off."

"Maybe she isn't because I made her an accessory," Tracy said, raising up.

"I don't think so. She only plays with people she likes."

"Smart girl."

He grinned. He waved for Cookie to come over from her alcove, but she wasn't about to budge. Tracy got up and began to dress. Cory wasn't about to budge either, even though the cement floor was cold against his naked body. He was content simply lying there, watching her dress.

He also observed the spider, still on the ceiling. It continued to make little progress in its wanderings. A step or two here, then a stop. A couple of steps in a different direction, another stop.

"I do like your place," Tracy commented, standing in front of him, only partially clothed. "It fits you."

"There anything else you liked?" he asked, grinning again.

"Oh sure," she replied, leaning down, picking up her glass and taking another sip from it. "I liked the lemonade."

✦ ✦ ✦

Cory tossed the ball into the air, swung the bat and lifted a fly to left field. Perry, positioned there with his glove on, took half a dozen steps in. Then he turned and ran back. Too late, the ball landed over his head. In truth, had he stayed where he'd started, the ball would have come right to him. Glumly, he retrieved it and tossed it back toward Cory.

It was two days after the party and the rain had been replaced by sunny weather. Cory had spent much of yesterday getting his car repaired. Perry had called an hour ago, right after Cory finished the morning's training, and suggested they get an early start, since he was on spring break. Once he and Cookie got to the apartment, Cory hoped to run into Tracy, but she didn't appear.

"Try again, Perry," he encouraged.

Cory hit a second soft fly. This time Perry started back. Another mistake. The ball landed about twenty feet in front of him. As he went to get the ball, he had his head down.

They'd already tried other positions—the infield in particular—with minimal success. Occasionally Perry had been able to snag a grounder, but his throwing arm was weak and of course his impaired vision caused him to misgauge distances. Almost every time, he threw significantly short of the target.

Fortunately, none of this affected his batting, which continued to improve. He'd mastered the techniques Cory had shown him. Even with Cory pitching harder and from farther away than previously, Perry rarely missed making good contact, and his confidence grew. Too bad when Cory tried the same techniques with Perry's fielding, distances were simply too great.

"Try one more," Cory called out.

Unhappily, Cory could hit a hundred more and it probably wouldn't help. The fly he did hit went slightly to Perry's left. The ball hooked, though, so that despite Perry starting in the correct direction, it curved back the other way and landed to his right. Cory didn't want the boy getting too discouraged. While Perry retrieved the last hit, Cory got Cookie from under a tree and they walked out to join him.

"I think that's enough for today," he told the boy.

"I like baseball," Perry shrugged, handing Cory the ball. "But maybe it's time to try something else."

"Oh?"

"I'm just not very good at this. Sometimes a man has to face facts."

"At age eight?"

"I'm almost nine."

"That still gives you some time," Cory chuckled. "Anyway, you've become a terrific hitter."

"Yeah, but I can't play in the field."

"So you could be a designated hitter," Cory countered, aware that this was the first time in his presence Perry had been negative. "In the American League, remember?"

"What if a National League team drafts me?"

"Might be a problem," Cory smiled. "They could trade you to the American League, though."

"Then you wouldn't come see me play."

"Why not?"

"You're a National League fan, remember? ... The Dodgers ... The D-Backs."

"If you played for the Yankees, I'd be a Yankee fan."

"What about the Texas Rangers?"

"Only if you played for them," Cory laughed.

That seemed to satisfy Perry. Cory handed him his bat and, with Cookie, they headed back toward where Cory had been hitting from, to get the rest of the baseballs. Cory had a thought.

"One thing I've noticed," he said.

"What?"

"You run very fast."

"Thanks."

"Maybe we could find you a race."

"But I'm not a horse," Perry disputed.

"Right ... They have special races for people. For kids."

"I could be like Bandit?" Perry glowed.

"Yeah. You could be like Bandit."

"Great."

"In a lot of ways," Cory said, "you are like Bandit."

"You mean ... because of our eyes?"

"No. I mean because of your heart."

Perry looked at Cory questioningly, without replying.

"What I like most about Bandit is what I like most about you," Cory explained. "Both of you try hard and don't easily give up."

They'd reached the other baseballs and they picked them up. Cory put his arm around Perry and, along with Cookie, they walked off the field.

CHAPTER 22

"I DON'T WANT YOU GETTING THE wrong idea about the other night," Tracy said solemnly.

"How could I?" Cory grinned. "You were only feeling sorry for me ... Bandit running bad and my car breaking down."

"I wasn't feeling sorry for you."

"You like to roughhouse. And Cookie was no match."

"I'm not joking."

He could see that. He could also see she wanted to talk. They sat in a remote booth at the rear of a rather plain coffee shop near Santa Anita. Evidently her finally accepting a breakfast invitation months after his first one wasn't the triumph he'd hoped it would be. Maybe he should have surmised such when he hadn't seen her during the four days since that night. Not even to come by the barn to see Bandit while he, Cory, was there.

"You probably won't believe this," she sighed, "but I haven't been with anyone that way since my divorce."

"How long?"

"Three years."

She was dressed simply—jeans, sweatshirt, denim jacket, all in shades of blue. She seemed downcast, her eyes red, as if she'd been crying. None of this made her any less appealing. In fact he had to resist putting his arms around her and pulling her close.

Neither of them had looked at the menus that lay before them. Their waitress, fiftyish with a grumpy expression, came by to take their order, but Cory waved her away. Along with a frown, she did provide them each a cup of coffee.

"It simply happened," Tracy added. "I didn't plan it."

He nodded. Again he had to fight the impulse to hug her. A little girl and a woman, who looked like she was the little girl's mother, passed the booth on their way to the nearby restroom.

"I'm just not ready," Tracy went on.

"With me? Or with anyone?"

"With anyone. It's still too soon."

"After three years?" he questioned, frowning himself.

"Time isn't the issue," she said plaintively, gazing down at the table. "It's my fear."

"Of what?"

"Of what happened before happening again."

"Did he abuse you too?" he asked directly. "Or just Perry?"

"What he did to me didn't matter," she muttered, almost to herself. "I got myself into it. But Perry was innocent."

This time his reaction was even stronger. He really had to restrain himself from reaching out and kissing her like he'd done that afternoon at her apartment. No doubt the memory of her subsequent withdrawal prevented him. Instead, he merely touched her hand. Tears formed in her eyes and he almost felt like crying himself.

"I should have stood up to him," she declared.

"So that's why you made such a big deal about bullies. Kosko. Dobson."

"Yes."

"Why you wouldn't let us give in and sell Bandit. Even though they'd threatened you and Perry."

"Yes."

He squeezed her hand. Which only brought more tears. If he wasn't doing her feelings any good, at least he was beginning to understand them. Beginning to understand her.

"So," he said softly. "I guess we won't be doing what we did the other night anytime soon."

She shook her head.

"Can we at least have breakfast?" he asked.

"Now?"

"And whenever else you have time."

"Yes," she answered, and touched his arm.

Almost on cue, their waitress returned. She looked less grumpy as they began to order.

✦ ✦ ✦

About two weeks later, Cory got a call on his barn phone from a racing department official. An allowance race for which Bandit was eligible was being offered as a last-minute "extra race," one not originally scheduled. It had four horses, Bandit would make five and they would use the race if he were entered, according to the official. The problem was that it would be run three days before the Santa Anita Derby. No way Bandit could race in both.

Until this moment, Cory had given little thought to the Derby. He was aware of it, of course, and aware that Bandit had trained well since his awful San Felipe race—almost as if the colt were determined to make up for his dismal performance. Cory wasn't ready to make a decision, though. Which now he was being forced to do. He needed time, if only a few minutes.

"I'll have to poll my owners," Cory told the official, "in case they want to run in the Derby. I'll get back to you."

"How soon?"

"Give me twenty minutes."

✦ ✦ ✦

"Got a big decision," Cory told Tracy via phone minutes later.

"What?" she asked, sounding a bit rushed.

"Catch you at a bad time?"

"I'm leaving for Sandra's. Supposed to be there in half an hour."

"Could you call her first? Bandit can run in an allowance race. Or the Santa Anita Derby. Which would she prefer?"

"Don't have to call her to give you her answer."

"The Derby?" he guessed.

"Sure. But I'll call her anyway. And call you back if I'm wrong."

"Thanks."

"You talk to anyone else?" she questioned.

"Only Tiger. He picked the Derby. Likes the idea of Bandit being a long shot. Maybe cash a nice bet."

"Figures."

"What about you?" he quizzed.

"You're the trainer. Leave it up to you."

"Wish you'd leave other things up to me," he teased.

She laughed. And promised again to call right back if she were wrong about Sandra's choice. When he hung up, Carlos was standing nearby, in their office doorway.

"Boss, I am sorry. I cannot help overhear. Maybe we do the wrong thing if Bandit, he run in the Derby."

"Maybe you're right."

"I think he have a good chance to win the allowance race."

"I know."

"The purse, it is much smaller. But I rather have something of a little. Than nothing of a lot."

Cory nodded. He'd rarely seen Carlos so adamant. He'd always left entry decisions to him, Cory. But then this was one of the few times he'd owned a share of one of their horses.

"Maybe he get hurt in the Derby, Boss."

"He could get hurt in either race," Cory quickly countered.

"There will be more horses in the Derby. Better horses, Boss. Maybe he is not ready for that."

"Maybe not. But there's only you and me … and possibly Tracy … in favor of the allowance race. The three minority owners. So we'd better convince Stan."

Cory walked out of the office, got a carrot and brought it to Bandit's stall. The colt gobbled it up so eagerly Cory had to get him another. He realized he was delaying, hoping that Tracy would call back with the news that she was wrong about Sandra preferring the Derby. Then he remembered his promise to notify the racing official within twenty minutes. He fed Bandit the second carrot and returned to the office, making a mental note that he owed each of their other horses two carrots.

Stan answered his phone seemingly before it rang, as though expecting Cory's call. No doubt Tiger had gotten to him first, and the old man was ready.

"The Derby," he asserted.

"You sure? We might be over our heads. Asking for trouble."

"I'm sure. Won a claiming race. Won an allowance race. Never won a stakes race."

"But this is no ordinary stakes," Cory debated. "This is the Santa Anita Derby."

"Better yet. I've never won a derby."

"Okay," Cory said, shrugging at Carlos, who had reentered the office, "I guess you'll be there for the race."

"With bells on my shoes," Stan retorted.

CHAPTER 23

"HEY, LOOK," STAN ANNOUNCED EXCITEDLY. "Bandit's gone up to thirty-three to one."

"His trainer's thirty-three to one," Cory joked. "The horse is no more than ten."

"Hear that, Tiger?" Stan proclaimed. "The trainer ain't runnin'. Our horse is. Let's get back to them windows."

With that, Stan and Tiger got up and left Sandra's box. As he'd warned, Stan did have bells on both of the black-and-white sneakers he wore. All of Bandit's owners, plus Perry, were there for the big race. So were about forty thousand other people, not in the least discouraged by a cool afternoon, unseasonably so for early April in the L.A. area. Perhaps Stan's bells, jingling loudly as he went to make more bets, lightened the mood in Sandra's box. Everyone seemed much more enthusiastic than before Bandit's last race. But then today their horse was running in the Santa Anita Derby.

"How's your grandson?" Cory asked Sandra, seated in front of him. "Potato Number Two."

"Oh," she laughed, "he's fine. Doesn't need an operation after all."

"That is good," Carlos chipped in.

Stan's jingling bells heralded Tiger and his return. Just in time, because the horses were approaching the gate. Bandit had the number-one post, fine with Cory since the colt had won his only race for them from that position.

Cory knew there were other reasons, aside from Bandit's trainer, that the colt was thirty-three to one. Along with most of the field from the San Felipe, there were two other formidable opponents. Both were eastern-based, stakes-winning colts. One, Something's Happening, was last year's Breeders Cup champion two-year-old, and was the nine-to-five favorite. Carlos's preference for the allowance race certainly appeared prudent right now.

"Look at that." Stan nudged Tiger after they'd sat back down. "Isn't he thirty-five to one now? Let's go get some more."

"Nah. Wanna watch the race."

"Whatsa matter?" Stan complained. "You sick? Never had to twist your arm to make a bet. You might be sorry."

"How sorry could I be?" Tiger shot back. "Winner's purse is almost half a million. How come you gotta make every last buck?"

"Money's money."

"Wasn't it you said there's more to life than bettin' horses?"

"Not at my age," Stan quipped.

Cory shook his head at their repartee. All the talk about money and purse size only made him more nervous, however. When Tiger mentioned the winner's cut of almost half a million, he realized that was probably more than the total combined earnings of all the horses he'd ever trained.

"Buena suerte, Boss."

Carlos's customary good wishes, spoken from the seat beside him while the horses entered the gate, didn't diminish Cory's tension. Had he let down his longtime sidekick by not standing up to the other owners? Spurning a much easier race to be thirty-three—no, thirty-five—to one. What if Bandit did get hurt in this race because he, Cory, hadn't heeded Carlos's warning? He would never forgive himself.

Bandit broke sharply when the gates opened for the mile-and-an-eighth contest, like he had in the San Felipe. This time he didn't get pinballed though, and secured a nice stalking position in third place, in the clear. The large crowd gasped when the outside horse in the field of eleven veered sharply toward the outer rail before his jockey could straighten him.

Meanwhile, Bandit proceeded comfortably in third as the pack rounded the first turn and began the long backstretch. Jockey Espinoza eased him out away from the rail, forcing any horses wishing to pass to try it on their inside, where Bandit could see them. Cory saw how easily Bandit was running, three lengths behind the two leaders and three lengths in front of the fourth-place horse.

For some reason, he peered briefly at Perry, sitting between Tracy and himself. The boy seemed transfixed, despite it being doubtful he could make much sense of the race from such a distance. In truth, when Cory looked closer, he saw that Perry had both eyes closed. He sat absolutely motionless, as if he were casting some type of spell on the outcome of the race. Or, possibly, was he simply meditating?

When the horses reached the far turn, Bandit began to move up. Cory felt a tightness in his chest and he had trouble breathing. He knew there would be no excuses this time. No ankle swelling, no missed training. Actually they'd trained Bandit hard prior to this race. Harder than ever before. Long gallops. Fast breezes. And he'd seemingly thrived on all the work, if eagerness and appetite were any indication.

At the top of the stretch, Bandit caught the leaders. Would all the hard training pay off? Above the mounting crowd noise, Cory heard Stan and Tiger yelling from behind him. Sandra stood up in front. As Bandit took the lead, Cory reached past Perry and held Tracy's hand. The crowd noise grew deafening. Then Cory saw a horse coming from behind on the outside. It was Something`s Happening, and his challenge was becoming more prominent with each stride. Cory knew Bandit couldn't see him. Espinoza was riding furiously. The wire came just in time.

One-Eyed Bandit had won the Santa Anita Derby.

✦ ✦ ✦

"Told you we shoulda bet more," Stan harangued Tiger as the track photographer snapped the winner's circle picture. All the owners, plus Perry and Espinoza, still aboard Bandit, were there.

"Ease up," Tiger growled. "Size of the purse doesn't matter to you?"

"What's the size of the purse got to do with the size of the bet?" Stan reasoned.

Cory laughed heartily. He still held Tracy's hand, and Perry was atop his shoulders. He thought the incessant debate would have ended by now, especially given the difficult trek from Sandra's box to the winner's circle. Fortunately, Sandra knew a couple of track ushers who'd guided them through the large throng.

After the picture, Espinoza jumped down from Bandit and shook everyone's hand before going over to the scales to weigh out. Carlos led Bandit away, toward the receiving barn, to be tested. Espinoza left for the jockeys' room.

Cory didn't know exactly what to do. He knew that he didn't want to let go of Tracy's hand or put Perry down, because contact with them meant he hadn't lost touch with reality, that what had occurred in the last few minutes wasn't merely a dream, that their horse really did win the Santa Anita Derby. He also knew that he felt like flying and they kept him from soaring off into space. Then he remembered that a track official had interrupted their path to the winner's circle and told him that the trophy presentation would take place in the media room. So he did know exactly what to do now.

Before going over to Sandra, Stan and Tiger, nearby, to inform them of the presentation, he hesitated. Sandra was standing between them, and Cory was momentarily reluctant to intervene, in case she was adjudicating their ongoing debate.

✦ ✦ ✦

"When will you send your horse to Kentucky for the Derby?" a television reporter asked Cory in the media room.

"Forgive me," he mumbled uncomfortably. "I haven't thought that far ahead."

Of course he hadn't. How could he? Were it up to Carlos and him, they wouldn't have even entered the Santa Anita Derby. Let alone win it. Therefore he wouldn't be standing in front of numerous members of the media, in this nondescript room tucked off in some obscure corner of Santa Anita he'd never seen before. Fortunately he was flanked by Tracy, Perry, Sandra, Stan and Tiger, all looking thrilled to be here.

The trophy presentation had already occurred. Indeed, their award, a huge engraved bronze statue of a horse, sat on a table before them. Cory did feel bad about one thing—Carlos, tending to Bandit, couldn't be on hand.

"You *are* planning on Kentucky?" another TV broadcaster inquired.

"Forgive me," Cory repeated, gesturing toward the other owners, "we just haven't thought that far ahead."

"A former claiming horse with only one eye," a woman with a tape recorder asserted. "Will these factors influence your decision?"

"I don't see where either has anything to do with it," Cory said, bristling at Bandit being denigrated in any way, especially with Perry present.

Because this type of interrogation was new to Cory, it undoubtedly increased his discomfort. Sure, he'd dealt with media people before, but never en masse like this. And never with microphones stuck in his face, cameras whirring, tape recorders clicking.

"Forgive me," he uttered for the third time. "Why don't you talk to the other owners now? I've got to go to the barn and check on our horse."

He quickly headed for the door, to the garble of numerous questions being hurled his way.

✦ ✦ ✦

"He looks like a million," a short, wiry man, gazing at Bandit cooling out on the hot walker, greeted Cory at the barn ten minutes later. "Ran like a million, too."

"Things went his way," Cory replied. "You here for a reason?"

"A million reasons."

"I'm missing something."

"My client's been in the game forty years," the man remarked. "Owned some nice horses. None of them ever ran in the Kentucky Derby."

Cory glanced at Carlos, standing near the hot walker, for any indication he knew this guy. Carlos simply shrugged in response. Their veterinarian drove by at that moment and clasped his hands together above his head triumphantly. Cory waved back.

"Dobson send you?" he asked the man.

"Don't know Dobson."

"What about Kosko?"

"Don't know any Kosko."

"You know about the colt's eye?"

"Everyone knows about the colt's eye," the guy confirmed.

"Doesn't matter to you?"

"Of course it matters to me," the man conceded. "But like I said, my client's getting on in years and wants a horse to run in the Derby."

"I'll talk to my owners."

Before turning to leave, the man handed Cory a business card. Below his name, Carlton Brannon, which Cory didn't recognize, was written the sum one million dollars.

✦ ✦ ✦

"Forgive me, Boss. I cannot help overhear."

"You sound like me with the media," Cory laughed. "Forgive me ... forgive me."

Carlos, of course, not being at the interview, didn't understand. Five minutes had passed since Brannon left. Enough time for Cory to give Carlos a celebratory handshake and hug. And for them to elicit simultaneous shouts of joy at their astonishing victory. And for Cory to offer Bandit, still attached to the hot walker, three carrots and two effusive pats on the shoulder.

"What do you think?" Cory asked Carlos, his expression turning as serious as his compadre's.

"I think if we sell Bandit for one million dollar ... I can bring my family here to live."

"So you want to sell."

"No, Boss. I do not want to sell. But I do want to bring my family here to live."

"Might be hard to convince Sandra and Stan. From the looks on their faces in the media room."

"I know, Boss. It will be hard."

Carlos went to Bandit. It was time to detach him from the hot walker.

✦ ✦ ✦

"Looks like I'm on a roll." Cory beamed.

"No question," Tracy concurred. "Winning the Santa Anita Derby."

"Not that." He grinned. "Two breakfasts with you in less than two weeks."

She laughed. Indeed, they *were* having breakfast again. The morning after the big victory, at the same plain coffee shop, in the same rear booth. This time, however, they were far more relaxed and had even managed to order before their same grumpy waitress became very grumpy.

"You talk to Sandra," he suggested. "I'll talk to Stan."

"About what?"

"About the million-dollar offer we got for Bandit."

"Wow! You really *are* on a roll. But I'm sure Sandra will want to turn it down."

"I'm sure I can get lots more. Guy sounded pretty eager."

"Wouldn't matter," she answered. "She's already talking about Kentucky. Turns out she's never been to the Derby."

"It would be quite a coincidence."

"What would?"

"If I could get two million," he replied. "Remember when you said you didn't care if we got forty times our investment? That night we all met at Sandra's. Well, do the math ... Two million is forty times our original fifty thousand."

She shrugged. The waitress brought their food. They'd each ordered oatmeal, eggs and toast. Cory observed that the waitress didn't frown. Actually, she even smiled and asked if she could bring them anything else.

He also observed Tracy. She had on the same low-cut navy-blue top she'd worn that morning he'd galloped Sandra's little filly. So far he'd confined himself to only a couple of glimpses at it.

"So ..." he ventured, looking her straight in the eye. "I guess you just didn't like me."

"When?"

"That night at my trailer."

"Oh," she gulped. He couldn't tell whether she'd reacted to his statement or to some oatmeal that was too hot to swallow. "I liked you. I just didn't like what we did."

"You sure?" he persisted. "I mean ... I think you didn't like *me.*"

"Not true. I did like you. *That's* the problem."

"Wait a minute ... let me understand this," he said, swallowing some oatmeal himself that was too hot. "Your liking me is the problem?"

"Yes. If I didn't, I could simply walk away."

"Isn't that what you're doing?"

"No. I'm here, aren't I? Having breakfast with you, like we agreed."

He certainly couldn't dispute that. Made all the more evident by his ongoing difficulty keeping his eyes off her navy-blue top. Anyway, when he'd invited her to breakfast, he'd hoped it could be their own little celebration for Bandit's triumph. Plus he wanted her opinion on what to do regarding Bandit.

"How do *you* feel about selling him?" he asked.

"I'd vote to keep him. But like I've said before, you're the trainer."

"It's a lot of money."

"It's always been a lot of money," she claimed. "And we've said no before."

"Not to a million dollars. Or maybe two."

"Somehow," she sighed, "I think there's more to all this than money."

He nodded. A fly had landed on his egg and he fanned it away with his hand. An obese man in the booth next to theirs tried to get up after finishing his meal. Finally, following a second attempt, he managed it and began to waddle toward the exit.

"I know you mean what you say," Cory offered.

"I try to."

"That night at my place," he stated. "I meant what I said."

"You mean about Cookie approving? That we passed her test?"

"No, not that ... That other thing ... About love."

"But that was just ... the heat of the moment."

"It was," he smiled.

"I thought so."

"But it also applies to before ... and after ... and now."

"Oh," she said.

✦ ✦ ✦

"This is where we first met," Stan told Cory. "Almost a year ago."

"I know."

"Right in this exact spot."

"Seems strange not to have horses and people around," Cory mused.

"I can live without the people," Stan remarked. "But the horses ..."

The old man gazed off into the distance. The two of them leaned side by side against the white railing of the outdoor Hollywood Park paddock. The afternoon was perfect—warm, a slight breeze and smogless—and if Cory remembered correctly, the old man wore the same black threadbare corduroy sports coat on that first occasion that he was wearing today. Cory had called him right after breakfast with Tracy. Because he and Cookie were long overdue to visit Janice, in the vicinity, and he knew that Stan normally bet the Santa Anita races at Hollywood Park, he suggested they meet at the paddock here to discuss the offer for Bandit.

"A million bucks," Stan marveled at the sum Cory had revealed during the phone call. "Hard to believe."

"We wait ... I'm sure they'll up it. Maybe to two."

"Anyone want to sell?"

"Carlos."

"He the only one?"

"So far. He wants to bring his family here."

"You know," Stan spoke a little hoarsely. "I helped Tiger out while back."

"Oh?"

"I'll do the same for Carlos."

"Not sure that's fair to you."

"You know what I'm gonna say." Stan grinned. "Sounding like a broken record ... Can't take it with me."

Cory smiled at him. In the background, he heard the Santa Anita announcer over television, alerting spectators that the horses for the third race were approaching the starting gate. It still felt strange for the paddock to be absent of horses and people.

"Plus I got another reason," the old man continued. "Much more important."

"Oh?"

"Chemistry!" Stan declared.

"Chemistry?"

"Yeah. Chemistry. We're a terrific team. All six of us. I don't want anyone leaving. We all go to Kentucky, and we all go as a team."

Cory didn't reply. The Santa Anita announcer began to detail the horses entering the gate.

"Way back in high school," Stan went on. "I tried out for football. Too small, though. Couldn't even make the junior varsity. They stuck me on the B team with all the other castoffs. None of us quit, though. We all stayed together. Had a terrific season. Didn't lose a single game. I remember it like it was yesterday."

"So we're like ... the B team," Cory said.

"Yeah. The B team."

"I'll talk to Carlos," Cory offered.

"Tell him I'll help him."

They shook hands and Cory headed for his car. Time to take Cookie, waiting there, to visit Janice. The Santa Anita announcer began calling the race over TV. Cory was interested in only one race today, the eighth, and he anticipated coming back here to watch it simulcast, provided they finished at Janice's in time.

Nearing his car, he thought about how well Stan had expressed things—the six of them were a terrific team. A very diverse cast of characters. Given the fact they'd all encountered their share of adversity, the name "the B team" seemed a perfect fit.

✦ ✦ ✦

"He is right, Boss. We must all stay together."

"He said he'd help you."

"No. That is okay. I will wait."

It was the next morning at the barn. Cory yawned. He was tired because he'd stayed up late last night. He had watched the race over TV at Hollywood Park, as he'd hoped. But then he'd returned to Janice's and taken her and Cookie out to dinner at a restaurant with an outdoor patio for Cookie. And had their own small celebration for Bandit's win.

"What about your family?" Cory asked Carlos. "What if something happens to Bandit and we wind up with nothing?"

"That is what bother me, Boss. That he will get hurt. People, they say horses, they go to Kentucky and they get hurt bad. Even they die."

"Can't disagree. And not only in Kentucky, but all the triple crown races. Especially in recent years."

"We must not let something happen, Boss. You and me, we must not let something happen."

Cory shrugged at Carlos's determination. And hoped his compadre wasn't making a terrible mistake in not accepting help from Stan.

CHAPTER 24

CORY OBVIOUSLY VALUED STAN FOR FAR more than naming them the B team. The old man had been instrumental in Carlos and his success in California. He was their first owner here. Every horse they'd claimed for him won at least once. And he'd introduced Cory to Tiger, without whom they'd never have even considered acquiring Bandit.

The run of good luck involving Stan continued. They claimed another horse, Avid Dancer, who won by three lengths on claim day. And Stan introduced Cory to a potential client, who lived in the same senior residence as Stan. Actually, it was the same guy to whom Stan had loaned his Racing Form on Thanksgiving, when he'd invited Cory, Carlos and Tiger to his place for dinner.

Cory and Carlos's good luck with Sandra continued as well. Her little filly—whom she eventually withdrew from the Pomona sale and named Charming Location, in honor of her former profession, real estate—finished third in her first race, boding a promising future. And Turbulent Flight won again, his second consecutive victory.

In fact, things were proceeding so well right here that Cory began to question going to Kentucky.

✦ ✦ ✦

"Still can't believe it," Sandra sighed. "Kentucky after all these years."

Tracy smiled. Yet beside the touch of excitement in Sandra's tone, Tracy now knew her well enough to detect the hint of sadness also. Like why couldn't this have happened before, while Phil was alive?

The two of them sat in Sandra's spacious living room, surrounded by the paintings of her horses. Tracy hadn't yet mentioned her own painting. She knew she would. But not now, this wasn't the time.

They were filling out applications for an upcoming horse sale. Sandra had recently accepted an offer on her farm, and since she had no place of her own to board her horses, it was now imperative that they aggressively reduce inventory.

"It *is* hard to believe," Tracy agreed, referring to Kentucky. "Like a dream ..."

She was about to say more, something expressing how lucky they were. But she sensed Sandra's further discomfort, so she stopped. Instead she focused on their work. She wanted to finish today and it was after one o'clock, nearing time to stop and go pick up Perry from school.

Following the initial adjustment, she'd really grown to like the work. More accurately, she'd really grown to like Sandra, admiration and respect being significant components. No doubt it was Tracy's imagination, but Sandra reminded her of what little she remembered of her own mother before she died. Her real mother, not the woman who became her stepmother.

"Glad Cory talked us out of keeping the little filly in the sale," Sandra said, perhaps deliberately steering the conversation away from Kentucky. "She ran too well the other day to sell."

"Pardon me, Sandra ... I don't think he exactly talked us out of it."

"You mean because he refused to breeze her when you asked him to?"

"I mean because he was being stubborn."

"Patient," Sandra corrected, causing them both to laugh. "I remember having a conversation like this with *him*."

"Me too," Tracy giggled.

"Speaking of Cory ... Mind if I say something?"

"Mind if I work while we talk?" Tracy asked.

"Of course not."

A brief silence ensued while Sandra evidently collected her thoughts. Tracy caught an error on one of the applications, of an incorrect birth year for one of their horses. Carefully she whited out the mistake and wrote in the right year.

"I've tried to push myself more lately," Sandra confided. "Take a few chances."

"What's that have to do with Cory?"

"How about you?"

"Me what?" Tracy questioned, not following Sandra's thought process at all, yet beginning to feel a little uncomfortable.

"Taking a few chances."

"Like how?"

"Like with Cory," Sandra asserted.

Now Tracy understood Sandra's direction. And was starting to feel *very* uncomfortable, realizing that she'd likely have to defend herself. She decided that she might as well begin to do that now.

"We've been having breakfast together," she ventured.

"At your place?"

"No, no. In a coffee shop."

"That doesn't sound very risky."

"Well ..." Tracy admitted, "truth is ... I haven't had much luck picking men."

"Seems like he's picking you," Sandra pointed out. "I see the way he looks at you. And at Perry."

What could she say? She knew Sandra had cut to the core. Disturbing, because it was one thing for Cory and her to confront her fear. It was another for others to recognize it.

"Let's make a deal," Sandra suggested.

"What?"

"From now on we *both* take more chances."

Now Tracy was the one who was sad. In fact, she could feel tears in her eyes. Sandra got up, came over and hugged her.

✦ ✦ ✦

On his way out of a grocery store after buying Cookie some dog food, Cory noticed a poster advertising a junior Olympics. Conducted by a local recreation department, it would take place on the last Saturday in April, about two weeks away. The list of events included a fifty-meter dash for youngsters nine and below.

He immediately thought of Perry.

✦ ✦ ✦

Several envelopes lay on the barn office desk. Cory took one and walked over to Bandit's stall. The colt, standing near the rear to avoid the heat of the noon sun, came to the front when he saw

Cory. They stood nearly together as Cory took out the contents of the envelope.

"Dear One-Eyed Bandit," Cory read aloud. "Thank you for your great performance in the Santa Anita Derby and for being such a wonderful representative for all of us with a handicap."

Charming Location, in the next stall, began to whinny. Cory folded the letter and went over to her. He scratched her behind her left ear, a gesture he knew she liked. Cory's cell phone started ringing in his pocket, but he decided against interrupting the scratching to answer it.

The letter was far from the first Bandit had received. In fact, this week he averaged about a dozen a day. Delivered by a Santa Anita public relations rep, most were addressed to Bandit, in care of the track. Some correspondents requested a picture and the track obliged by sending a photo of the colt crossing the finish line in the Derby.

"In this world which can often be unfriendly to those of us with a handicap," Cory resumed reading after he'd stopped scratching Charming Location and returned to Bandit, "you have given us hope that we too can thrive. Good luck in Kentucky." He didn't read the signature because he couldn't quite make it out.

If there was still doubt about Bandit and him going to Kentucky, Cory realized it was steadily dissipating.

✦ ✦ ✦

"Thought I'd check," Cory said. "See if it's okay with you."

"What's okay?" Tracy asked.

"That besides baseball, Perry try some running."

"He mentioned it the other day. Told me you spoke about it with him."

"It okay?"

"Long as it's okay with him," she replied.

"There's a race coming up. Maybe I could show him a couple things."

She nodded. But her attention seemed more focused on the field in front of them. Tee-ball tryouts were taking place, and Perry was about to bat. She and Cory, plus forty or fifty other spectators, were sitting in the third-base bleachers. Because Perry was now eligible for the league's older division, his season this year began much earlier than last.

Perry stepped into the batter's box and faced the ball on the tee. He swung quickly and confidently. The ball flew on a line, into left center field. If batters were running the bases, it would have been an easy double, maybe a triple. Tracy clapped, as did some of the other spectators.

Since there were so many trying out, nearly eighty, each youngster got only two swings. Perry stepped away from the tee while a coach placed another ball on it. Because the afternoon was warming, Perry fanned himself with his left hand. Or possibly he was brushing an insect away from his face. He moved back to the tee. Again he swung quickly. Another liner, this one landing fair down the left-field line. What would have been another easy double.

"Nice going, Coach," Tracy grinned at Cory as Perry dropped his bat and headed over to get his glove.

"His fielding's another story."

"Maybe with more practice."

"I have my doubts."

"How about tomorrow night?" she asked, a slight twinkle in her eye.

"For practice?"

"No."

"What then?"

"A movie."

"The three of us?" he queried.

"No. Just you and me."

"What about Perry?"

"It's Sunday night," she answered. "He can stay with my friend. I've got her kids tonight."

He didn't reply. Really, he didn't know what to say. Was this a "date"? What else could it be?

"An ominous silence," she said. "Thinking of an excuse not to go?"

"No."

"Then say something."

"This sounds like more than breakfast."

"Make your own interpretation," she giggled.

✦ ✦ ✦

Cory didn't like the idea that the draft for teams took place right after tryouts, right on the field, in front of all the kids. All the more when number seventy-five of the seventy-eight players was selected, and Perry hadn't been. Clearly every coach knew of Perry's eye and none wanted him on their team.

Not that his fielding performance had helped. Cory was right—Perry needed more than practice. It was pretty much a duplication of the recent fielding session Cory had with him. Perry bobbled all three grounders hit to him, then threw wildly after retrieving them. And didn't come close to snagging either of the fly balls lofted to him.

Number seventy-six was picked. It wasn't Perry. Even from a distance, as Perry sat across the field in the first-base dugout, Cory could make out the disappointment on his face.

"This is cruel," Cory fumed. "No reason to humiliate a kid."

"I just hope he isn't last," Tracy sighed.

Number seventy-seven of the seventy-eight was selected. It wasn't Perry.

✦ ✦ ✦

Stan felt angry too. He knew that eventually it would come to this, but the timing was awful. Winding up in a hospital bed the afternoon your new horse is running.

Four hours ago, he'd been fine, sitting on the bus bench near his residence, waiting for the bus to come and take him to Santa Anita to meet Tiger before the race. Suddenly he'd felt tired. And faint. Next thing he knew he was on the pavement, looking up at several people. He could hear a siren far away. Moving closer. He realized it was from an ambulance, coming for him.

"But Avid Dancer is running," he remembered telling someone.

When the ambulance arrived, he'd tried to get up and let everyone know he was okay. He couldn't move though. Riding to the hospital, he'd actually considered asking the ambulance personnel to take him to the track. He was too tired to talk, however. Definitely a rarity for him. Now at least, lying in bed, he felt stronger.

The phone on his bedside table rang. He'd reached the Santa Anita press box a little while ago, hoping they'd call him back right before the race and let him listen to it over the phone. Maybe this was them. He grabbed the receiver and put it to his ear.

"Press box here," a voice divulged brusquely, before he could say anything. "They're in the gate. Good luck."

Stan could hear the phone placed down on the other end, he assumed next to a TV. The guy apparently didn't do a good job putting it down, though, because Stan heard vibration, like the receiver was rolling around. Although he could hear the track announcer, his voice was garbled. So garbled, in fact, that Stan could only make out the sound of his own horse and how he was doing.

"Avid Dancer is running fifth ..."

How could Stan expect his horse to perform well without him, Stan, being there? Without being able to place even a small bet on him? He was still so angry that he nearly slammed the phone down.

"Avid Dancer continues in fifth ..."

A nurse entered the room and shoved a pill into Stan's mouth. Which he felt like spitting out onto the floor.

"Avid Dancer is moving up on the outside ..."

When the nurse offered him a glass of water, he brushed it aside. Couldn't she tell he was listening to his horse run? Finally she left the room.

"Into the stretch, Avid Dancer is taking the lead ..."

Stan began rooting aloud. Fortunately he'd swallowed the pill, otherwise he *would* have spit it out. In the background over the phone, above the announcer's garbled voice, above his own voice, he did manage to hear the crowd noise swelling. Obviously they were cheering for his horse.

"At the finish ... it's Avid Dancer in front ..."

Stan let out a whoop. He nearly dropped the receiver. His luck was holding—if it could be called luck to be stuck in a hospital bed while your horse wins.

A doctor came into the room. He wore a white frock and was youngish, tall and unusually thin. Maybe he'd heard Stan shout and thought he needed help. But no, he carried a clipboard with some papers attached.

"Want to talk about test results, Stan?" he asked.

"No, Doc. Not now. Much rather talk about race results."

✦ ✦ ✦

"Got your message," Tiger proclaimed breathlessly, bursting into the hospital room. "Also got your bet down."

He pulled a large sum of money from his pocket and dropped it on the bed. Stan had been asleep and was very groggy. But not too groggy to now understand how his horse could have won.

"Congratulations," Tiger continued. "You won the bet. The purse. Plus plenty money on the claim."

"The claim! You mean they claimed one of my horses again!"

"Yep. Dobson again. Still tryin' to get even for Bandit, I guess."

"Man!" Stan exclaimed. "What I got to do to keep a horse?"

"Don't complain," Tiger advised. "Just keep winnin' races."

"How'd you get my message?"

"Circuitously," Tiger laughed. "After you called the press box, they got ahold of Carlos. Who told Cory. Who told me. Prob'ly everyone at the track knew you couldn't make it today."

"Guess I'm famous."

"Out there you are. Long as your horses keep winnin'."

"You get a bet down too?"

"Big time," Tiger grinned. "Hey, you okay? What you doin' in here?"

"Little fainting spell," Stan admitted, reluctantly.

Clearly he could have revealed more. Told Tiger of the condition undoubtedly causing it. And that time was likely short. But these were supposed to be happy days—winning races, cashing bets, Kentucky Derby. Why spoil things being morbid?

"When you gettin' out?" Tiger asked.

"Few days."

"In time for Kentucky?"

"Plenty of time," Stan assured him.

Stan was feeling tired again, though. So he closed his eyes and immediately dozed off.

✦ ✦ ✦

When he woke, the money was still there, on the bed. Tiger was still there too, perusing a Racing Form. He had turned on a light, because it was becoming dark outside.

"Hey, no train to catch?" Stan asked groggily.

"Made a deal for you," Tiger answered, ignoring the old man's question.

"Yeah?"

"Liquor store up the street carries the Form. Owner loves horses. Told him yours is in the Kentucky Derby."

"Yeah?"

"He was impressed," Tiger said, his nose still in the racing newspaper. "Promised to deliver the Form right here to you every morning."

Stan smiled. Then he closed his eyes and started to doze off again.

✦ ✦ ✦

This time Tiger was gone when Stan awoke. He'd left the Racing Form on the bed, though, on top of the money.

CHAPTER 25

"FEELS LIKE WE'RE IN HIGH SCHOOL," Cory laughed.

"Yes, to me too," Tracy agreed.

Indeed, pretty much everything they'd done so far on their "date" might have been done by a couple of high school kids. He'd picked her up at six thirty in his old Chevy—a high school jalopy if there ever was one—and they'd driven to the movie theater. Soon after the film began, she took his hand and held it. Following the movie, they'd gone for a drive down a main boulevard and listened to some old songs on his car radio. Now they sat in his front seat, parked at a drive-in restaurant that had enabled them to order hamburgers, fries and milk shakes right to the car.

"I liked the movie," he said, munching on his hamburger.

"Me too," she concurred, drinking some of her shake.

"You know which part I liked best?"

"Which?"

"The part right after the beginning."

"When?" she inquired.

"When you held my hand," he smiled.

✦ ✦ ✦

As they walked up the sidewalk to her apartment, Cory wondered what would happen next. While driving back here, he'd offered to pick up Perry. Tracy had declined, however, insisting that dates and kids don't mix. Did that mean she had something in mind for them now? Something that Perry couldn't be party to?

She brushed up against him when they reached her door. He had to remind himself to be patient, to not throw his arms around her right then. She had on a dark turtleneck sweater, which seemed soft, warm and inviting. Thoughts of them cuddling on her couch raced through his mind. She unlocked the door, then turned toward him.

"Well … good night," she said softly. "I had a nice time."

"Me … too," he muttered, unable to hide his disappointment at apparently not being invited inside.

"Want to do this again?" she asked.

"Sure," he mumbled.

"Next Sunday?"

"Okay …"

He turned to leave. But her cozy turtleneck caught his eye again. He turned back toward her.

"Can I … at least … kiss you good night?" he managed.

"Sorry." She smiled. "Not on our first date."

"But we've … already …"

"I know," she interrupted. "The night we got the cart before the horse."

No question they were playing by her rules. He turned to leave again. But something was bothering him. He turned back toward her once more.

"So we're … dating," he said, though it was more a question. "Like normal people."

"Yes."

"Can I ask you something?"

"Sure."

"Does this mean we stop doing breakfast?"

"No," she laughed.

This time, after turning to leave, he kept going.

✦ ✦ ✦

"On your mark," Cory called out. "Get set … Go!"

He clicked his stopwatch. Perry stumbled a little as he started. Then he sped up. Cory was amazed at how fast he was. Nearing the finish, where Cory stood, Perry got a bit tired, though. Cory pressed his stopwatch again, recording Perry's time.

They were in the same park where they'd practiced baseball so often. Cory had paced off fifty meters, the distance of Perry's race in the junior Olympics. After sprinting past Cory, the boy slowed down and walked back to him, puffing from the exertion.

"Slightly under eleven seconds," Cory told him, looking at the stop-watch. "Not bad. Looks like we've got some work to do, though."

"I think I can do it faster," Perry said hoarsely.

"I know you can. You got tired at the end. And we can improve your start."

They addressed the latter issue first. Cory kneeled down on his left knee, his right leg slightly in front. Then he raised up his buttocks, maintaining balance by placing both hands, fingers extended, directly in front of him on the ground. He raised up further, supporting much of his weight on his fingers. He next showed Perry how to "explode" into a fast start by propelling himself forward with his fingers, feet and legs, all at once.

Perry tried it. Cory could tell by how readily Perry positioned himself, that he would quickly master the technique.

✦ ✦ ✦

Cory and Perry left the park with Cookie about forty-five minutes later. The second part of the workout—dealing with Perry's fatigue —hadn't been so easy. Cory introduced him to the idea of improving his stamina by running as fast as he could for distances slightly longer than fifty meters.

Perry, as usual, was a willing pupil. Cory started him at sixty meters. By the end of their session, Perry insisted on increasing to a hundred, and Cory had a weary youngster on his hands as they walked back toward the apartment.

"When is my race?" the boy asked.

"In less than two weeks."

"Will you come?"

"Afraid I can't. I'll be in Kentucky with Bandit by then."

"Oh."

"I have confidence in you."

"Thanks. Can you keep training me?"

"For a few days," Cory replied. "But you're on your own next week. You up to it?"

Perry shrugged. Cory pointed to a little market across the street, where they could get cold drinks. No question Perry could use one.

✦ ✦ ✦

"How about a little *send-off* before you and Bandit leave?" Sandra suggested via phone one morning. "At my place. For all his owners."

"Nice sentiment," Cory responded. "But I'm worried about Stan."

Indeed he was. He told her how he and Carlos had gone to visit Stan in the hospital and didn't like what they saw. How tired and weak he looked. How, even though Stan wouldn't admit it, they surmised he had cancer because he was in the cancer ward. And how it didn't seem likely he'd be up to any kind of social gathering anytime soon.

"I wouldn't feel right ... our having something without him," Cory explained.

"I understand," Sandra replied. "I'll try and go visit him, too."

✦ ✦ ✦

"Have the vet look at Turbulent Flight's knee every day," Cory told Carlos in their barn office a couple of mornings before Cory and Bandit were to leave for Kentucky. "It gets any worse, we'll prob'ly have to lay him up."

"Okay, Boss. I will tell the vet."

"I'll phone you twice a day while I'm gone."

"You do not have to, Boss. The horses and me, we will be fine."

"Not worried about you," Cory snickered. "It's me. Might get lonely back there."

"Boss, please ... we must not let something happen to Bandit back there. Please take good care of everything."

Cory nodded. Indeed, he'd already started taking good care of everything, at least regarding arrangements. The van company they used in California had booked transportation for Bandit and him to and from the airports, and helped get them a flight to Kentucky. Cory had contacted Dan McFarlane, an old trainer friend of his in Arizona, who now trained in Kentucky. McFarlane offered him a stall for Bandit in his barn at Churchill Downs, plus one of his best grooms. He also put him in touch with someone in the racing office there, who reserved a hotel room near the track.

"Don't worry about entering any our horses here," Cory told Carlos. "I'll take care of it from there."

Before Carlos could respond, a knock at the office door interrupted them. It was an exercise rider. Cory had sent out word that he'd be gone at least two weeks and needed a replacement. Prior to leaving, he wanted to try out prospects.

A week ago, prompted by all the attention Bandit was attracting, Cory had hired a new groom. They were in the big leagues now, about to compete in America's premier race. No sense letting the entire world know that their survival here depended primarily on economizing. Especially since, thanks mainly to Bandit's big win, they could now afford some help.

Cory escorted the rider—who was unusually tall for his profession—over to Charming Location. The new groom had her ready for the track, and he led her out of her stall. Cory boosted the rider aboard the filly, and he began to follow them toward the track. No question the rider looked good on a horse. But Cory couldn't avoid comparing him to Tracy, who, of course in his mind, looked much better.

✦ ✦ ✦

"All Perry talks about lately is his big race." Tracy smiled. "When he gets to be like Bandit."

Laughing, Cory replied, "He can run almost as fast."

"He's happy you've been training him. Makes him feel even more like a horse."

Cory laughed again. Perry and Cookie were hiking on ahead, through a grove of sizable trees. Cory and Tracy followed. The four of them had driven into mountains north of Santa Anita. The same mountains from which the track's scenic turf course seemed to extend.

They'd just finished a picnic in a picturesque canyon, cut short by cool, windy weather and the ubiquitous colony of ants. Between Cory's preparations for Kentucky and Tracy's normal busy schedule, they hadn't been together since "movie night." Despite it being Sunday, her regular occasion for child care, they'd decided to take Perry and Cookie with them.

"Thanks for looking after Cookie while I'm gone," Cory said.

"Perry wouldn't have it any other way. But I know you'll miss her."

"And I know you'll miss Bandit."

He'd been aware for a long time that his last statement was true, but he'd had no idea how true until a couple of hours ago, after he and Cookie arrived at the apartment to pick up Tracy and Perry. She had led him directly to her garage, which she'd converted into a studio. There she showed him numerous paintings and drawings of Bandit. Their detail and clarity were incredible. The ones he liked best had her and Perry beside the colt.

"I'll miss him," she acknowledged after a considerable pause, during which he'd pointed to a pair of baby deer in the distance, scampering up a canyon wall.

"Well," he replied, "you could reconsider ... about you and Perry coming to Kentucky. At least for the race ..."

"'Fraid not," she sighed. "Too costly."

"What if I chipped in?"

"Thanks for offering. But you know how I feel about Perry and school. He'd probably miss a couple of days. Louisville's not the easiest place to fly to."

"Stan'll be disappointed," he coaxed. "If he's able to travel, that is. He'd want us all together."

She shrugged. He reached for her hand as they continued walking. Her hand was cold, colder than his, he was sure. He considered putting his arm around her, but he liked holding her hand and it would be awkward to do both. In truth, what he'd really prefer would be to entice her off into the foliage surrounding them, and snuggle, keep warm and do who knows what else. Of course he realized, Perry being present, that wasn't possible.

His thoughts turned to Cookie, on ahead. Although he contemplated taking her with him to Kentucky, he had decided against. Finding a hotel that would accept dogs might be difficult. Plus he wasn't certain how long they'd be gone. Should Bandit run well in the Derby, they'd likely move on to the other triple crown races—the Preakness in Maryland two weeks after the Derby, and the Belmont in New York three weeks later—creating further accommodation issues.

"Looks like a ready-made family," he said, gesturing toward Perry and Cookie.

She glanced at him, smiling. Her light-green eyes sparkled in the late-afternoon sunshine. He chanced a kiss on her cheek. It was cold also.

"You supply the kid," he continued. "I supply the dog."

"That's not a proposal?" she teased.

"Maybe." He winked. "Or maybe just an observation."

"I'm sure you'll like Kentucky."

"I hope so."

"You might not want to come back."

"To California?" he asked.

"To Perry and me."

"I'll be back."

"What makes you so sure?"

"Cookie." He winked again.

PART FIVE

CHURCHILL DOWNS

CHAPTER 26

"NEED ANYONE TO STAND IN FOR you for Derby festivities," Dan McFarlane offered while slapping Cory on the back, "I'm your man."

Cory backslapped back. Not only was he happy to see Dan in his current habitat, his beautifully manicured barn in the Churchill Downs stable area, but he welcomed his friend recalling his aversion to social events. He also appreciated that, despite it now being twilight, well beyond the man's normal workday, he had waited for Bandit and him to get here. Plus he'd made sure an extra feed tub was prepared. And now that Bandit was standing comfortably in a stall, actually served it himself.

"Thanks," Cory said as the colt began eating.

"Pleasure. Never fed a Derby horse before."

"Gonna hold you to your offer. I'll train our horse. You go to the parties."

"Deal," Dan laughed, slapping Cory's back again.

They had known each other a long time. Since shortly after Cory, as a teenager, moved to Arizona with his father. Dan employed Cory's father as a jockey and exercise rider, and Cory occasionally hung around Dan's barn at Turf Paradise. Both he and his father were very disappointed when Dan moved his stable to Kentucky a few years ago.

Nearly all the horses in the Kentucky Derby lodged in the high-profile "stakes barn." Predictably, Cory preferred lesser status. So he had contacted Dan—now into his forties, yet sporting the same tall, athletic build and boyish good looks Cory remembered from his youth—and he quickly obliged.

"The trip okay?" Dan asked while Bandit continued his meal.

"Long and tiring."

"You look it. Seems he held up better than you."

"'Cause I doubt he worried about me like I did about him."

"Can't blame him for that," Dan opined. "You don't have to run a mile and a quarter in a couple weeks."

Cory probably felt even more tired than he looked. He'd been up since three o'clock this morning. With Cookie at Tracy's, unavailable for "snooze button" duties, he'd set two alarm clocks. He got to the barn at four, the van left at four thirty and the flight at seven.

Fortunately, other than one minor incident, the trip had turned out routine, if traveling eleven hours with a racehorse could be termed routine. The incident occurred when their plane, with fourteen horses aboard, encountered several severe air pockets in mid-flight. Once the turbulence subsided, Cory rushed from his seat in the rear of the craft, to Bandit's stall in the middle. All the horses had broken into a chorus of whinnies, loud and clear. All except Bandit, that is, who, when Cory reached his stall, looked at him with a welcoming but bored expression.

Their arrival at Churchill Downs was the high point of the day. Like during his first glimpse of Santa Anita, Cory got goose bumps when he saw the renowned twin spires atop the white-framed grandstand. And the long, wide homestretch of the racetrack itself, which he'd viewed before only on TV, seemed both longer and wider in person. He was even inspired by the sight of the huge green infield inside the racetrack, where thousands would frolic on Derby day.

"They got you in that hotel with all the other visiting dignitaries?" Dan inquired.

"Unfortunately," Cory answered, an eye on Bandit, nose still in the feed tub. "Least that's what the racing-office guy told me."

"Poor you."

"No worries. I'm pretty good at making myself invisible."

"Right," Dan laughed. "Especially with me serving as your stand-in."

✦ ✦ ✦

Cory's new residence was certainly appropriate for "visiting dignitaries." Not only was the twenty-story skyscraper close to the track, but it presented a splendid view of it as well. Several spewing fountains embellished the spacious lobby and four restaurants graced the premises. All hotel personnel wore jockey outfits, complete with cap.

Cory had requested and received a middle-floor room at the opposite end of the hall from the elevator, as remote as was possible in his opinion. Predictably, the room was lavish, with Victorian motif and four-poster bed. Good thing Churchill Downs had contracted a reasonable rate with the hotel for "visiting dignitaries," otherwise there was no way Cory could afford this.

"We offer shuttle service to the track anytime you wish it," the desk clerk, adorned in lavender jockey silks and cap, had told him when he checked in.

"Thanks for letting me know," he'd replied, "but I'll be walking over. Good exercise."

✦ ✦ ✦

"Don't see many claiming horses in the Derby," a newspaper columnist informed Cory. "And they rarely do well."

"Not so loud," Cory grinned, pointing to Bandit in his stall nearby. "He might hear you."

Cory of course was aware of his sarcasm, but this particular theme was growing tiresome. He and Bandit had been here three days and he'd been interviewed about a dozen times, each interrogator making the same allegation—Bandit didn't belong. And several implied that Cory didn't either, calling the Santa Anita Derby the only significant win of his entire training career.

"You going to mention his handicap?" Cory asked, this also being a recurring topic.

"You mean his eye?" the columnist bit, no doubt relieved that he'd been spared introducing a delicate subject.

"No," Cory smiled. "Having me as his trainer."

The columnist's face, already ruddy complected, grew redder. So far he'd gotten nothing he could use. Cory didn't care though. No way he'd accept insults, either toward himself or the colt. If they didn't meet media criteria for Derby participants, too bad.

"You've had some success in California," the columnist said, evidently not giving up. "Any particular reason?"

"Yes."

"What?"

"Forgive the expression," Cory chuckled. "Blind luck."

That answer ended most interviews. Today's was no exception.

✦ ✦ ✦

"Might get lonely back there."

Cory's comment, made to Carlos before he and Bandit left, turned out to be prophetic. Not only did he miss the activity each morning at their barn, but he was especially lonely for Tracy, Perry and Cookie—perhaps explaining his sarcasm, that plus his anxiety over facing the biggest race of his career, wondering whether he and Bandit really did belong there.

Having idle time definitely didn't help. Other than training Bandit each morning and enduring whatever interviews the Churchill Downs publicity department cast upon him, he essentially had the day to himself. It would have been nice to socialize with Dan more, except Dan had a barn full of horses and their owners to deal with, and didn't have time.

One morning Cory rented a car and drove to a renowned Kentucky breeding farm. From there he went on to Keeneland, a beautiful track about seventy-five miles from Churchill, for an afternoon of racing (the Churchill season wouldn't begin until the weekend). He found neither activity fulfilling, however. He'd never paid much attention to breeding, and he'd come there neither to claim nor bet on local horses.

Twice he took a bus into downtown Louisville and wandered around, ending up at a movie both times. He also tried to help Dan around the barn, but wound up only getting in the way. He did manage to keep up on the southern California races—now at Hollywood Park, since the long Santa Anita meeting had ended— by watching simulcasts on TV at Churchill.

As promised, he phoned Carlos twice a day. And maintained contact with the Hollywood Park racing office, in case any of the horses needed to be entered. Of course he called Tracy and Perry regularly. And Stan once a day to check his progress. Unfortunately there wasn't much, other than he might soon be transferred from the hospital to a convalescent facility. He even phoned Sandra and Tiger two or three times each, to let them know Bandit was training well.

No question, time dragged. As it did, a prevailing thought ran through his mind. He missed California and all the elements of his life there.

✦ ✦ ✦

"How sad," Sandra said as she and Tracy left the hospital after visiting Stan. "I don't think he has much time left."

"Then why are they talking about moving him?" Tracy puzzled.

"Maybe because they can't do much for him here. Except try to make him comfortable. And the other place can do that better."

"Shame he can't go to Kentucky," Tracy lamented.

Somewhere in the distance, church bells chimed the noon hour. They walked toward Sandra's car in the parking lot. They still had plenty of work to do at Sandra's house, especially since she was leaving for Kentucky the first of the week.

"Shame *you* can't go to Kentucky," Sandra said, varying Tracy's comment only slightly.

"Cory feels the same way."

"Then why not go?"

"Well, what I didn't tell Cory ... Perry's been having some trouble with his schoolwork. I don't want him falling behind. Plus I've got an art exhibit coming up. The week after the Derby. I still have a lot to do. Need these weekends to catch up."

"Do you paint?"

"Yes."

"I didn't know that," Sandra said almost apologetically. "I'd like to see your work."

"Any time. Bandit's my main subject now."

"Oh," was Sandra's only response, as they reached her car.

"I shouldn't say this," Tracy sighed. "But with Stan not being able to go ... least he won't know that all of us wouldn't have been together anyway, if he went."

Sandra shrugged, looking like she didn't quite understand Tracy's logic.

✦ ✦ ✦

Having parked his rental car close by, Cory walked briskly across the large park located very near Santa Anita. Actually, he could even see the outline of the track's aqua-green grandstand. The afternoon was warm and he could feel himself perspiring beneath the heavy shirt he'd worn to protect himself against the Kentucky chill early this morning.

He checked his watch nervously. He hoped he was on time. His flight had landed in L.A. half an hour late. Conceivably, all the traveling he'd done today would be wasted effort.

He spotted Tracy sitting on a brown blanket thirty or forty yards away, wearing jeans and a tan top, holding Cookie in her lap. He looked for Perry, but couldn't see him. Instead of a direct path to Tracy and Cookie, he took a circular one, coming up from behind them. As he approached, he was sure neither of them saw him. When he reached the blanket, he simply sat down.

"What are you doing here?" Tracy exclaimed, clearly flustered.

"Came for Perry's big race." He winked, patting Cookie.

"But you're in Kentucky," she stammered, touching his arm.

"Apparently not," he laughed. "I'm right here with you."

No question about that. And it hadn't been easy. Very early this morning, Saturday, one week before the Derby, he'd breezed Bandit a solid mile. Afterward he watched him cool out on the hot walker, stopping it twice to thoroughly inspect him. Satisfied with the workout and Bandit's physical condition, he alerted Dan that he'd be gone most of the next two days. Dan told his barn foreman and Bandit's groom to watch the colt closely and they promised to notify Cory of any concerns.

Cory had taken a shuttle to the airport and boarded a plane. A special weekend fare made the flight affordable. Likewise a rental car in L.A. Maybe, aided by the favorable time change, he wasn't too late for the race.

"Where's Perry?" he asked, still patting Cookie.

"There," she pointed to a group of youngsters gathered across the field. "I still can't believe you're here."

That seemed apparent. She touched his arm repeatedly with her fingers, as if contact verified his presence. Her eyes emitted a gleam that he'd witnessed only once or twice before. Perry evidently spotted him, because he waved. Cory waved back.

"Guess I made it on time."

"Barely," she smiled.

The youngsters lined up for the race. There were about twenty. The starter, a graying fellow in a red jacket, put a whistle to his mouth. Cory, still patting Cookie, reached for Tracy's hand and held it.

He watched Perry crouch into the starting position he had taught him, and felt himself become nervous. He crossed his fingers on his right hand, the one not holding Tracy's. He knew that this was Perry's big moment. His chance for success, after all the failures caused by his limited vision.

The starter blew his whistle. Perry exploded forward, taking the early lead. A couple of kids collided and fell. After twenty-five meters, the halfway point, Perry led everyone by at least two meters.

"Go Perry!" Cory heard himself cheering louder than he ever remembered cheering for Bandit. "Go! Go!"

But then a taller, bigger boy started to gain. With ten meters left, he caught Perry. Cory gasped out loud. Was Perry going to fall short in this, his big chance for redemption?

Cory wondered if Perry was tiring, like he had in their first workout. He quickly found out. Right near the finish, Perry spurted, flashing across the line a full meter ahead of the tall boy.

Perry had won the race.

✦ ✦ ✦

"Wait till I tell Bandit about your big win," Cory told Perry early that evening.

It was the fourth time Cory had said that. This time they were in the apartment with Tracy and Cookie. All of them, including Cookie, had just finished devouring a huge pizza they'd picked up on the way here.

Perry grinned, for the fourth time. Around his neck, he still displayed the blue ribbon and medal awarded him following the Olympics.

"Thought you might be getting tired," Cory said. "When that big kid caught you."

"No," Perry insisted. "Not after I trained like you showed me."

"I'll tell Bandit that too."

"When that guy caught me, I thought of Bandit and what he'd do. That gave me energy."

"Wow," Cory said.

"Plus I closed my eyes. It helps me run faster."

Cory laughed. He also yawned. Despite it being only seven, he felt tired. The time difference, the day's activity and getting up early this morning all were catching up with him.

He gathered Cookie's belongings. He and Tracy had already agreed that Cookie would spend the night with him in the trailer. He would bring her back in the morning, before going to the airport.

He tried to attach her leash to her collar. She rolled away from him, though. He tried again. This time she barked at him. Then she raced around the room.

"Looks like you're sleeping alone," Tracy teased.

"Few days away," he complained, "and I'm a forgotten man."

"I'd offer you my couch," she giggled, "but that's where she's been sleeping."

He didn't reply. Instead he simply put down Cookie's things and headed for the door. Perry joined him there, of course to shake his hand.

"Oh, before you go," Tracy giggled again. "Maybe you'd like to walk her."

"Think she'll let me?" Cory muttered.

"Sure." She smiled. "Long as Perry and I go too."

She got Cookie's leash and handed it to Perry. Cookie calmly allowed him to attach it to her collar, and he led her to the door. Then, still smiling, Tracy gave Cory a plastic bag so that he could retrieve any contributions Cookie might make to the neighborhood.

✦ ✦ ✦

"Hate this place," Stan croaked once Cory entered his room in the convalescent facility the next morning and sat down beside him.

"Not much to look at," Cory agreed.

"Not talkin' 'bout looks. Talkin' 'bout what they let me do. Or don't do. Don't even let me call my bookie."

"Any chance they'll let you travel?"

"To Kentucky? Hardly let me travel to the bathroom."

No surprise to Cory. Not with Stan's appearance. Pale, gaunt, barely able to keep his eyes open. Several pillows were positioned around him, evidently to prop him up.

This was the third residence in which Cory had seen Stan. None of them were much to applaud, but this was the worst of the three. The senior complex at least had a feeling of camaraderie. The hospital, where he and Carlos had visited him about a week and a half ago, had a sense of efficiency. This place seemingly offered neither. "Drab" would best describe it. A single story with long hallways and nondescript rooms, in need of fresh paint both inside and out. Inhabitants barely alive and apparently waiting to die. What Cory knew of Stan didn't fit this scene.

"I'll watch the race right here on TV," Stan groaned. "If they let me."

"So the B team won't be all together," Cory said plaintively.

"Guess not," Stan sighed. "Except in spirit."

"In spirit," Cory repeated glumly.

✦ ✦ ✦

Cory wanted to make sure that at least one key member of the B team, besides himself, would go to Kentucky. Carlos. Before visiting Stan, he had gone to the barn. After training, he and

Carlos sat down and wrote out a schedule for the next week, for their two horses here.

On Friday, Charming Location and Turbulent Flight, knee much better, would breeze at Santa Anita. Both, overseen by the new groom and exercise rider (Cory did hire the tall one), would merely walk on Saturday and Sunday because after Friday's training Carlos would fly to Kentucky. He'd return late Sunday, in time for the horses to get back to full training Monday morning.

They'd also briefly discussed transferring the horses to Hollywood Park and training there during the incipient three-month season. Their decision was unanimous, neither of them wanted to go. All the more with Cory being gone for an indeterminate length of time.

Their little meeting adjourned with Cory stating that he would buy Carlos's ticket to Kentucky when he got to the airport later this morning.

✦ ✦ ✦

"Everyone sleep well?" Cory asked Tracy by phone, once he got to the airport.

"Like logs."

"How's Perry?"

"A little tired from all the excitement yesterday. But still thrilled about the race."

"Nice."

"He did say something to tell you if you called."

"Oh?"

"That he's not sure he beat that kid because he closed his eyes … or because he thought of Bandit … or because of all the help you gave him."

"What do *you* think?" he asked.

"Maybe a mixture of all three."

"Sounds right to me," he concurred. "A mixture."

After hanging up, he anticipated having things to think about during the long flight back to Kentucky. Besides what Tracy had just told him, Perry having his eyes closed during Bandit's Santa Anita Derby win. Plus how gratified he, Cory, felt over being a part of Perry's terrific victory.

CHAPTER 27

THOUGH NEVER ACTUALLY A JOCKEY at Churchill Downs, Cory's father had been there as a young man during Derby week. He was the regular exercise rider for a horse eventually finishing fifth in the big race. It was one of his proudest periods and he often told Cory about it. Especially of the lavish dinners, parties, receptions and other festivities leading up to the Derby. How, as a mere exercise rider, he'd managed admittance to all the activities, he never revealed. But Cory assumed that it had plenty to do with his father's conviviality.

Were Cory himself more sociable, he was certainly in the right place. Particularly with Bandit a genuine conversation piece. No matter what position one took on the colt—from criticizing his presence to deeming him inspirational—he was a ready topic. Except Cory didn't care to discuss him, no more than he cared to party.

He did make two exceptions to the latter aversion. One was slight—the annual post position draw party. It wasn't at all festive, other than cake and ice cream being served. Cory drew the fourth choice among the twenty participants, and selected the number-eight post. He figured that would give jockey Espinoza various options in a very large field, without having to commit early in the race to a particular strategy.

The other exception occurred after Sandra called him from a breeding farm near Keeneland, where she was staying during Derby week. She mentioned a dinner exclusively for owners of horses in the Derby, offered by Churchill Downs, to be held on

Thursday, two days before the race. He'd received an invitation from the public relations department prior to returning to California, but had decided to pass it along to Dan—as he'd already done with several other invitations.

When Sandra insisted on his attending, however, he knew he'd have to change plans.

✦ ✦ ✦

"I, for one, admire your work with the one-eyed horse," a portly man, sitting across the table from Cory and Sandra, complimented him. "I'm not sure there's ever been another in the Derby."

Cory nodded. He was uncomfortable, though. Of course any allusion to Bandit's handicap continued to bother him. But he was far more uneasy about something else. The man wore a tuxedo. Sandra had on a long vintage light-blue chiffon and silk evening gown with elbow-length darker-blue gloves. Everyone else at the table, like the hundred or so others assembled for the dinner, was impeccably dressed too. Meanwhile, having forgotten to pack his lone sports coat, he wore ordinary khaki slacks with a plain brown shirt and jacket. Everybody in the room looked very much like an owner. While he could barely pass for a poorly-dressed trainer.

The room itself was also intimidating. It was huge, with large multicolored chandeliers hanging from the ceiling. The racetrack finish line was immediately below. Because it wasn't dark yet, there was a great view of the massive infield. Cory quickly visualized the thousands thronging there for the Derby, reminding him that the big race was only two days away.

A waiter delivered mint juleps to the table. Cory, despite rarely consuming alcohol, barely waited for the others to be served before taking his first gulp.

✦ ✦ ✦

"Thank you," Sandra said as she and Cory left the room after dinner.

"For?" he questioned. "I wasn't much company."

"For making me part of this," she explained, ignoring his statement.

"But you invited *me*. I wouldn't have come if you hadn't insisted."

"No, I mean the race ... the Kentucky Derby."

"If any of us belongs here," he answered, "it's you."

A puzzled look was her only response. They were headed down a long hallway, to the elevator.

"Stan calls us the B team," he continued.

"The B team?"

"A bunch of castoffs ... Misfits who couldn't make the varsity."

"But we have a horse in the Derby," she countered. "We're entitled to be here."

"You're entitled to be here," he corrected. "A person of style ... Dignity ... Distinction ... Exactly what the Derby stands for ... As for the rest of us ... ?"

The elevator's arrival interrupted his comments, however. He requested that the operator take them to the ground floor. On the way down, the car whirred, almost like a nightingale tuning up for its evening melody. The operator smiled and tipped his cap as they strode out into the night, which had turned cool. As they walked toward her car, she took from her purse a scarf—also blue, like her gown and gloves—and wrapped it around her neck.

"All I know," he said, continuing his prior theme, "is that you're a welcome addition to the team."

"And all I know," she stated emphatically, "is that Phil and I tried for years to develop a champion. It took you and this ... this unusual team of yours to finally get us here."

In the dim light of the parking lot, he saw tears in her eyes and knew enough not to reply. Apparently this was her moment to try and make sense of what had happened. The death of her husband. Followed by, almost as a memorial, this trip to Kentucky.

"Can I give you a ride to your car?" she asked, once they got to hers.

"No thanks. I walked over."

"Take you back to the hotel?"

"Rather catch some fresh air."

"See you Saturday," she said as she got into the car.

"Aren't you staying in the hotel tomorrow night? That's what the track PR guy told me."

"No. Change of plans. Some guests are staying in my hotel room instead. See you Saturday."

"Saturday," he repeated, and she started the car.

✦ ✦ ✦

"You're not exactly giving us guys from Arizona a good name," Dan winked at Cory the next morning at the barn.

"What I do?"

"You mean besides tormenting the media all the time?"

Cory laughed. Nearby, in virtual accompaniment, a big black bird screeched. The sun shined brightly, promising a warm day. Cory had checked the forecast for tomorrow, Derby day, and found clouds predicted, but no rain.

"Needed me as your stand-in last night," Dan smiled. "Word is, you fell a little short of the dress code."

"'Cause I didn't wear a tuxedo?"

"Or even a tie."

"Well," Cory laughed again. "They all say we got no chance in the Derby. And don't even belong here ... Might as well try and look the part."

It was Dan's turn to laugh.

✦ ✦ ✦

Cory spotted Carlos entering baggage claim at the Louisville airport that night, and started zigzagging through the very crowded room to greet him. Even from a distance, Cory could see that Carlos looked tired, no doubt from a long day of travel. They shook hands and began to work their way over to the carousel conveying luggage into the area.

"I hope you have plenty room, Boss. In your car."

"I don't. Rental company only had subcompacts left."

"That is not good."

"You bring that much stuff?"

"It is not for me, Boss."

Someone tapped Cory on his shoulder. He quickly turned. And saw why Carlos was concerned. Tracy and Perry were standing there. Cory blinked twice, to make sure.

"What're you doing here?" he stammered the same words Tracy had used when he surprised her in the park, before Perry's race.

"You came for Perry's big race." She smiled. "Least we could do is come for yours."

He should have corrected her by saying "ours," but his mind was elsewhere—on how pretty she looked in a turquoise blouse, on how glad he was to see her and Perry, on how much he wanted to hug her, which he clumsily managed by throwing his arms around her and at the same time shaking Perry's hand. Carlos grinned at the three of them before resuming his course to the luggage carousel.

"Don't worry about Cookie," Tracy said once Cory released her. "She's with a friend and her two kids. I think Cookie likes them better than she likes Perry and me."

"Great," Cory remarked sarcastically. "Prob'ly never want to see me again."

✦ ✦ ✦

"Stan, he call this morning, Boss. He wish us luck ... He sound so weak, I do not think it is him."

Cory shrugged, purposely not mentioning his own recent visit with Stan. He glanced at Tracy, sitting beside him in the front as he drove them all to the hotel. Carlos and Perry were in back. It turned out there was room for all of them and their luggage in the tiny car, though just barely. It also turned out that the guests Sandra had referred to after dinner last night, who'd be staying in her hotel room, were none other than Tracy and Perry.

"Tiger, he call too, Boss. He say he will surprise Stan and watch the race on the TV with him."

"Everyone's full of surprises," Cory said, glancing at Tracy again.

"You should talk," Tracy replied, sticking her tongue out at him.

"Tiger, he sound sad, Boss."

"Won't be the same without them," Cory uttered softly, practically to himself. "Least you three and Sandra are here."

He looked once more at Tracy, still not quite believing she and Perry had come.

✦ ✦ ✦

"What time is it?" Tracy mumbled into the phone after struggling out of bed in the dark to answer it.

"Five thirty," Cory replied on the other end.

"Two thirty California time," she muttered after calculating quickly.

"Time for the track."

"But the race isn't till this afternoon," she objected.

"I'm jogging Bandit a little this morning. Thought you might want to come."

"Long as you don't mind someone half asleep."

"I don't mind."

"You want Perry too?" she asked.

"Of course. I'll knock on your door in half an hour."

✦ ✦ ✦

It was slightly past dawn as Cory, Tracy and Perry ambled from the rental car, which Cory parked in the stable area lot, toward Dan's barn. Cory probably would have suggested they walk from the hotel instead of driving, were it not so early. That, plus his so rudely waking them.

Carlos had wanted to come also, but with him looking so tired last night, Cory insisted that he go back to sleep in their room. While walking, Cory noticed that the sun wasn't visible because of the cloud cover. Evidently the forecast for today was accurate. On their way, despite the hour, they encountered numerous horses headed for the track for their morning exercise.

"Let's you and me be trainers today," Cory told Perry as they neared Dan's barn.

"Yeah," the boy enthused, clearly wide awake and eager to see Bandit.

"We'll let your mom exercise Bandit."

He glanced at Tracy when he said this. She looked back at him —strangely. But he'd already observed that she had on an outfit that he'd seen her ride in before. Tan jeans, matching boots and top. Brown and white down jacket.

"For good luck," he said before she could speak. "And for old time's sake."

"But I'm not in shape," she protested. "Haven't ridden since the last time for you."

"We're talking simple jog," he emphasized. "Not even once around the track. Besides, I'd like you to speak with Bandit."

"About what?"

"About how proud we are of him. No matter how he does today."

"Don't have to ride him to tell him that."

"But it'll mean more to him ... Your coming all this distance."

She didn't respond, even to question what might be considered dubious logic. They reached Dan's barn. When they got to Bandit's stall, the groom had him ready for the track. Tracy greeted the colt affectionately and immediately rubbed his forehead. Cory picked out a carrot from a nearby bin and gave it to Perry so he could feed it to Bandit.

"You'll have to lend me your helmet," Tracy said resignedly.

"With pleasure," Cory replied, handing it to her.

"And give me a leg up."

"With more pleasure," he joked.

The groom led Bandit from the stall once Perry offered the colt the carrot, and Cory hoisted her aboard. Dan, returning to the barn from watching a set of his own horses train, waved at Cory. Tracy rode Bandit toward the track and Cory began to question what he was doing. Entrusting a million-dollar horse to someone who hadn't ridden for several months. With the Derby mere hours away.

Sure, one could explain his actions by saying he'd gotten caught up in the excitement of the big race. Or the excitement of having Tracy and Perry here with him. But he knew that there were far more significant reasons involved.

"I'm a trainer. No more, no less."

These words, which he'd spoken to Sandra at her house when he declined her job offer, came back to him. He also recalled telling Sandra that day about his marriage. How Susan had accused him of being much more married to the horses he trained than to her.

He sensed he was different now, though. That he had changed significantly. That, at least around Tracy and Perry, he'd become more than a trainer. And that he knew exactly what he was doing when he asked Tracy to exercise Bandit this morning.

He was certain that what was happening at this moment was more important than anything that might happen later. Yes, he was proud of Bandit. But he was also proud of Tracy—and Perry, walking beside him, toward the track.

He wanted them both part of anything he did.

✦ ✦ ✦

The brief workout finished, Tracy rode Bandit off the track. No question in Cory's mind, time had changed nothing. It might as well have been the first time she rode for him. While she'd jogged the colt, head right next to his, she could've been whispering in his ear. She still fit him perfectly, completely in sync with his gait.

"You speak to him?" Cory asked once she and Bandit joined Perry and him on a roadway leading back to the barn.

"I did."

"He understand?"

"He did," she smiled. "He appreciates your sentiment. And so do I."

As if to emphasize what she'd said, she reached down from atop Bandit and touched Cory's hand. At the same time, he put an arm around Perry.

"I know a place," Cory announced, "that serves great waffles."
"Oh boy!" Perry exclaimed. "Can I have one?"
"And some pancakes, too," Cory winked at Tracy.

CHAPTER 28

GETTING PERRY HIS WAFFLE AND PANCAKES wasn't easy. Nor was doing anything else anywhere near Churchill Downs that day. Crowds were overwhelming. They had to try more than half a dozen restaurants before finally finding one with less than an hour wait.

Roads were clogged. They spent forty-five minutes getting back to the hotel, and—after relaxing with Carlos, who looked much more rested, then napping, showering and changing clothes—even more time returning to the track. That was because they started out driving before doubling back on account of the congestion, and walking over instead. Good thing the big race wasn't until late afternoon, or they might have been pressed to make it.

Despite all these preliminaries, Cory still wasn't prepared for what they encountered once they got inside the track entrance gates. Movement was almost impossible and they had to edge their way through the throngs to locate an usher who could point them to their seats. After they finally reached them, Cory gazed out at the massive infield—the same one he'd viewed at the elegant dinner two nights ago—now packed with all the people he'd visualized then. A race was run and the noise generated by the crowd—predicted at a hundred fifty thousand—was deafening.

The sheer magnitude of everything, plus the day turning sunny and much warmer than forecast, got the best of him. He began to perspire, and experienced lightheadedness and claustrophobia. After watching only the single race, he convinced Carlos, Tracy and Perry to walk with him to where he anticipated they could get some peace and quiet—the stable area, to visit One-Eyed Bandit.

✦ ✦ ✦

"They surprised me," Sandra told Cory at Bandit's stall, gesturing toward a group of men, women and children standing nearby. "Had no idea they were coming."

"Oh?"

"My son flew his family in from the east coast. My daughter from the west. Everyone simply showed up at the farm last night. Without even calling."

"Kind of like Tracy and Perry," Cory grinned. "Thanks for giving up your hotel room."

"Good thing I did. My family might never have found me."

"I'm sure they would have found you. Weren't they in touch with the people you were staying with?"

"They were," she smiled. "My friends ... they knew all along. Those culprits."

"Those culprits," he repeated, smiling back. "Like you and Carlos. Keeping Tracy and Perry a secret from me."

She laughed. She'd already introduced her family to Carlos, Tracy, Perry and him. Son Phillip, his wife and four children. Daughter Becky, her husband, their three kids. Cory was especially happy to meet Potato Number Two, a small thin boy with glasses. Tracy was clearly thrilled to meet everyone and gave each a big hug when Sandra introduced them. Cory had never seen Sandra— dressed in emerald green, the color of their silks—looking so radiant. Following the intros and some brief conversation, she and Cory had eased away from the others, to Bandit's stall.

"Everyone's already met Bandit," she informed him.

"He behave himself?"

"Perfectly. He let all the kids pat him on the forehead. For luck."

"Nice."

"I was able to pull a few strings and get seats for my family in our section. I hope you don't mind."

"More the merrier."

"You know something?" she asked after a short hesitation.

"What?"

"Phil's here too. I can feel him with us."

"I'm sure he is," he replied.

He expected a tear or two to roll down her cheek, but none did. Nor was there the slightest trace of melancholy in her voice.

"We were just heading over to the races when you got here," she said. "You all want to go with us?"

"No, we'll wait and go over with Bandit later," he answered, patting the colt on the forehead himself.

✦ ✦ ✦

"Do you want I take Bandit over, Boss?"

"No," Cory had answered. "You're an owner today."

If Cory had sounded cool and nonchalant when he, Carlos, Tracy, Perry, Bandit and the groom (who, rather than Carlos, was leading the colt) began the long hike from the barn to the paddock, he was far from it. Now, about halfway to their destination, as they walked on the track itself and approached the throngs along the outer rail, he was even less so. Sure, he had every right to be nervous before the biggest race of his life. But besides nerves, a sense of dread gnawed at him. Spawned by the recurring thought of the last several days—maybe he and their horse really *didn't* belong here. Maybe they were about to be humiliated.

The afternoon had at last cooled, yet he still perspired. He took hold of Tracy's hand and put his arm around Perry. Neither act helped to calm him. Nor did the sight of beautiful and varied flowers and foliage they passed along the way.

When they reached the first of the crowd near the rail, something he hadn't expected occurred. Bandit's name was called out. Once, twice, a third time. Applause broke out. It grew in volume. Everyone was cheering for Bandit, loud and clear. A one-eyed horse in the Kentucky Derby.

Cory looked at the colt. Bandit nodded a couple of times toward the crowd, as though acknowledging their appreciation. He did it coolly, matter-of-factly, like there was no doubt that he deserved this adulation. He proceeded on nonchalantly toward the paddock, as if this entire festive event was no more than a stroll in the park.

Tracy tightened her grip on Cory's hand. Cory glanced at Carlos, who winked back at him. Obviously both Tracy and Carlos recognized what was happening.

Cory could question the legitimacy of his own presence here all he wanted, but there appeared no doubt in Bandit's mind that he, Bandit, belonged. Nor in the minds of the multitudes applauding him.

✦ ✦ ✦

"Stay close to the winner's circle."

If Bandit was one cool customer, so was his jockey. Now as Cory, Carlos, Tracy and Perry started from the paddock toward their seats, Cory chuckled at Espinoza's words spoken when Cory boosted him aboard Bandit after saddling the colt for the race. He also chuckled as he caught himself visually checking the distance between their seats and the winner's circle.

They didn't get very far from the paddock, though, when they were forced to pause. In fact all movement throughout Churchill Downs appeared to stop. A band on the track, wearing blue regalia, began playing "My Old Kentucky Home."

Seemingly everyone present started singing. Women bedecked in glorious hats. Children dressed formally. Men waving their hands in time to the music.

Cory looked at the band and the track. He felt tears come to his eyes as he saw Bandit step onto the track.

✦ ✦ ✦

Just before they got to their seats after struggling through the crowd, Cory glanced at the odds board. Bandit was thirty-three to one, the same as right before the Santa Anita Derby—which of course Cory interpreted as a positive. It also reminded him of the last-minute betting flurry Stan and Tiger undertook before that race. And brought a smile to his face as he recalled their squabbling after Bandit won, over whether they should have bet more. But it also saddened him because he couldn't avoid pondering Stan's current condition and the reality he and Tiger wouldn't be here for the big race.

Cory considered making a bet for Stan, for good luck. After all, he knew the old man steadfastly believed there was no way a horse of his could win without his having money on him. While debating to himself, he saw Sandra and her family sitting in the row in front of the one he, Carlos, Tracy and Perry had occupied earlier. He could only shake his head at Sandra's ability to get seats for her family at the very last instant like this.

He also saw an elderly man sitting near her, about a dozen seats in from the aisle. The fellow was looking straight ahead, out at the track, slouched over a little, elbows on his knees. Cory probably wouldn't have noticed him, except he resembled Stan slightly. Actually, the resemblance was more than slight.

Tracy, Perry and Carlos edged past some people in their row, before Cory followed. The closer he got, the more the elderly man looked like Stan. Then he saw someone resembling Tiger sitting on the other side of him. No, it couldn't be. Stan was in a convalescent facility and Tiger would be watching the race there with him, on TV. Yet it *was* them. It definitely was. Tracy recognized them too, and gave each a big hug.

"What're you two doing here?" Cory exclaimed, using the same phrase that had become so common between Tracy and him lately.

"Got a horse in the Derby," they retorted, in unison, like the reason was evident.

"You fly in?"

"Too far for the bus," Stan cackled.

"You should've called. Would've met your flight."

"Took a cab," Stan said. "Wanted to get right over here and make our bets."

Cory thought about his internal debate over whether to wager for Stan. Maybe something told him that he really didn't have to. That somehow Stan would take care of it himself. Even if he had to depart a sickbed and fly more than halfway across the country to do it.

"That convalescent place?" Cory asked. "They release you?"

"Not exactly … Took couple days off."

"They don't know you're gone?"

"Prob'ly do by now," Stan laughed.

Tracy gave Stan another hug. Carlos shook both his and Tiger's hand. As did Perry, of course. Sandra, sitting directly in front of them, turned toward Cory.

"I would have told you at the stable," she admitted, "but they wanted to surprise you. Besides, I still had some strings to pull to get them seats."

"Glad she's a member … of the B team," Stan said.

"Glad you're a member, too," Cory replied.

Stan laughed again. This time, however, his laugh was weak. Like it came from someone who had just escaped a convalescent facility. And he certainly looked the part. Pale, haggard, wearing clothes that hardly fit. Someone who definitely shouldn't be there.

CHAPTER 29

"THE HORSES ARE ENTERING THE STARTING gate for the Kentucky Derby."

Cory rarely listened to the track announcer when one of their horses was running. He preferred to focus on their horse exclusively and the announcer named all the others, creating a distraction. But he listened today. With so many horses in the race (normally twenty, no exception this afternoon), he didn't want to risk losing Bandit in the collection.

"One-Eyed Bandit goes into gate eight."

"Buena suerte, Boss."

Carlos was sitting on his right, and Cory touched his wrist. Tracy and Perry were to his left, and he gently squeezed her hand. To their left were Stan and Tiger. Sandra looked over her shoulder at Cory and silently mouthed, "Good luck."

"The flag is up," proclaimed the announcer.

Cory watched Bandit, standing patiently in the gate while the horses near him fidgeted nervously. The crowd buzzed expectantly. Cory knew from watching the Derby so many times on TV that the moment the gates opened, the buzz would quickly become a roar.

"And they're off!"

The horses burst forward. Bandit got bumped by the horse on his right, whom he probably never saw. But it only seemed to anger him and propel him ahead. With the field so large, early position was critical. Success depended—much more in this race than most—on avoiding trouble and not being crowded, especially for a colt with limited vision. As the cavalry charged right in front of their seats, down the long homestretch for the first time, Espinoza maintained a path out away from the rail.

"Into the clubhouse turn," the announcer blared, then rattled off several names Cory couldn't make out, followed by, "One-Eyed Bandit is sixth."

Cory became concerned that Bandit was up too close, only seven or eight lengths behind the leaders. Then he remembered that the colt was near the front during the early part of the Santa Anita Derby, and things had worked out fine. Plus he was running smoothly, effortlessly, displaying the same long, fluid stride he showed the very first time Tracy breezed him.

"Down the backstretch ... One-Eyed Bandit is moving up." These were the only words Cory could distinguish, as the crowd noise ascended. He didn't have to hear anything, though, to recognize Bandit, still on the outside, spurting past horses. Cory took a deep breath. He sensed that Espinoza had the horses in front of them measured. Was anyone coming from behind? No, no one that Cory could discern.

"Into the far turn ... One-Eyed Bandit is third."

The crowd noise reached a crescendo. Sandra stood up in front of Cory. He felt himself rise too. Tracy and Carlos got up also. They were shouting, Tracy in English, Carlos in Spanish, although, with all the noise, he couldn't be sure.

For some reason, as he'd done at almost the identical stage of the Santa Anita Derby, Cory peered at Perry. Like then, the boy seemed transfixed. He had both eyes closed and was sitting absolutely motionless, as if he was meditating. And maybe casting some type of spell on the race. A magical spell?

Cory flashed back to his phone conversation with Tracy before his return flight to Kentucky. When they discussed Perry's junior Olympics win. How Perry couldn't decide whether he'd beaten the other kid because he closed his eyes, or because he thought of Bandit or because of all the help Cory had given him.

Cory would toss one more possibility into the mix. Magic. It wouldn't take much to convince him that Perry was a magical kid. Especially with the unique powers his mother had regularly demonstrated. Nor would it extend his imagination much to view Bandit as a magical horse.

"Into the stretch, One-Eyed Bandit takes the lead. It's a length ... now it's two. He's drawing away from the field."

Was this really happening? Cory closed his eyes, then opened them again to make certain. Maybe Bandit, like Perry now and in his junior Olympics race, had both his eyes closed too.

"Seventy yards to go ... It's still One-Eyed Bandit in front."

Then Cory saw a horse loom out of the pack. Almost in fear, he stopped listening to the announcer. Bandit was tiring, his long stride shortening. He neared the finish. The other horse kept coming. Cory tried closing his eyes for an instant, but that horse wouldn't go away. The noise was deafening. The horse caught Bandit a few feet from the wire and flashed past. One-Eyed Bandit had finished second in the Kentucky Derby.

Cory shook his head. So close, so close. His emotions had plummeted from such an incredible high at the anticipation of winning, to such a dreadful low. Like someone had just kicked him in the stomach.

He knew the others must be disappointed too. Particularly Stan, who had escaped a sickbed and come all this distance. He turned to console the old man. And was horrified by what he saw.

Stan was slumped down in his seat, head in his lap. He looked asleep, but Cory was afraid he was unconscious. Or worse. Tiger crouched over him and shook him gently. Stan didn't move.

"He okay! He okay!" Cory yelled to Tiger, trying to be heard above the crowd.

"Don't think so!" Tiger yelled back.

Cory shouted and waved toward an usher, but feared that with all the noise and excitement from the race, he'd neither be heard nor seen.

✦ ✦ ✦

Riding in the back of the ambulance with Stan, Tiger felt scared. Scared by the sound of the siren wailing as they tried to work their way through all the traffic around Churchill Downs. Scared that the traffic would prevent their getting to the hospital on time. Scared by how pale the old man looked and how labored his breathing appeared. Scared he should never have helped him escape the convalescent place.

All he had to do was tell Stan every flight to Louisville was booked. Or all the taxis in L.A. were tied up that late at night because of some big film event. Or the back exit to the convalescent facility was locked.

Stan was strapped onto a bed, an attendant beside him, regulating an oxygen mask covering the old man's face. Tiger sat on a bench nearby, which was attached to the side of the vehicle. A medicinal smell was prominent. The ambulance hit a bump, likely a pothole in the road. The attendant removed the oxygen mask.

Tiger saw Stan open his eyes for the first time since the attack began, then shut them. They hit another bump. Stan opened his eyes again and blinked once or twice. This time he kept them open. Tiger moved quickly to him, bending over the bed. He was sure the attendant would shoo him back to the bench, but he didn't. Surprisingly, the old man nodded to him, as if recognizing him.

"We goin' the airport?" Stan wheezed above the siren noise.

"No," Tiger said, relieved that the old guy had spoken.

"The track?"

"No. The hospital."

"The one we left?"

"No. Local."

"But I wanted to buy everyone dinner," Stan protested weakly.

"It'll have to wait."

✦ ✦ ✦

"What you all doin' here?" Stan inquired hoarsely, looking up from his hospital bed. Cory, Tracy, Perry, Sandra, Tiger and Carlos surrounded him.

"Called a special meeting," Cory answered. "Of the B team."

Stan seemed to grin. Or maybe he was simply maneuvering facial muscles from the discomfort of all the tubes stuck in him. Regardless, he closed his eyes and appeared to doze. Pretty much what he'd been doing the last five minutes or so, ever since the others joined Tiger, after their traffic-infested taxi ride.

"Doctors say anything?" Cory asked Tiger.

"'Fraid so."

"What?"

"That we shouldn't have made the trip."

"Maybe they're right."

"Maybe," Tiger replied pensively. "But how do you deny a man his dying wish? How do you tell him he can't go the Derby … when his horse is in it?"

Cory shrugged. Of course he understood. How could he not? No matter that they didn't win the race. No matter that Stan looked at least a dozen years older than not much more than an hour ago.

A nurse came into the room. Cory thought she might ask them to leave. Instead she checked what he assumed was a heart-monitoring device and scribbled something on a chart beside Stan's bed. Shortly after she left, Stan stirred and opened his eyes. Slowly he looked around the room.

"Still havin' the meetin'?" he wheezed.

"Yeah," Tiger answered.

"Sorry," Cory said to Stan.

"For what?"

"For you coming all this way to be disappointed."

"I'm not disappointed."

"We didn't win ..."

"No," Stan agreed, sounding a little stronger, "we didn't win. We finished second ... In the Kentucky Derby. Not bad for the B team."

Cory smiled. He glanced at Sandra, Tracy and Tiger, and they were smiling also. Carlos reached over and touched Stan's shoulder. Predictably, Perry took Stan's hand and shook it.

"Anyway," Stan went on, "Tiger and me, we made us a nice bet. Some to win, but most to place." He looked at Tiger. "What he pay?"

"Don't know," Tiger responded. "Didn't have a chance to collect. Got a little busy ... with other things."

"You can cash later. They won't run outta money."

"For sure."

Stan looked around the room again before speaking. "Wanted to invite you all to dinner tonight. But if this place is anything like the hospitals in L.A., the food's lousy."

Cory could only shake his head.

✦ ✦ ✦

"It was a good race, Boss."

"It sure would've been nice to win," Cory lamented.

"I think he will win the next race."

"The Preakness."

"Yes, Boss. Someone, they tell me that race, it is not so long."

"It's a sixteenth of a mile shorter. That distance today, we'd have won."

Carlos shrugged. They were in their hotel room, following dinner with Tracy and Perry in the hotel dining room. After dinner, while Cory walked Tracy and Perry back to their room, Carlos had called home.

"You talk with your wife?"

"I talk with her, Boss. She is very happy. She say she see the race on the television. She say she see you and me on the television."

Carlos seemed happy too. Although Cory's feelings about the race were mixed, bittersweet—disappointment at not winning, yet elation at Bandit's sensational performance—he tried to put them aside and focus on his compadre's contentment.

"So we did the right thing when we came to California," he ventured.

"I think we do the right thing, Boss ... when we claim Bandit."

✦ ✦ ✦

"I feel bad for Stan," Tracy said.

Cory was driving her, Perry and Carlos to the airport early the next afternoon, following another meeting of the B team in Stan's hospital room. Everyone had been present, plus Sandra brought her daughter Becky and Potato Number Two.

"I think this is what he wants," Cory replied solemnly.

"To be stuck here?" she retorted. "In a hospital room."

"Maybe this is where he wants his life to end."

"But why?"

"Kentucky ... it's the heart and soul of American racing."

Silence ensued and as he drove into the airport parking lot, Cory sensed nothing more would be said on the subject.

✦ ✦ ✦

Cory watched Tracy watch Perry and Carlos go through the airport security gate. She'd given the boy strict instructions to stay with Carlos until she met them in half an hour at their departure gate. Once they disappeared down a long corridor, she took Cory's hand and led him toward the front of the terminal.

He wondered where she was taking him and what she had in mind. The airport was so crowded that it reminded him of Churchill Downs yesterday. Seemingly everyone was displaying Derby souvenirs—hats, shirts, jackets, all with Derby insignia. It was noisy too, almost as if another big race were about to be run here.

At the front of the terminal, Tracy guided him to the left. He assumed that she wanted to get away from the hordes. Sure enough, she pointed to a quiet corner, near a couple of airline counters that were apparently closed for the day. An overhead loudspeaker summoned a certain passenger to baggage claim.

She didn't say anything to him when they got to the corner. Although several seats were available, she remained standing. She let go of his hand and put both arms around him. She looked up at him, her light-green eyes aglow. Then she kissed him. A tender, lasting kiss. He had trouble breathing. Or maybe he simply held his breath, in surprise.

"What was that?" he managed, once she released him.

"Your kiss good night. The one I didn't give you on our first date ..."

"What's it for?" he asked, still unsettled.

"For all you are. And for all I feel for you."

Then she turned and began to walk off. He started to follow. She wouldn't let him, though, motioning insistently for him to stay. He stood there watching her head back toward the crowds and the flight to California. Finally, when he could no longer see her, he began walking to the parking lot.

CHAPTER 30

STAN'S ATTACK AND BANDIT'S NEAR MISS weren't the only bad news Cory had to deal with. When he got to Dan's barn the next morning, an overcast Monday, he discovered heat in Bandit's left front foot. He probed the area with his fingers, and the colt flinched like he was in pain.

Since Bandit showed no sign of distress when he'd examined him thoroughly yesterday morning, the day following the race, Cory grew suspicious. Any injury from the race would likely have shown itself then. Bandit's only exercise yesterday had been a simple walk, nothing that would cause damage.

Cory's thoughts turned to Kosko and Dobson. Could they somehow be involved? Did their sphere of influence extend clear to Kentucky? Or was there a new set of Koskos and Dobsons to contend with here?

Cory decided that, rather than leap to potentially false conclusions, he'd start at the logical beginning. He went right to Dan, who immediately called his veterinarian.

✦ ✦ ✦

"No way we can hold your job. Either you're here or you lose it."

Tiger listened over his cell phone to his boss's angry words. It was barely nine in the morning, six California time, yet the restaurant was already open. In fact Tiger was supposed to be there at this very minute. Not to mention tomorrow and Wednesday mornings. After they'd given him the weekend off for the Derby, he certainly couldn't expect much leniency. Especially at the last minute like this.

He had to make an instant decision, consequently. Obviously he couldn't get there today. But tomorrow was possible, and he could negotiate for that now. Only one person had been a real friend to him lately, though. Had helped him financially and otherwise, when he really needed help. No way could he abandon that friend here in a Kentucky hospital, seriously ill and essentially alone.

Without saying so much as a single word to his boss, he simply flipped his cell phone shut.

✦ ✦ ✦

"Let's give it a day or two," the veterinarian suggested, "before we make a final diagnosis."

"No x-rays?" Cory asked.

"Not now."

"You don't think anything's broken?" Cory questioned cautiously.

"If I did, I'd x-ray."

"What about exercise?"

"Walk him if you want. Nothing more."

The vet, named Rick Clouse, pulled his raincoat tight around his neck and began to move away from Bandit's stall. He was bulky and handsome, likely in his late thirties. The overcast of earlier this morning had turned into a steady light rain. Cory recalled that Bandit's prior problem, the ankle swelling caused by Kosko's men at Santa Anita, had also seemingly prompted inclement weather.

"Care to speculate on what's wrong?" Cory pressed Clouse.

"If we're lucky, no more than an abscess. Gotten a lot of those around here lately."

"Medication?"

"You can poultice him if you want."

"Sure," Cory said, feeling a little relieved. "Anything else I can do?"

"Not now. Why I want to wait a day or two. See if something else shows up."

Cory watched him slosh off into the rain. He decided to give Bandit the day off from walking. He assumed that the colt wouldn't want to be out in the rain any more than he did.

✦ ✦ ✦

"How come you're still here?" Stan croaked after waking from a deep sleep.

"Who's gonna make your bets this afternoon?" Tiger shrugged.

"What ya mean? We got racing today?"

"Right here at Churchill. Special Monday card. Plus simulcasts from all over the country."

"Got the entries?" Stan inquired.

"Better yet ... Got the Form."

He gave it to Stan. Tiger noticed that the old guy's hands were shaking when he took it. Though he could hardly hold it up, he began browsing through. Tiger glanced at the room's only window.

"Pick mudders," he advised. "Been raining all morning."

"Still can't believe that race the other day," Stan sighed as he put down the Form. "Almost shocking that field. At thirty-three to one."

"Right."

"Tell ya one thing. Won't be no thirty-three to one in the Preakness. Or the Belmont."

"Right," Tiger repeated impatiently. "Hey, cut the chatter and pick them mudders. First post's less than an hour."

Stan nodded and got back to the Form. It crackled in front of him as his hands kept shaking.

✦ ✦ ✦

"He looks better," Clouse declared. "Much better. I can tell you've been poulticing him."

"I have," Cory confirmed.

It was now Wednesday, two days after the vet's first exam. Two days that had passed very slowly for Cory. Besides visiting Stan and Tiger at the hospital and phoning Carlos, Tracy and Perry, he had spent most of the time brooding. This morning was crisp and sunny, a welcome relief from the humid light rain that had fallen most of the past forty-eight hours.

"Still don't want to x-ray?" Cory questioned. "Just to be safe."

"No reason to. It's like I thought. A simple abscess. Just needs a little time for the inflammation to subside."

"How much time?"

"Hard to say for sure," Clouse replied, rubbing his chin. "Maybe a week. Maybe longer."

"Can I train him at all?"

"I wouldn't. Not while his foot's still inflamed."

"Ten days till the Preakness," Cory said hopefully. "Any chance?"

"Doubtful. But let's see how he comes along."

The vet turned to leave. The incident with Kosko and his men ran through Cory's mind. Maybe someone wanted to keep Bandit out of the Preakness.

"Before you go," Cory said. "Can I ask another question?"

"Sure."

"Any possibility this is a setup?"

"Setup? What do you mean?"

"In California, this colt was the victim of some characters making it look like he had an injury ... when he didn't."

"I heard about that," Clouse remarked, rubbing his chin again. "Made one of our professional publications."

"Oh?"

"Anyway, to answer your question ... I doubt this is a setup. Like I told you the other day, I've seen too many this type of injury lately. But I can do a test to see if there's foreign substance in his foot ... If you want."

"I want," Cory quickly replied.

"Okay. I'll draw some blood later. Should hear back from the lab in a day or two."

The vet, instead of rubbing his own chin once more, rubbed Bandit's. Then, like two days ago, Cory watched him slosh off, the ground still wet from all the rain.

✦   ✦   ✦

Someone tapped Tracy on the shoulder as she stood near the front of the art gallery, a large, stark multi-cornered room. She turned around. And was astonished to see Sandra standing next to her.

"Thought you weren't getting back from Kentucky until tomorrow," Tracy beamed.

"Didn't want to miss your show."

Although they'd conversed daily by phone since Tracy's return —reviewing the condition of each of Sandra's horses—Sandra hadn't mentioned getting back early. And Tracy couldn't recall giving her the date and place of the show. Then she remembered telling her almost a couple of weeks ago that the only gallery near Santa Anita held an exhibit the second Thursday of every month. Evidently, along with her numerous other abilities, Sandra possessed ample skill as a detective.

It was a two-person show. The other artist, a graying middle-aged woman, did motels. Apparently she was obsessed with them, like Tracy was with horses. That is, with Bandit, the subject of the entire dozen-piece collection she was presenting. Unfortunately neither artist had attracted many spectators, so that Sandra stood out among the few people there.

"You didn't tell me you have so much talent," Sandra complimented.

"Bandit brings out the best in me," Tracy smiled.

"I think he brings out the best in all of us."

Someone else approached Tracy, with a question about the composition of the paint she'd used. Sandra went over and stood before a large portrait of Bandit looking out at the viewer from his stall at Santa Anita. Tracy had adeptly presented the angle of his gaze and highlighted his good eye in such a way that one hardly noticed the bad one.

When Tracy finished with the inquirer, she observed that Sandra hadn't budged from in front of the picture of Bandit.

✦ ✦ ✦

"Got the results back from the lab," Clouse said. "Showed nothing unusual."

"No setup, then," Cory replied.

"No evidence of any."

It was Friday morning, two days since the last time the vet had seen Bandit. He'd called Cory yesterday, to tell him he'd been summoned to a breeding farm on an emergency. And wouldn't be back until evening. The two of them bent over Bandit's ailing left front foot. Clouse probed it with his fingers. Bandit flinched only slightly.

"Much better," the vet declared.

"You know what I'm going to ask."

"The Preakness?"

"Yeah. Eight days away. Any chance?"

"Maybe," Clouse answered. "He keeps coming along like this."

"Can I train him?"

"Foot's still a little tender. Let's give it another day or two."

Warm, sunny weather had dried the ground around Dan's barn. This time, when Clouse left, he made no sloshing sounds.

✦ ✦ ✦

"Oh, forgot to tell you," Tiger told Stan, "Cory and Sandra came by yesterday morning."

"What was I doin'?"

"The usual. Sleepin'."

"Oh."

A nurse came in the room with Stan's breakfast, placing it on a tray in front of him. She went over to the window and drew the curtains. As she left the room, Stan stuck his tongue out at her.

"Want some this slop?" he asked Tiger.

"No thanks ... Sandra told me to tell you good-bye."

"She goin' back to California?"

"Went. Said somethin' about Tracy and some art show."

"When you goin' back?" Stan inquired.

"I'm not. Stayin' right here."

"You must like the Kentucky races."

"Yeah," Tiger muttered after pausing. "I like the Kentucky races."

He placed a Racing Form in the middle of the bed, so Stan could look it over whenever he wanted. The nurse returned. Evidently she'd entered the wrong room, though, because she turned almost immediately and left. But not before making a face at Stan, apparently for not touching his food. Of course he made a face back, prior to her getting out the door.

"Found me a little place last night near the track," Tiger disclosed.

"Yeah? What about your place in California? All your clothes and things?"

"Not gonna worry about that right now."

"You got money?" Stan asked.

"Sure. From Bandit's purses. Cory said my share of the Derby's 'round twenty grand. And I still got some left from his Santa Anita races."

"Way you bet," Stan needled, "won't last very long."

✦ ✦ ✦

News of Bandit's foot leaked out to the media. Reporters constantly dogged Cory for information about how serious the injury was. What he was doing to treat it. And, of course, whether Bandit would be able to run in the Preakness.

At least now Bandit's eye was no longer a focal point. And no one was questioning whether they belonged there, either.

CHAPTER 31

"GREEN LIGHT," CLOUSE TOLD CORY.

"For this morning?"

"For this morning."

"I'll have his groom get him ready for the track," Cory said excitedly.

Clouse nodded. The two of them stood outside Bandit's stall, the vet having just finished probing Bandit's foot. No flinching. It was Sunday, eight days after the Derby. Six days before the Preakness. Cory sensed that the race was still possible. Provided everything went well.

"One thing's bugging me," Cory admitted.

"What?"

"He's been off his feed."

"No surprise. Injury usually affects appetite. I can see he's lost a lot of weight."

"I know," Cory agreed.

"Derby takes it out of them too. Especially when they run as hard as he did. Most of the Derby horses I've treated ... they need at least a week to recover and get back to eating regular."

"So he's right on schedule," Cory joked.

"Only if he starts eating soon."

Cory gazed at Bandit. He hoped that the colt was as eager to get to the track as he was.

✦ ✦ ✦

So far, the workout had gone poorly. "Sluggish" and "indifferent" best described Bandit. In fact, when Cory rode him to the track, the colt had been so lethargic that Cory half-expected him, like a pony at a rental stable, to try and double back to Dan's barn.

It was supposed to be a simple jog. Pretty much what Tracy had ridden him through on Derby day. It turned out anything but simple. Early in the workout—while cantering down the back-stretch along the outside rail, heading clockwise, the direction opposite most of the other horses on the track—Bandit gawked at a bird flying overhead and nearly ran into the rail. Negotiating the last curve, leading into the stretch, he stumbled, recovering barely in time to keep from tossing Cory.

Now, nearing the finish of the workout, Cory looked for something, anything, to offer the slightest cause for optimism. He would have welcomed Lasting Impression's routine of snorting and kicking. And yes, even jumping, like the day he'd dumped Cory at Santa Anita. Any sign of positive energy. The ideal would have been for Bandit to turn his jog into a slow gallop.

Cory clucked to him. He gently dug his heels into Bandit's sides. Neither act elicited response. If anything, the colt slowed down, and trudged the final yards of the workout.

As they came off the track, Bandit was puffing. The eight-day inactivity had obviously taken its toll. Cory couldn't help thinking of the last time Bandit missed some training. When he had the phony swollen ankle before the San Felipe Stakes, the worst race of his life.

✦ ✦ ✦

"Thought I'd better discuss the Preakness with you," Cory told Sandra by phone the next day.

"But I don't know much about race strategy," she replied.

"Not race strategy. The race. Whether Bandit should even run."

"Is something wrong?" her voice displayed concern.

"He's not himself. I exercised him this morning for the second time since the Derby. He went even worse than yesterday. And yesterday was bad."

"Oh, no," she said.

"Another thing … Stan can't travel to Maryland in his condition. Tiger'll probably stay behind with him. Gonna be tough for Tracy and Perry to get away again. Carlos has his hands full with the horses in California. That leaves only you and me."

"So …" she sounded sad. "Your … B team won't be together."

"Right."

"And Bandit might not be up to the race."

"Right," he repeated. "And I wanted you to help me decide."

"You're the one who's developed him into a possible champion. Please, you decide."

"I'll be in touch," he said.

✦ ✦ ✦

"Nothin' against your hospitality," Cory told Dan the next morning in Dan's barn office, "but Bandit and me ... we're movin' on."

"Maryland ... and the Preakness."

"No ... California ... And some R and R."

"Really. That abscess gettin' the best of him?"

"Not so much him," Cory confessed. "Me. I don't want to put him through what I'd have to put him through to get him ready."

"I understand. But what about all that big money? Plus what you make him worth ... you win one those big races."

"There's plenty big races later on. He means too much to me to rush him."

"You becomin' sentimental in your old age? What would your father say about gettin' attached to a horse?"

"I think even he might get attached to this one," Cory responded.

Dan's assistant trainer entered the tiny room, with a question for Dan about whether to take one of their horses off a medication he was on. While Dan answered, Rugged Landing, for some reason, came into Cory's thoughts. Despite it being more than a year ago, Cory was surprised at how fresh the images of the horse's tragic ending were.

"You check with your owners?" Dan asked, once his assistant left.

"A key one. She left it up to me."

"You're pretty sure you're doin' the right thing."

"Yeah," Cory replied. "Pretty sure."

"You'll have to face the media," Dan warned. "Among other things ... prob'ly call you a coward."

"They're prob'ly right."

"But then you don't much care about the media."

"Not like I care about this colt," Cory remarked, realizing he was sounding sentimental again. "Actually, this time ... I'm gonna try to behave myself. Unless you want to stand in."

"No. It's all yours. I don't think I could behave myself with those guys."

"I'm gonna do my best to behave myself," Cory said, sounding resolute.

✦ ✦ ✦

"When you leavin' for the Preakness?" Stan asked Tiger hoarsely later that morning.

"Not goin' the Preakness."

"You're not goin' with Bandit?"

"Bandit's not goin'."

"Since when?"

"Since he's had a little foot problem and Cory's not takin' any chances."

Tiger then filled him in on what had happened with Bandit the last week or so. He went on to tell him that Cory planned to give Bandit time off until late in the year. And how Cory had come by the hospital earlier to let them know, and to say good-bye.

"What was I doin'?" Stan wheezed.

"One guess."

"Sleepin'?"

"Good guess."

Stan closed his eyes and began breathing heavily. Tiger expected he'd hear him snoring any second now, sounds he'd heard all too often lately. He anticipated him sleeping for hours, until he woke him to get his racing selections for the day.

"Sometimes people change," Stan whispered, surprising Tiger.

"Yeah?"

"Yeah. But it isn't easy."

Tiger had no idea what Stan was talking about. He'd heard sick people sometimes became delusional and he reasoned that's what was happening now. Maybe he should alert a nurse, just in case.

"All my years at the track," Stan continued whispering. "See the same faces there every day."

"Yeah?"

"Once in a while ... I hear about people stopping ... Deciding there's more to life."

Tiger smiled, beginning to understand. He recalled their conversation at Santa Anita two or three months ago. The day Tall Order won.

"You're still a young guy," Stan went on. "Whole life ahead ..."

Tiger didn't answer. Again he saw Stan close his eyes and heard his heavy breathing—he must be falling asleep once more. Maybe he should leave now. Go back to his little place. He could return later and get the old man's picks.

"I have faith in you," Stan whispered again, once more surprising Tiger.

Then Tiger did hear the old man snoring. He got up and went to the door. He turned to say something. He knew it was useless, however. He knew from recent history that once Stan began snoring, he'd sleep for hours.

Tiger went down the hall. He passed the same nurse who regularly brought Stan his breakfast, at whom Stan regularly stuck out his tongue. Tiger thought she might make a face at him, like he'd seen her make at Stan, but she apparently didn't even recognize him.

He stopped at a restroom. Once inside, he locked the door behind him and moved to a large mirror to comb his hair. Before taking his comb from a pants pocket, he looked carefully in the mirror. At the reflection of his own face.

Stan was right. He *was* still a young man.

✦ ✦ ✦

"Could he run in the Preakness?" a bespectacled man with a notebook asked Cory.

"Yes. But I think your question's missing a significant word."

"What's that?" the man queried.

"Could he run *well* in the Preakness?"

"Okay … Could he run *well* in the Preakness?"

"Not likely."

"What about the Belmont?"

"Same answer," Cory replied. "Not with that race being a mile and a half. Much farther than the Derby and Preakness."

About a dozen media persons stood with Cory on a grassy patch near Dan's barn. The press conference, arranged by the Churchill Downs publicity staff, had begun a few minutes past its scheduled noon start time. "High noon," as Dan had joked. Dan himself stood off to Cory's right, within earshot, evidently as some sort of moral support. Or maybe because he was curious.

Cory had already detailed Bandit's ailment. Publicity personnel helped by passing out literature, complete with diagrams, on foot abscesses in horses. Cory had also divulged Bandit's recent missed training and lethargy.

"What about all his admirers?" a man with a cane inquired. "They'll be disappointed he's not running."

"I feel bad for them," Cory acknowledged. "All the support they've given. Letters, cards, e-mails. At least fifty a day lately. But let me ask you something ..."

"Yes?"

"How would all those people feel should something terrible happen to him in one of those races? Like what's happened too many times in recent years."

The guy shrugged. A rooster scurried across a nearby roadway, cock-a-doodle-dooing as he went. Cory hadn't seen roosters before at Churchill. He glanced at Dan, who appeared to be frowning. Not from the rooster, he assumed.

"Those are grueling races," Cory stated. "Back-to-back-to-back. Hardly any time between. Lot of horses never race again."

"So you're advocating a change in the format," a young woman with a tape recorder suggested.

"I am."

"Despite it being this way for decades."

"I am."

"Even though," the bespectacled man said, "this setup makes winning the triple crown one of the most difficult and supreme accomplishments in modern sports."

"At what price, though," Cory submitted, "to the horses?"

Cory anticipated more questions, but none were forthcoming. The rooster scurried across the roadway again. Gradually the media persons dispersed. Cory walked over to Dan, who had stopped frowning.

"You did it," Dan said.

"I did what?"

"You behaved yourself through the entire interview."

"That why you were frowning? Didn't think I could do it?"

"No," Dan laughed. "It was that rooster. I was trying to decide who was more impressive. Him or you."

✦ ✦ ✦

"Make your picks?" Tiger asked.

The position of the Racing Form—in the middle of the bed, exactly where Tiger remembered leaving it—was pretty good indication that Stan hadn't. A nurse, one that Tiger hadn't seen before, brought in lunch and placed it on a tray in front of Stan. The fact that she wasn't one of his regular nurses in no way prevented Stan offering his customary parting gesture—a nasty look plus an extension of his tongue.

"Better get with it," Tiger admonished. "Already missed the first race."

"Give me ten minutes."

"Way you been picking lately," Tiger cackled, "don't need ten seconds."

PART SIX

GOLDEN GATE FIELDS

CHAPTER 32

Dear Stan,
    Since those last days in Kentucky, I've tried to figure out how to be in touch with you. I can't think of any other way except to write you a letter. And mail it, even if I don't know what address to use.
    Today I'm at Golden Gate Fields, near San Francisco. You'll be happy to know that this is my first day at a track since our last days in Kentucky. And I didn't make a single bet!
    I'm here for two reasons. Bandit ran for the first time in five months, since the Derby. And Cory and Tracy just had their wedding, right here at the track. In fact, I slipped out of their reception to write you.
    Bandit ran great. He won easily, by nine lengths. Looks like he's better than ever. Cory wants to run him in the big winter races at Santa Anita.
    The wedding was held a couple hours after the race. Right in the same winner's circle Bandit went into earlier. Tracy told me she'd grown up near San Francisco and always loved the area, so when they decided to get married, she wanted the wedding to take place in this vicinity. Maybe not at a racetrack. But it did seem fitting, and Cory told me that, in order to get Bandit to run here, Golden Gate Fields made a lot of the arrangements for the wedding.
    Guess what! Tracy picked me to walk her down the aisle. Which in this case was the track itself. She wore a beautiful wedding gown. Emerald green, the color you picked out for our silks. And did she look great!

Carlos was Cory's best man. He was real happy. His two daughters, Rosa and Luisa, were Tracy's bridesmaids. His wife Alicia played "Here Comes the Bride" on a piano the track had rented and moved to the winner's circle. His family is all together now. Carlos bought a little house not far from Santa Anita. For the down payment, he used his share of Bandit's purses, plus the money you left him.

Perry had two jobs at the wedding. He was ringbearer and he watched Cory's dog, Cookie. What a great kid. Always smiling and shaking everyone's hand. He told me he's like Bandit because he runs in races himself. Junior Olympics, things like that. He's been in four so far, and he's won every time. But he still wants to play baseball, he said. When I asked him for who, he told me he has his eye on the Texas Rangers.

The wedding had a very funny moment. After the justice of the peace asked if anyone objected to the marriage, Cookie started barking. She went to Cory with her leash in her mouth. They had to hold up the ceremony while he took her down the track. When they came back, we all cheered.

Sandra was Tracy's matron of honor. All seven of her grandchildren came to the wedding. She looked great in her own emerald green gown, a little lighter shade than Tracy's. After the wedding, Sandra told me that when I'm in L.A., to come visit her at her house. She said she wanted to show me the six portraits of Bandit she bought from Tracy, that now hang on her living room wall.

You'll be happy to know that Cory and Carlos now have twelve horses in their stable at Santa Anita. Three times what they brought to California from Arizona. And Cory tells me they've got some good ones. Horses he thinks will soon win.

But Bandit's still their leader. And it seems he's more popular than ever. Because of him, Golden Gate Fields had its biggest crowd in years today. And Cory says the fan mail keeps rolling in.

So, as you can see, everyone's doing well. Yet, even with all this joy today, there was sadness. It just wasn't the same without you. Cory said he kept looking around, hoping you'd somehow magically appear. So did I. Still, even though we all knew you wouldn't be here, I could feel you with me. Like I have so often since those last days in Kentucky.

You and I joked a lot. Of course neither of us ever took it serious. But I am sorry for one thing I said. You remember when I told you that where you're going, they don't allow horses? That was wrong. I know that where you are now, they race seven days a week, twenty-four hours a day. Otherwise this life makes no sense.

As for me, it wasn't hard to get here, to Golden Gate Fields. I now live in the San Francisco area. I'm going to a community college near Stanford. You might recall that I told you I was supposed to go to Stanford on a football scholarship a few years ago. Before I blew out my knee.

I know it's a long shot, but I've been thinking about Stanford and trying to play football again. As Cory once suggested, I've been working out lately. If I learned anything from you and your B team, it's that there _is_ more to life than betting horses and anything's possible. A one-eyed horse can go to the Kentucky Derby. And even finish second there. Maybe I can still go to Stanford.

Anyway, you never know, Stanford might even have a B team.

Your friend always,
Tiger

Made in the USA
San Bernardino, CA
16 June 2017